PRAISE FOR *UNTIL MY SOUL GETS IT RIGHT*

"Berner has a talent with prose that flows smoothly and puts the reader right where they belong, inside the character's head. *Until My Soul Gets It Right* is another winner."

—*BigAl's Books and Pals*

"No one got one single thing out of me for two-and-a-half days because I could not get my nose out of the books."

—*Empty Nest blog*

"*Until My Soul Gets it Right* by Karen Wojcik Berner is a novel of self-discovery, sin, redemption, and forgiveness—and also wicked fun."

—*Donna's Book Pub*

"I read it entirely in one day, I just couldn't put it down! Catherine Elbert inspires you to go out and do the things you want to do."

—*Goodreads reviewer*

"...a series about a book club with each book centered around a different member of the club—genius!"

—*Kritter's Ramblings book review blog*

"This excellent addition to the series will endear readers to the Bibliophiles indefinitely!"

—*Lovey Dovey Books*

YOU CAN'T RUN AWAY FROM YOURSELF

*U*ntil My
—Soul—
Gets It Right

THE BIBLIOPHILES: BOOK TWO

Karen Wojcik Berner

KAREN
WOJCIK
BERNER

Until My Soul Gets It Right
Copyright © 2012 by Karen Wojcik Berner. All rights reserved.
Second Print Edition: May 2013

www.karenberner.com

ISBN-13: 978-1-4751-8903-2
Cover and Formatting: Streetlight Graphics

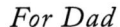

For Dad

PROLOGUE

CATHERINE COLLAPSED ONTO HER BED exhausted, a chocolaty brown comforter enveloping her. Her mind was swirling. Her head ached. Too much Sangria, but, what the hell? She felt like celebrating. Shakespeare was undisputed, big-time theater, even if she only had a few lines.

It was nice of her friends from the book club to come. Even Annie Jacobs was there. Crazy Edwina Hipplewhite and her sunflower hat! Omigod. *They're good people, though.* Her father's expression flashed into her consciousness. Her family, if you could still call them that, would never have come to a Shakespeare in the Park. Like the moron brothers would understand even one line from *As You Like It*.

Come to think of it, her family would not relate to anything in her present life. Living in the Chicago suburbs. Acting on the weekends. She even owned a Bears jersey. That's the thing that would probably piss them off the most. *Cheeseheads.* Catherine could say it now. She had no intention of going back to Burkesville, Wisconsin, again.

Not that they would welcome her home with open arms anyhow.

CHAPTER ONE

*I*T TAKES A LOT OF effort to be ordinary-looking. Catherine performed the same morning routine the pretty girls did. The same shampoo, conditioner, blow dry, style, spray. The same moisturizer, concealer, foundation, blush, eye shadow, eyeliner, mascara, lipstick. She checked herself out in the mirror. *Ugh, still me.*

Still a senior in high school who hesitated to use the term "farm girl" for fear of it being too clichéd after her English teacher defined the term as "the lack of thought." Clearly, nobody aspires to be a stereotype, but, really, is everyone that original?

Who hasn't grown up knowing the bitchy cheerleader, a dumb jock, the computer nerd, an overbearing mother, a distant father, a misunderstood old person, or an alienated artist, writer, musician, or dancer? If everybody knows these people, are they really clichés or merely categories? Maybe the various cities, towns, neighborhoods, and blocks are really replicating microcosms? The same strands woven together to create one large tapestry of life?

Anyhow.

Still living in boring-as-shit Burkesville, Wisconsin. The

entire town consisted of a bank, post office, drug store, gas station, church, two schools, and four taverns, all within a four-block area. Anyone could walk through it in about two seconds unless old Ben got a hold of you. Ben practically lived on the third-from-the-left bar stool at Pat's Bar and Grill, Burkesville's only real restaurant.

One day, Catherine and her friends were there for pizza and old Ben started blabbing to anyone who'd listen about how Bart Starr was the greatest quarterback who ever lived. Then this guy, Ernie, who usually goes to Padowski's, but it was closed because the furnace broke, piped up with "Well, what about Dan Marino?"

Ben turned to Ernie like he was going to beat the shit out of him for even thinking of someone besides Starr, (a) because he's a Miami Dolphin and (b) he's not a Packer. Heaven forbid! Like there aren't any other teams in the NFL. Catherine could not have cared less about the Packers. Who would wear green and yellow together anyway? Vomitosis.

———⁂———

"Ma! I hate sunny-side up." There was something about the way the yolks jiggled, like teasing, googly eyes. *Eat me, Catherine. Eat me.*

"Everyone else likes them well enough." Vintage Clara Elbert. Don't deviate from what the men in the family want for breakfast. Eggs. Bacon. Homemade bread, toasted. Would it kill her to buy some fruit?

By nine o'clock on Saturday morning, her father had already put down fresh hay for the pigs and milked the cows. "Here ya go, Clara," he said, placing a filled pitcher in front of her.

"Thanks, Hank. Boys, wash your hands."

No matter how old the brothers were, Clara always referred

to them as "the boys." Of course, since they acted like little kids, maybe she was right. Catherine fiddled with her eggs, eventually covering the oozing yolks with bread. "So, Mr. Leary is nagging me about 'my future plans.' How am I supposed to know what I want to do with my life? I'm only seventeen."

Clara scoffed.

Russell smirked. "Yeah, like you're so good at makin' decisions."

"Remember Dairy Queen?" Laughing, Peter pulled his sleeve over his left wrist and ran it across his face. Ma shot him a pulverizing look. He grabbed his napkin and wiped his mouth properly.

"I mean, really, even if I do go to college, what am I supposed to major in?"

Hank glanced at his wife, then at the boys. "You could work with us here."

How could she tell her family that staying on Elbert Farm was the only thing Catherine was certain she could never do?

————⁕⁂⁕————

With February looming, its contemptible blend of pink hearts and dateless nights, the only bright spot in Catherine Elbert's endless gray winter days was the spring musical. Three years of paying dues were about to end. Seniors were guaranteed to get the leads. She was a dancer in *Li'l Abner*, a chorus member in *Hello, Dolly!*, and had two lines in *Bye Bye Birdie*. This year, she would be the one coming on stage last for curtain call, receiving a huge bouquet of roses, bowing her head in appropriate humility, and then rising to continuous applause.

The choir had begun rehearsing the *Oklahoma!* score two weeks ago in anticipation of tryouts. Anyone interested in solo work was welcome to book a time before school with Mr. Gusselman. So, every morning at seven thirty, Catherine began her day singing "Out of My Dreams" and ended it running lines with Beth, who would rather skydive than get up on stage. She was happy running the crew, safely tucked backstage.

At three o'clock on Tuesday, the usually dark auditorium had become a flurry of activity. Every few rows, seemingly schizophrenic teenagers mumbled lines to themselves. On stage, dancer hopefuls practiced a combination step. Mrs. White, the elderly organist from St. Agatha's Church, was brought in as an accompanist, so Mr. Gusselman could focus on his directorial duties. He sat with student director Ted Swanson ten rows up, dead center.

"Denise Nelson. Please come to the stage. Denise Nelson. You're up," Ted yelled through a megaphone.

Catherine slipped into the seat next to Beth. "How's it going so far?"

"Pretty good. Nobody as good as you yet, but Denise is up next."

"Hey, Smellbert." Bill Davies biffed her on the back of the head as he worked his way through the row behind.

"Cut it out, juvenile."

Bill faked a "What did I do?" smirk that made Catherine flush.

"So, are you ready?"

"Ready as I'll ever be. Besides, my competition is pretty lame." He sat back, kicking her seat as he crossed his legs.

Bill was right. Arrogant, but correct. The only other boy with a decent voice looked like he would be more likely to play "Curly" from *The Three Stooges*.

"So, Bethie. Do you think our little smellbag has a chance?"

"Absolutely. She's gonna nail it."

"Bill Davies to the stage. Bill Davies."

Bill rose. "Break a leg, Smellbert."

"Yeah, you too." Her stomach churned with about fifty thousand butterflies.

"Catherine Elbert. Catherine Elbert to the stage."

Now the waiting began. Clara told her daughter there was nothing she could do about it, so she might as well get on with things, but Catherine couldn't help but wonder if it went well. Mr. Gusselman was smiling, but then he had started talking to Ted halfway through the song. What was that about?

Before she leaned her head against the window of Bus 79, Catherine checked for splattered bug remnants. Halfway between Burkesville High School and Elbert Farm was the only true Victorian house in or near the town, quite possibly in all of Muskegee County. It was built in 1892 by a gentleman from Milwaukee who supposedly made his money in beer. Probably one of the Pabst relatives. Sophomore year, her class toured the Milwaukee mansion on a field trip. Dumbass Mike Wurhauser kept asking the tour guide where all of the beer was, like the Pabst family had the brewery in their basement or something.

The Pabst mansion had a gorgeous, ornately carved staircase in the foyer, perfect for grand entrances. Catherine imagined herself, long skirt flowing as she descended, extending a gloved hand to greet guests. "Hello, Mr. Taylor. How wonderful to see you." "My dear Mrs. Banks, you look beautiful this evening."

The Gazette reported that the people who bought it were going to turn the Burkesville Victorian into a bed and breakfast. One time when the bus drove by, there was a little girl in a floral pinafore dress jumping rope on the front lawn. Her mother, clad in a denim jumper and straw hat, watched nearby as she trimmed away the overgrowth. Today, ladders and furniture were strewn about the lawn. A sofa, almost identical to the one Great-Grandma Gribbons had given Clara, sat on the front porch.

No one knew much about the family. One of the ladies who sat behind the Elberts in church had told Clara that the missus was wife number two and was way younger than the man. Hank had heard the guy had taken early retirement from a bank in Milwaukee to settle into a more peaceful life in the country. If "peaceful" was a synonym for "boring," then maybe he got it right. Otherwise, he was delusional.

The newspaper also stated the bed and breakfast would be opening on Memorial Day, and that the owners "were hoping to draw boaters from Lake Sikapu in the summer and to capitalize on some of the Sleepy Hollow Fall Festival traffic," which was a mile or so down Route 36. Catherine wished she lived in Sleepy Hollow, even if it wasn't the real one. At least the name suggested a link to literary greatness, not like Burkesville, with absolutely no associations whatsoever.

Visitors flocked to Sleepy Hollow every weekend in October to view the fall colors, purchase corn stalks, hay bales, and Halloween costumes at Johansen's Pumpkin Farm. If they were lucky, they might even catch a glimpse of Ichabod Crane out for a stroll or run into Katrina Von Tassel, both played by the Johansens themselves.

When the Elbert children were little, Hank made them pose for pictures next to the "How Tall This Fall?" wood cut-out of a scarecrow holding a measuring stick. The photo collection of little Catherine only went from barely standing at two to age seven, the year Peter hurled a pumpkin at Russell's head for calling him a baby. Hank sped to the emergency room, where the doctor informed a distraught Clara that her eldest son had a concussion. Peter was banished to his room for one week, and that was the end of the Fall Festival excursions.

From then on, Halloween costume choices consisted of whatever was leftover from last year at the Quickie Mart, which turned itself into a lame "Halloween Spook-Quarters" every October. Clara Elbert was not about to drive all over Muskegee County for some outfit Catherine would wear only once.

Consequently, when she was eight, Catherine was a ballerina. Year nine, Sleeping Beauty, who really had the best gig of any fairy tale princess, slumbering away while the prince had to go fight that awful Maleficent and her dragon-and-thorn extravaganza. Best gig, worst costume. Cheap fabric and a plastic mask that damn near suffocated Catherine when she was trick-or-treating. Year ten, a godforsaken butterfly. By the time she was eleven, Catherine had had enough with the cheap crap and bought her own costume with leftover birthday money from Aunt Ida. She was Lizzie Borden.

The bus left her off at Blather's Hill. Elbert Farm was about a mile up the road. Most days, Catherine enjoyed this solitary walk before the onslaught of parental questioning. It gave her time to process the day's events, figure out what to tell Beth on the phone after dinner, and what to keep from her mother. She threw Clara a bone every once in a while to delay the incessant nagging about future plans. Like they ever had to make such a decision. Hank inherited the farm from Grandpa Elbert, and he and Clara got married a month after high school graduation.

Catherine stopped to breathe in the fresh, non-farm-animal air courtesy of the World's Largest Christmas Trees, huge pines that divided their house from the soy bean field. When she was little, Catherine had asked her parents if they could decorate them for the holidays.

Russell laughed. "Yeah, right."

"How stupid are you?" Peter added.

Hank cut in. "Cat, honey, it would be impossible to run electricity all the way over there."

"Those trees were planted ages ago to block the farmhouse

from the wind, not for your own personal decorating pleasure, missy." Clara gave an exasperated sigh and left the room.

A faint clucking came from the chicken coop. Winter was a good time on the farm. The frigid air canceled out a lot of the animal smells. Next door, the pigs lay asleep, as they were apt to do in the late afternoon. Pigs are actually some of the cleanest animals on the farm. They change the straw for their beds every day and never poop where they sleep. Poor misunderstood creatures.

"It's you and me, Penny." Catherine petted the over-sized swine slumbering near the sty's fence. Each Elbert, from as far back as anyone could remember, was either a farmer or a farmer's wife. Even on the Gribbons' side, Ma's relatives. Didn't any of them want to be a teacher? A banker? A truck driver? An artist? Butcher? Baker? Candlestick maker?

Clara left the large farming to Pop and the boys, but was totally in control when it came to cooking ingredients, which were grown in a small garden plot to the side of the house. There were vegetables and a few herbs, even an occasional flower or two—nothing fancy. One of Catherine's chores was to weed the thing, cringing every time she donned those dumb denim overalls and gardening gloves so thick with mud that even industrial-strength detergent could not remove. Somehow, dirt always got through the gloves anyway and jammed under her fingernails. Gross.

"Cat, is that you?"

"Yeah. It's booger-freezing cold out. Can we have some hot chocolate?"

"Watch your tongue. Don't have time for hot chocolate. I've got these clothes to fix, and then I need to get dinner started."

Why mending holes would take precedence over a nice, hot afternoon beverage she did not know, but then again there was little about her mother Catherine understood anyway. The sewing could have waited, but Clara Elbert operated on an internal time clock from which there would be no deviation.

The telephone rang.

"Hey, Miss Catherine."

"Hey, can you hang on just a second? Ma, I'm going to take this in my room. Would you hang it up when I yell down?"

"Who is it?"

"Beth."

"Didn't you just see her less than an hour ago? I'll tell you, frivolous time-waster, the telephone."

"I got it." Click. "Okay, my mom's off. So how are things with our dear Fred?"

"Nonexistent."

"But I thought you said the situation was heating up."

"Only because we are chemistry lab partners."

"Give it time. Pretty soon, he'll be igniting your burner."

"Stop it." Beth giggled. "Oh, crap. My mother's yelling for me. Call me after dinner." Hank had mercifully bought Catherine her own phone for her sixteenth birthday. Well, not really her own line, just a phone for her room, but she was the first one of her friends to have one. You would think it was 1946 instead of 1985. Beth was still stuck talking right in the middle of the kitchen where her entire family could hear every word.

She was pretty quiet about anything related to guys, but last week Beth let it slip she thought Fred Schmidt was cute. She would never ask him out or anything, so Catherine got him to build sets for the musical after overhearing Mr. Jones talking to Pop about Fred building bookcases for him. Beth was always the stage manager, so that would give them a chance to work together after school, romantic strains of Rodgers and Hammerstein music floating sweetly in the air—albeit blended with the buzz of circular saws—but maybe Fred liked that sort of thing. They would be dating by prom!

CHAPTER TWO

"Now class, get out your notebooks. Come. Come. Hurry up now. We have much to cover." Miss Keller floated among the desks, turquoise scarf billowing in her wake. She was at least two hundred and fifty-six, but somehow had never learned how to properly apply powder foundation. A pink line was visible, clear as day, separating her face from her neck.

"Mike, be a dear and turn off the lights. Thank you." She wiggled her plump toosh into a chair and turned on the overhead projector. "Art can stir up many emotions. Wouldn't you agree? One person can love a painting, while another can loathe it. Some unfortunate souls are indifferent to it."

The Scream flashed onto the screen.

"What do you feel when you see this?" Miss Keller scanned the room.

"Like I do every day I'm in this hellhole."

"Very funny, Mr. Berger, and, rest assured, you are not the only one."

Bill Davies put both of his hands behind his head, yawned broadly, and swept his right hand across Catherine's desk, knocking her spiral to the floor. "Oops, sorry."

"Thanks a lot."

"Anytime."

Bill's blue eyes were the color of the Blessed Mother's robe in the stained glass behind the altar at St. Agatha's. Catherine had logged in many hours—thousands now—staring at it while Father Wilhelm droned on about purity or piety or some other "P" word. Cerulean blue, according to the sixty-four box of Crayola crayons from grammar school.

Miss Keller changed the transparencies. "Okay, how about this one?"

Omigod! Same prim expression. Same angular sternness.

"Can anyone tell me what this painting is called?"

Rose Slattery's hand jolted up. "It's *American Gothic* by Grant Wood."

"Very good, Miss Slattery."

"I saw it once. At the Art Institute in Chicago."

"Really, what did you think?"

They were off, beginning their private conversation as they often did during class time.

No one else cared. The man on the screen looked like Clara in drag. The dark, defiant eyes. The thin, tight mouth. His entire essence of being shouted "What are you lookin' at, missy?"

Bill turned around and mimicked Miss Keller. "So, what do you think, Miss Elbert? How does it make you feel?"

"Gross. How 'bout you? Maybe if you're lucky, you'll end up with a farm of your own and a lovely wife like her by your side."

"No thanks." Bill was not from a farming family like the other boys. His father owned Paulie's Petroleum and Quickie Mart. "Davies" was before "Elbert" in the Burkesville High School senior class alphabetizing routine, had been since the second day of seventh grade when Mr. Manning walked the new kid into homeroom, and Bill had stood in front of the class shuffling sideways, blond hair blocking his eyes like a sheep dog. No "Eden" or "Eggert" had ever moved in to shake up the seating arrangement.

"Mr. Davies? Miss Elbert? Would you care to join us?"

While more paintings flashed on the screen, Catherine occupied herself with another art form. How Bill's shoulders filled his mesh Packers jersey just right, despite its horrendous colors. How he cocked his head to the left when thinking. Sometimes when he leaned back in his seat, she hunched forward, rested a cheek on her left arm, and pretended to be especially interested in something Miss Keller said. He was so close, the smell of gasoline drops from his shoes wafted up her waiting nostrils. One time, Catherine reached out, longing to trace the number on his jersey, when, all of a sudden, he shifted back, and her pen poked right through the mesh.

"Ouch. What are you doing, Smellbert?"

"Um, my pen sort of..."

"Mr. Davies. Miss Elbert. Do I need to separate you?"

Friday morning, Beth ran to Catherine's locker. "Did you see? The cast list is out."

"What? It wasn't supposed to be posted until Monday."

They sprinted through the hall, steamrolling Phil Martin who always seemed to be in the way, and fought to the front of the small group assembled. "Okay. Okay. Let's see. Bill Davies—Curly. Figures." Feigning nonchalance was all she could do.

"Here's you!" Beth's finger pointed further down the sheet. "Catherine Elbert—Ado Annie."

Ado Annie? Not Laurie? No duets with Curly?

"Denise Nelson—Laurie. Gary Derekson—Will."

The little sophomore? Sure, he was a decent dancer, but a sophomore?

"Mike Wurhauser—Ali Hakim." Beth paused. "Cat, are you..."

"Just dandy. I get to play opposite Gary Frickin' Derekson and shit-for-brains Wurhauser, while Denise Nelson gets Bill. Yeah, I'm great."

"It's not the ideal cast, I know, but…"

Catherine stormed toward the music room.

"Cat, wait!"

"Sophomore? Dumbass? Slut-bag Denise?" She burst through the door.

Mr. Gusselman was sitting at his desk. "Ah, my Ado Annie. Congratulations, Catherine."

"But why?"

"It's the best female role, don't you think? And with all of your pizzazz, I thought you could really sell it."

"My pizzazz?"

"Anyone can play the ingénue, my dear Catherine. It takes true talent to play a character with a capital 'C.'"

"I guess I didn't think of it that way."

"Besides, you get a fabulous solo. You'll knock 'em dead."

"I will? Yes, I will."

"So, what was it you wanted?"

"Wanted? Oh, um, well, when do rehearsals start?"

"Monday after school."

"Okay, see you then." She dragged Beth out the door.

Stupid Denise. Stupid Gusselman. Stupid musical. Denise and Bill sang "Winter Wonderland" in the Christmas concert. That's probably what gave Gusselman the idea. Denise had the blonde hair, the body. All straight brown hair and dirt brown eyes got anyone was a one-way ticket to second banana. And no Bill.

What was she going to do now? Ma always said never lower yourself for a boy. "If he wants to see you, he'll call. If not, you're just a nuisance." Was she right?

But Ado Annie, the comic relief? "Best female part," Gusselman had said. "Pizzazz," he said. Of course, one *would* need more talent to pull off that role.

Catherine imagined the review of *Oklahoma!* in the school newspaper. "Denise Nelson and Bill Davies were passable as Laurie and Curly, but the real stand-out performance was delivered by Catherine Elbert as Ado Annie. Is Hollywood next for this budding talent?"

"What are you smiling about?" Peter punched his sister in the arm.

"Oh, I was just thinking that your I.Q. is so low, it's subterranean."

"Sub what?"

"Precisely."

Catherine threw her backpack and coat on the kitchen table.

"Hang those up." Clara Elbert was stirring something in a large bowl, from the looks of it, chocolate chip cookie dough.

"Hello, Ma."

"Hi, yourself."

"I have some news. You know this year's musical is *Oklahoma!*, right?"

Nothing registered on Clara's face.

"Well, anyhow, I got the part of Ado Annie. Can you believe it? It's the second female lead. Isn't that awesome?"

Her mother kept stirring.

"Why don't you get an electric mixer? You look like your arm's gonna fall off."

"Tommyrot. What do you think, we're made of money? Besides, if a wooden spoon was good enough for my mother, it's good enough for me."

"Rehearsals start Monday. Every day after school from three to six."

"That's suppertime. I guess one of the boys could pick you

up. I'll hold dinner a bit, but not too long. You'd better be on time."

"Thanks."

Catherine stuck her finger in for a taste as Clara poured the dough into a flat pan. "Out of there, missy, it's raw."

"It's awesome. Hey, we should check out cookie dough ice cream sometime. I bet it's tasty."

"Probably filled with salmonella."

Every Friday night during Lent, the Muskegee County VFW Hall held a fish fry. Not ones to dine out, this was considered a splurge for the Elbert family, an event for which the men would actually put on clean flannel shirts and, on rare occasions, even shave. Tonight, Clara wore her beige dress with doubtfully leather belt and flat beige ballet slipper shoes.

"Wouldn't hurt you to put on a dress every once in a while, missy." She gathered up her purse and coat, clucking disapproval at her daughter's sweater and jeans.

"Let's go! What's takin' so long?" Hank was already at the door. "I'm leavin'. Anyone who cares to join me should get their sorry butts out the door now."

Peter and Russell ran after him, zipping up their coats, visions of dollar beers dancing in their heads.

If I could just stay in here a little longer.

Clara grabbed her daughter's arm. "Nice try. We are going out as a family tonight and that includes you."

"Oops, sorry, Cat. No room here." Russell smirked claiming the station wagon's middle seat. "Looks like you're ridin' in the back."

Next to him, Peter stretched out his legs and arms.

"Catherine! Get in the car." Hank started the engine.

"But..."

"I don't care. Just get in."

It took her three tries to open the back door to the family's 1972 Ford Country Squire station wagon. Ma refused to buy a new car when they only used it for groceries or when all five of them went to church, so they were stuck with this rusted-out shitmobile. Three vehicles plus farm gear were plenty for anyone. Blah. Blah. Blah.

The VFW was booming. The parking lot was almost full when the family arrived. Sadly, it was Frankie Dubrowski Polka Night, and music was blaring through the open doors. "And here's a little one I wrote last year. We debuted it at the Central Wisconsin Polka Festival." A smiling Frankie fingered his accordion. Behind him, the drummer and bass guitarist kept the oompah beat. The trumpet player joined in. Their collective age had to be at least three hundred.

The Elberts made their way to an open table near the back. *Ouch! What the hell?* Two short, round, gray-haired ladies whirled past. The one in the "Polkaholic" shirt elbowed Catherine in the ribs mid-turn.

"What can I get for you?" Stacy Schmidt fumbled for a pen in her apron. "Oh, hey Catherine."

"Stacy? What are you doing here?"

"Trying to make some extra money." She leaned down and whispered, "Once they get blasted, the tips are great." By the look of things already, tonight would be very profitable.

"Mr. and Mrs. Elbert. So nice to see you again."

"Hey there, Stacy. How are your parents?"

"Good, good. What can I get for you?"

"How about four Miller High Lifes and a soda for Catherine?" Most Burkesville residents were not even aware there was a legal drinking age in Wisconsin, but somehow Clara and Hank Elbert were right on top of it. Hank ordered breaded perch, walleye, and bluegill, plus fried cheese curds and potato pancakes for the family.

Peter elbowed Russell. "Check it out."

A girl meandered through the dancers, her blonde hair teased up, forming a mini-plume, much like a chicken. She wore a tight, light pink t-shirt and denim miniskirt, despite the six inches of snow still on the ground from Wednesday's storm.

"Denise Nelson? Are you kidding me?"

Jonesy, who owned the neighboring farm, pulled up a chair and began talking with the parents. The brothers were still ogling Denise. Catherine sat there, pretending to be interested in her soda, hoping the food would come soon so she would have something to do. She set off to find the washrooms.

"Smellbert! Fancy meeting you here." It was Bill Davies.

"What are you doing here?"

"My folks love Frankie Dubrowski." He shrugged. "I had to eat somewhere. This beats my cooking."

Maybe this evening would not be a total waste after all. She attempted a subtle sideways glance down to create the illusion of modesty while actually checking out how his Lee jeans hugged his hips. Clean Lee jeans. She imagined his hands caressing her cheek as he bent his head toward hers...

"Smellbert? Hello? Anybody home?"

"Huh? Oh, sorry. Couldn't hear you. The music's too loud. What did you say?"

"I said the only thing I can cook is scrambled eggs. Not much of a supper."

"Hey, Cat. Dinner's at the table. Who's he?"

"Oh, Bill, this is my brother, Peter. Peter, this is Bill Davies. He sings in choir with me."

Peter gave him the once-over. "Nice. Let's go, Catherine."

"Um, bye, Bill."

"Maybe I'll see you later, Smellbert."

"Choir, huh?"

"Come on, you two, sit down before it gets cold. Catherine, here's a napkin."

A half-full pitcher sat next to Russell. Apparently, they had abandoned ordering only one beer at a time.

"Found our little Cat talkin' to a Tinkerbell choir boy." Peter shoved three fried cheese curds into this mouth.

"He's not gay, you idiot. Not every guy who sings in the choir is gay."

"Sure about that?"

"Shut up. And what if he was? Who cares? God, you're such a moron."

"Simmer down. You're in a public place. Sometimes you kids act like four-year-olds. Now, who was it?"

"Bill Davies."

"The kid from the Quickie Mart?"

"Yeah, Pop."

"Paulie, now he's good people. Just the other day, Jonesy was tellin' me how he ran out of gas a little up the road from him. Paulie helped him push his truck to the station, then gave him a free Coke to boot."

Maybe I'll see you later, Smellbert.

Hank suddenly rose. "May I have the pleasure of this dance, my dear?"

Clara blushed and held out her hand.

"You go, Pops!" Russell and Peter held up their cups in a man salute. "Down the hatch!" In unison, they chugged their beers and slammed the cups down on the table. "Waitress! We seem to have run out."

"Damn if I didn't know it was you two with your hands in the air, waitin' for more beer like two schoolboys." Skip Nagurski slid into one of the empty chairs. "Good evening, Lady Catherine."

"Uh, yeah." She pretended to be interested in the perch.

"You keep eatin' that way, your fine young bottom will be as big as Lake Sikapu."

Catherine left, very aware of Skip's eyes on her behind.

Scanning the crowd hoping to spot Bill, she saw father's head above the crowd and moved sideways for a better look. He was holding Clara's waist, cupping her small hand in his. The only other time Catherine had seen them dance was at Cousin Tess' wedding, but that had to have been at least five years ago. Her mother was not musical. She did not play any instruments or even listen to the radio. Hank whistled or hummed when he worked, but the only time Clara sang was in church.

Catherine spied Bill Davies' curly blond head. *You've got to be kidding.* He was slow-dancing with Denise Nelson, holding her close, stroking her back.

"Why, Catherine, my love. Would you care to take a turn?" Skip Nagurski grabbed her hand, bringing it to his lips.

"Yuck, no way," she said, rubbing the spittle on her leg.

"Your loss." Skip sauntered back toward the Elbert brothers.

Life really did suck.

———— ❧ ————

Catherine woke to thudding sounds and tried to find the clock. *Three in the morning?!?*

"Oh man." Peter was grasping Russell's shirt. "How did we get here?"

"Skip drove. Get off me, you reek. How many beers did you have?"

"You shhhould talk, you assssssshole. Oh man, I'm gonna be sick." Russell began pulling an ashen Peter up the stairs, trying to stay focused on keeping his brother from throwing up all over Great-Grandma Gribbons' heirloom rug. "Get out of the way, Cat!"

"Here it comes." Peter held his mouth and sprinted toward the bathroom.

"Shut up, you idiot. You'll wake Ma and Pop."

The doorknob from their parents' bedroom twisted.

Catherine ran into her room. *Dumb bastards.* She could hear Peter flushing the toilet, and then Ma's voice in the hallway.

"What's going on in here? Peter, you sick?"

The next morning, Catherine bounded downstairs, smugness oozing from every pore. "Good morning, dear brothers. Rough night?" She pulled out a chair and slammed it down hard on the floor.

"Cut it out." Peter lifted his head from the table. A small brown throw-up chunk dangled from his bangs.

"You don't look too good either, Russell, dear."

"Gee, thanks. Ma? Can I have more coffee?"

Clara finished tying her apron and took his cup. "Anyone for breakfast? How 'bout some pancakes and sausage?"

"I think I'm gonna be sick." Peter took off for the bathroom.

"Stupid fool. Okay, who used my cup?"

"It's right here." Clara handed her daughter a black cup, on it was a smiley face with a shotgun hole through its forehead. "Ease up on your brother. He had a hard night."

"Oh, please, Ma."

"Boys like to go drinkin'. There's nothing you can do about it but hope they come home in one piece."

"But you would kill me if I did that."

"Girls are different."

Hank came in, rubbing his arm. "Pop, are you okay?"

"Oh, sure. It's just a big job for one, that's all."

"You did everything yourself?"

"Nah. Don't worry, Cat." Her father sat down at the table. Clara poured him a cup of coffee. "Boys will be boys. Can't help it. Why don't you help your mother with breakfast?"

CHAPTER THREE

"BAD CATHERINE. BAD CATHERINE." PETER'S face was scrunched. Lips pursed, his head bobbed from side to side with each syllable.

Catherine elbowed him in the ribs.

"Ouch, Catherine! Pop!"

"Catherine, cut it out," Hank barked from the driver's seat.

Peter was satisfied, for now. Russell shook his head when his sister turned toward him, but winked at Peter when she turned away. Even when Catherine stayed perfectly still, hands folded on her lap, Peter would begin his mantra, not quitting until the little girl found herself going straight to bed after dinner. The Elberts had a three-strike rule. One warning. One threat. One "up to bed with no dessert."

"Bad Catherine. Bad Catherine."

"Stop it, Peter."

"Ma! Catherine's pushing me!"

"Catherine, cut it out. That's two."

Served her right, the little interloper. They were just fine until she came along, messing up the balance of things. Peter moved in to seal the deal by pulling her hair and then flicking her forehead. "Bad." Flick. "Catherine." Flick. "Bad." Flick. "Catherine." Flick.

His little sister punched him as hard as she could.

"Pop! Catherine punched me!" Peter held his arm for sympathy.

"That's it, little missy. Straight to bed after dinner tonight. And, trust me, I won't forget. You'd better be perfect at Granny's or no supper either."

Peter gave Russell the thumbs up. They could always count on Ma to lower the boom.

One afternoon, Catherine was roaming around the house bored. She had already gone to Kindergarten and ate lunch. Her brothers were still at school, not that it really mattered. They never played what she wanted anyhow. Whenever Catherine asked them to play house, Russell and Peter laughed, saying they would never play a stupid girl game.

"Hey! I have an idea. Catherine, you can be the maid and clean our rooms for real if you want to play house so much. Now that sounds like fun." Russell strutted about, apparently the wittiest boy on earth.

Catherine looked around upstairs. Ma was outside somewhere, probably killing a chicken for tonight's dinner. She skipped into her parents' room, immediately drawn to the photograph on Clara's dresser. Her father was so handsome in his black suit and tie. A small carnation was affixed to his lapel, and his chin pointed slightly down toward Clara, who was quite a bit shorter than he. She stared straight at the camera, wearing an unadorned satin dress. A tulle veil sprouted out of her head, and she carried a bouquet of carnations and baby's breath. Catherine could not tell what color the flowers were since the photo was black and white. She asked her mother once, but Clara didn't remember.

Catherine picked up a silver-plated mirror and stuck her tongue out at her reflection. Why did tongues have those white bumps on them? Did they make food taste better? She grabbed the hairbrush and dove onto the bed, pulling out her ponytail's rubber band mid-air. Catherine turned over the brush. The silver was shiny and had little scroll decorations on it.

She looked at the ugly cross hanging over the doorway, the one Aunt Ida made out of white sea shells. Catherine knew she could make a prettier one, or at least a more colorful one, but then maybe it wouldn't match Ma and Pop's room. The walls were white. The two scraps of carpeting on either side of the bed were white. The lace that lined the tops of both parents' dressers was white. The two "doilies," as her mother called them, which protected the tops of the nightstands— from what Catherine did not know—were white. Only the patchwork quilt was not, but it had faded so much, it was now the palest of blues and pinks, conforming over time to the sterility surrounding it.

Catherine tied her ponytail back up and jumped off the bed. She smoothed the covers from her indentation and took any straight brown hairs out of the brush, tucking them in her pocket. She poked her head out the doorway. Still no sign of Clara. She walked down the hall.

The boys' door was ajar, so Catherine peeked inside. She proceeded cautiously, hopping over the G.I. Joes and tanks left on the floor from yesterday's war. *Ouch.* She pulled off the green Plastic Army Man stuck on her foot. Russell's Hot Wheels were lined up in order of coolness (his words) on his shelves, next to his *Speed Racer* poster. Catherine scanned the room. There it was, way up on the shelf across from Russell's cars—Peter's teddy bear, worn and discolored, with one eye popped off. Hank made Peter retire the bear the day after his seventh birthday. "Stuffed animals are for babies. No son of mine is goin' to play with sissy stuff."

His father wanted to throw the thing away, but Peter had cried so hard, he shook for an entire hour. The agreement was he could keep it, as long as it stayed on the shelf. What Hank did not know was that every night after Peter put his pajamas on, and while Russell brushed his teeth in the bathroom, Peter cuddled Huck and whispered his innermost secrets into the bear's left ear. Catherine knew this because one night she got up for a potty run and walked into the boys' room by mistake.

"Get out, Catherine!" Peter screamed and threw the bear at the wall, knocking two Lego towers he had just built off with a crash.

Clara sprinted upstairs. "What's going on?"

"Catherine scared me," Peter whined, tears pouring down his face.

"What are you doing out of bed, little missy?"

"I had to go potty."

"How did you get in here?"

"Wrong door. I didn't mean to."

"Go to the washroom and then get back to bed."

"Yes, ma'am."

"Come here, baby!" Peter ran into Clara's outstretched arms. "It'll be okay. Come on now, let's clean up this mess."

The door slammed on the little girl in the yellow-and-orange polka dot pajamas.

Bad Catherine. Bad Catherine.

Her brother had started again yesterday at the grocery store, and if there was anything her mother could not stand, it was getting hassled at the Piggly Wiggly. She rubbed her still-sore bottom. No chocolate layer cake and a visit with "the board."

When Russell was a toddler, Clara hung a seven-by-eleven-inch cutting board on the mudroom wall, close enough for easy access from the kitchen, but not prominently displayed, in case anyone might get the wrong impression that she and Hank were beaters. It was a reminder, that was all.

Bad Catherine. Bad Catherine.

She looked up at the shelf. How she hated that stupid bear! He was dressed in denim overalls and a red-and-white checked shirt; a little cowboy hat sat on his oversized head. His tag had read "Theodore" when Granny gave it to him, but Peter insisted on calling him Hucklebeary, Huck for short, after Clara read him Mark Twain as a bedtime story.

Bad Catherine. Bad Catherine.

Catherine moved the desk chair over near the shelves and stretched. *A little more.* She spied two books. Standing on her tip-toes, right atop *The Adventures of Tom Sawyer*, Catherine grabbed the hem of Huck's pant leg and pulled. She got down and looked out the window. Ma was weeding the garden patch. All she had to do was get past her.

Catherine put the chair and books back and shut the door, careful to leave everything how she found it. She tucked Huck under the very full prairie-style dress she received for her birthday last year and ran downstairs as fast as she could. The boys would be home soon. She scooted out the back door toward the pig sty.

———⌇⫶⟆⟆⫶———

Peter shot past Hank. "Russell!" he screamed. "I'm gonna kill you."

"I didn't do anythin'." The muffled response came from behind the bathroom door.

Peter began banging. "Where is he? I'm gonna beat the livin' crap out of you."

"Hey, hey." Hank grabbed Peter's hands. "Catherine's tryin' to sleep."

"I don't care. He took Huck, and I want him back."

"Huck who? What? The bear?"

A faint "I did not" came from the bathroom.

"He's lyin', Pop. Who else could have done it? Catherine's not big enough."

"Finish up, Russell, and get out here." Hank turned to

Peter. "Are you sure you didn't lose it? You aren't even supposed to be playin' with the damn thing."

A small twinge of guilt crept across Peter's face.

"You have been, haven't you?"

Peter looked at the floor.

"Tell me, boy. There's no sense in lyin'. I can see it all over your face."

"Well, um, just to say goodnight, only five minutes tops, I swear. I'm sorry."

Russell emerged discombobulated. "I didn't do it."

"You had to. Huck didn't walk out of our room."

"Pops, I swear." Russell held his hand over his heart and stared directly into his father's eyes. "I swear on a stack of bibles."

"You'd better not be lyin' to me, son."

"Then where's Huck?" Peter was sweating now.

The three searched the boys' room, but came up empty.

"Russell Adam Elbert. Peter James Elbert. Get down here now!"

The boys ran down the stairs, heeding their mother's call.

Clara held up a bucket.

"Oh my God." Tears formed in Peter's eyes.

Huck sat inside, covered in straw and pig excrement. An unbelievably horrendous stench wafted through the air. "I will ask you not to use the Lord's name in vain, Peter Elbert. Now, what in the Sam Hill is this doing in the pig sty?"

Russell's slightest of smirks did not go unnoticed and incriminated him despite his protestations.

"I'll get you for this, Russell."

"But, I didn't!"

"Stop your lyin'." Hank pulled out his belt.

Clara guided a sobbing Peter up the stairs.

From her bedroom, safely tucked under the covers, Catherine Elbert smiled and fell asleep.

CHAPTER FOUR

*A*MERICAN HISTORY. PAGE 156. "THE Suffragists." Why hadn't any of their ideas reached Burkesville? Guys could do whatever they wanted. Girls? Be good and maybe you will snag a husband. Such bullshit.

"Catherine! Come down here!"

Her parents sat on the living room sofa, arms folded across their chests. A video box lay on the coffee table, bearing the unmistakable smiling faces of Shirley Jones and Gordon MacRae.

"Oh, hey! You rented *Oklahoma!* Isn't it great?"

"Sit down." He did not look happy. "Your role is that Annie girl?"

"Yes, Ado Annie."

"I see."

Clara glared, fingering the plain silver cross around her neck.

"Your mother and I talked it over. You are not allowed to be in that play."

"What?"

"That's no proper character for a young girl to play. 'I'm just a girl who cain't say no'? The girl's a hussy. I won't allow my daughter to play a hussy."

"Hussy? What are we in 1955?"

"Catherine Elbert! How dare you talk to your father that way!"

"I don't believe this."

"Our minds are made up. You go tell that Gusselman you can't take the part. You tell him on Monday."

"I will not."

Hank would not be challenged. "You will, or I'll march into that school of yours and tell him myself."

"Are you telling me Peter and Russell can come home stinking drunk and that's okay, but I can't play a character because she might not be proper? No one in their right minds would think Annie is a slut. No one. She's just comic relief, that's all."

"You shut your mouth, young lady. You've said enough." Clara's eyes glistened. The boys would have never dared to talk to them this way.

"Oh no, Mother, I'm just getting started."

Hank rose. Father and daughter stood, face to face, inches apart. "Listen to me. I said the decision has been made."

"By people who can't even understand a..."

Slap! Hank's hand met Catherine's face with such force, the red outlines of his fingers were visible on her cheek.

"I hate you!"

"Get back here, missy."

"Let her go, Clara."

"You can starve for all I care." Clara's voice boomed up the stairway.

Catherine had cried for three hours straight, not bothering to go down for dinner. Her cheek was sore, though the redness had subsided slightly. She blared *The Wall* through her headphones, attempting to block out the sounds of the Neanderthal brothers downstairs. She was the one with the "A" grade point average, not that she tried or anything, it just sort of happened. They had barely graduated. Yet, she was completely screwed while they high-fived each other with each Bucks basket.

Ado Annie was a character. That was all. The stifling stupidity! The people of Burkesville were "good, honest, God-fearin' people." How many times had Father Wilhelm spouted that out during Sunday Mass, where most of the town sat, sanctimonious and smug, congratulating themselves on what pious lives they lead, all the while blanketing their hypocrisy in "traditional values?"

Yes, her parents would be among them this week, sitting in St. Agatha's mid-section—not too far up as to be pretentious, not too far back to appear unworthy—convinced they had saved their daughter from moral decline. Among Morris family, two rows up, whose patriarch, Charlie, tried to feel Beth up in his car when he drove her home from babysitting his children. Among Molly Smith, a row behind and to the right, known to come onto any man within striking distance after knocking down a few drinks at He's Not Here Tavern. "Let's just say it was quite a night." Jonesy had related to Hank, shit-eating grin on his face.

Charlie Morris and Molly Smith sat in their pews, thinking all they had to do was say they were sorry and God would forgive them. But Hank and Clara Elbert would never seek forgiveness for robbing their daughter of the one thing she truly cared about. And there would be no absolution. Any doubt of her leaving Burkesville was erased by Hank's own hand.

———⁓⁓———

"I can't believe it." Beth picked up her backpack and hit her head on the seat in front of her. "How are you going to tell Gusselman? He's going have a cow."

"All I know is I'm outta here." Bus 79 trudged through the snow down Route 36 toward Burkesville High School. A hat whizzed by Catherine's head, flung from the back of the bus somewhere.

"How? Graduation isn't until June. Can't go anywhere till you get that little piece of paper."

"I thought about it all weekend. I'm going to pick a college far away, and they'll have to pay for it."

The bus pulled up in front of school. "Well, another day in the shiter." Catherine set off for Guidance Counselor Leary's office.

———&———

"Look, it's the missy, coming down from on high to grace us with her presence. Can you believe it, Hank?" It was the first time in two days Catherine had joined her family for dinner, existing instead on a few bags of sour cream and onion potato chips and two grape sodas from the vending machines at school.

"What do you have there?" Hank gestured toward the small bundle his daughter had placed next to her plate.

"College brochures. I figure I'd better make a decision before I miss the application deadlines."

"Let me see here. Stanford. The University of Illinois. NYU. This is quite an assortment. You think you got the grades to get into these?"

"Mr. Leary thinks so. I met with him this morning. And these are a few others. Smaller schools. I have to figure out where I would feel comfortable. Maybe even the University of Wisconsin-Madison to stay more local."

"How do you think we can afford these?"

"Well, there are scholarships."

Peter reached over his sister. "Gimme the meatloaf."

"You're not smart enough for a full ride, that's for sure." Clara passed Russell the biscuits.

Disregarding the comment, Catherine turned back toward her father. "So what do you think, Pop?"

"I guess there has been some sort of misunderstandin'. When I said you could stay here or go to college, I meant college 'round here, not traipsin' all over the country."

"But, everyone else is..."

"God, you ungrateful child. I never even had the chance."

"Clara, please. Cat, Muskegee County is all we can afford."

Not hearing anything else, Catherine left the table.

"Where are you going? You haven't even eaten anything. You're going waste away. Do you have that anorexia or whatever it's called? Honestly, I don't understand that girl." Clara shook her head.

Each stair felt like another rock in Virginia Woolf's coat. The only thing Muskegee County Community College was known for was its agriculture major.

———— 𝒰\\𝒮 ————

Spring came, and with it, preparations for the planting season. Not quite warm enough to seed the oats, Hank had begun plotting which crops would be placed where after the fields were rototilled. Peter and Russell were fixing the silo's siding. The usual miscellaneous winter maintenance projects were almost done.

Since Burkesville high school was so damn small, the choir doubled as extras in the musical, so Catherine was forced to sing music from *Oklahoma!* every day during fifth period, whether or not she was allowed to be in the production. As if this were not torture enough, she also had to endure Mr. Gusselman's looks of exasperation each time her pizzazz-free replacement messed up. Opening night was only a week away, and Kit Matthews still could not remember it was "cain't" instead of "can't."

"Sweet Jesus, Miss Matthews. We've been doing this for eight weeks," he spat, glaring at Catherine over the piano. "Now, start again. One, two, three, four."

She watched from the wings as Kit fumbled through what was to be Catherine's moment of triumph. Bill presented his co-star with an enormous bouquet of red roses, kissed her hand, then hoisted it up as together they received a standing ovation.

"Hey, sweetie. You ready for pizza?"

"Sure, Fred, just give me a second." Beth slipped off the headset and laid it next to her script on the podium. "Cat, want to come?"

"No thanks. You go celebrate. You deserve it. Great job, guys."

"Don't forget to lock up then. Night."

The emergency lights and exit signs cast a surreal, greenish glow over the auditorium. Why had she come here tonight? Was she some kind of masochist? Her stomach felt raw. No matter how many fingernails she had chewed off, Catherine had to be a part of the musical, even if only from backstage.

Her feet dangled as she ran her fingers across the wooden stage, breathing in the still-lingering smells of pancake makeup, the dancers' sweat, a faint trace of roses. God, how she loved this auditorium! Even with its chairs so old, springs jammed into your butt in Row D. Even with its frayed and faded red velvet curtains. Even with its mediocre acoustics.

None of that mattered during a performance, waiting in the wings, sure she would forget her first line of dialogue.

One step on that stage and there were no more looks of Clara's disdain. No orders from her father. No brothers to set her up. The lights erased all of that, and she was free. She controlled her destiny. She commanded the spotlight.

Taking one last deep breath, Catherine rose and blended in with the darkness.

CHAPTER FIVE

"*I*'M DOING IT."
      "Okay. You go on now."
      "I really am."
"Sure you are."
"I'm leaving."
"Where are you going to go?"
"To Granny's house."
"You're going to walk all the way to Granny's house?"
"Yup."
"Luggin' that suitcase?"
"It's not that heavy."
"All right, then."
"Um, yeah, okay...Bye, Ma."

Seven-year-old Catherine Elbert trudged down the gravel road, pulling her magenta and green flowered suitcase that held her pajamas, Mrs. Beasley doll, toothbrush, and a change of clothes. Her tummy rumbled. She should have waited until after dinner to run away. In her haste, she forgot to pack something to eat.

Catherine would have to cross the tracks to get to Granny's, but she was scared of them. Betsy's cousin got hit by a train last year and was in the hospital for a long time. Catherine didn't know how long exactly, only that it was really long, like a week or something.

She kept walking. Peter had said Ma and Pop loved boys

better than girls. That he and Russell were more useful, smarter, and obviously more fun. When Catherine brought up that Ma was a girl, Peter only shook his head. She really didn't know anything, did she? Grown-ups didn't count.

A hoot from a nearby barn owl gave Catherine a start. She would never make it to Granny's before dark. She sat on her suitcase to rest. Why hadn't anyone come for her? She had to have been walking for at least six hours. Peter must be right.

Well, they would all be sorry when they stumbled upon her mangled, bloody body on the side of the road. Jimmy Jones was talking yesterday about a cougar he heard growling underneath his window, the next farm over.

Maybe she was adopted. That would explain a lot. Peter had Ma's emerald green eyes. Pop and Russell had the same round-shaped faces. She did not look like either parent.

Catherine shivered. It sure was getting chilly out here. She should have packed a jacket. The crickets were chirping. Fireflies took flight. The sun's forehead barely peaked over the horizon. She couldn't go home now. It would be giving in. Something tickled her. Catherine looked down and screamed. A huge spider was taking his after-dinner stroll on her arm. She flicked it off and sprinted toward the house.

All of Burkesville was on "Prom Watch." Who was pairing up with whom? What were the girls going to wear? How did the boys pop the question? The adults probably organized a pool, like for the NCAA Basketball Tournament, wagering on which couples would stay together afterward. What else did they have to do? They were already stuck with their spouses, why not root on the youngins and watch them screw up their lives?

Maybe the "Prom Madness" winners could receive a free wedding at St. Agatha's and a reception at Wally's Place?

Perhaps Paulie would throw in a year's worth of free gas for the newlyweds? So far, Denise and Bill were the front-runners, followed closely by Beth and Fred. The long shots were Rose Slattery and Mike Wurhauser, an unlikely pairing who had found a common interest in fishing, of all things.

Big surprise, no one had asked Catherine to the prom, a fact the brothers never failed to exploit every time she came within ten feet of them.

"What color's your prom dress, Cat? Oh, that's right. You're not goin'."

"Hey, Cat! Skip Nagurski wants to know if you'll be needin' his services come prom night. He's willin' to escort you for a small fee."

Since Bill and Denise were now musical sweethearts, there was no other male Catherine could imagine spending even an hour with, much less an entire evening. Beth had tried to fix her up with Fred's friend, Brian Reichmann, but as it turned out Brian had a severe allergic reaction to intelligent females.

Catherine's attempt at dating a Burkesville boy last year had ended in a knock-down, drag-out fight during dress rehearsals for *Bye Bye Birdie* because of ridiculous jealousy over her dance partner's hand placement. The entire cast launched into a rousing "Bye Bye Bauer," as the boy stomped out of the auditorium.

No, Catherine was alone in her room on prom night, plotting her escape. At the top of a piece of notebook paper, she wrote "Burkesville Exit Plan." Phase One: never work on the farm again. Begin dropping hints to the parents about the enormous cost of college books and gasoline. Once they were sufficiently freaked out, their benevolent daughter would "volunteer" to get a summer job outside the farm and receive a real paycheck versus working for Hank, who automatically deposited her wages directly into her college fund.

She needed to be able to control her own finances. That was of utmost importance. The parents would not be able to object, seeing as she would be paying for all miscellaneous college expenses. Unfortunately, there was no other alternative but to attend Muskegee Community College, at least for a while, which had to be better than hanging around here all day.

Clunk!

What the heck was that? Probably the morons downstairs. Catherine started filling out the Muskegee County application. Grade point average? Class rank? What did it matter? Muskegee never rejected anyone.

Clunk again.

A robin sat on a white birch tree branch. It looked straight into her eyes, then proceeded to shit, sending stream upon stream dripping down her window.

Last night's rain had flushed out unsuspecting worms from their soil abodes. They lay strewn about the sidewalk in front of Burkesville High School, a blackbird's breakfast buffet, a slimy pedestrian minefield. Why did it smell like fish? There was no lake within ten miles, yet the unpleasant odor prevailed, a reminder of why she had avoided summer road trips to Lake Sikapu since age thirteen. Well, that and the absolute boredom that was fishing.

Hank loved it, but none of his family did. Eventually, he gave up on the idea, probably because the three kids complained so much, they scared the fish away. In good years, he and Jonesy went up north to Rhinelander, coming home with full beards and smelling worse than the cows, but Clara did not mind as long as her husband brought back a cooler full of blue gills or perch, plenty for every Friday during Lent and then some.

Homeroom. Same announcements. Graduation robes. Prom tickets still left. "The following students please report to Principal Schmidt's office immediately. Albert Schneider. Mary Frankenvort. Catherine Elbert."

———

Hank glanced over the letter.

"Number three in your class? That's wonderful."

Even Mr. Gusselman had offered congratulations, uttering his first words to her since "What the hell are you talking about? You have to play Ado Annie! Are you *$#&!*$ kidding me?"

Hank raised his glass of milk and toasted, "To Catherine. I'm proud of ya."

Russell scoffed, "Oh, please."

"Gimme a break," Peter uttered through a mouthful of corn.

"Listen, compared to you two, she's Albert Einstein."

The brothers mimed gagging and turned their attentions back toward the meal.

Only Ma said nothing.

———

Clara swept with such intensity, no dust bunny stood a chance. "Ridiculous girl."

"Sweetie, it wouldn't hurt you to compliment Cat every once in a while."

"Why? Nobody bothered to ever give me any flowery words. I did what was asked of me because that's what a person's supposed to do."

"But she's not you, and, no offense, you weren't third in our class. You seemed more interested in other things, handsome things." He kissed her ear.

She swatted him. "Get out of there. I have a brain, too, you know."

"Of course you do. I only said…"

"You only said I was more interested in you than in my studies. Here, hold this for me, will ya?" Clara jammed kitchen debris into the dust pan.

Hank straightened up and emptied the contents into the trash. "I think Cat would like to hear you say it."

"Go call the boys. It's almost time for lunch."

———*U\S*———

It had stopped hurting so much awhile ago. Catherine assumed at one time her mother must have exhibited the usual maternal tendencies—blowing raspberries on her baby's soft, squishy tummy, crying with joy when she finally gave birth to a girl—but those propensities were now buried deep under Clara Elbert's fifty-one-year-old crust and would never be excavated.

Maybe people have limitations on how much they can love, and her mother's was used up before Catherine was born. Clara's heart was only so big, after all. Perhaps adding another person would have sent it into defibrillation. But this class rank thing, surely even Clara Elbert would know it was pretty cool, something that had never been done before in their family. Catherine wasn't asking for much. Just a hint of pride. A smile, even. Anything to acknowledge her as a valuable human being. Anything to replace the daily looks of scorn.

Did she think Catherine did not notice the pats on the shoulders she gave to Russell? Or the tiny laughs she and Peter shared? It was like the four of them were in on some private joke and no one cared enough to let Catherine in on it.

———*U\S*———

After some time, the parents actually agreed to Catherine finding outside employment for the summer. Phase One was put in action. Maybe she would be able to save enough money for books, gas, clothes, and the escape fund. If not, she planned on continuing to work throughout the school year, a small fact omitted from her conversations with Hank and Clara.

Beth had picked up a part-time job at Walgreen's, the only national chain in Burkesville. McDonald's was technically in Sleepy Hollow, just across Route 36, so it did not count. Yippee, Beth and Fred had won "Prom Madness," paying 20:1 odds to those who bet on them at Padowski's. Fred and his family were hard at work building the couple's future home on the northwest corner of the Schmidt property. After the wedding, he planned on farming and making furniture on the side for extra money.

Catherine wasn't sure how to feel when Beth shared her "good news" and asked her best friend to be "Maid of Honor," a title Catherine personally detested. Why is the male counterpart called "Best Man," which implies elevated status, while the female gets stuck with "Maid of Honor?" What, like Milk Maid of Honor? Meter Maid of Honor? Old Maid with No Honor?

To Beth's face, Catherine oozed happiness and joy, proclaiming that Beth had landed the best guy in all of Burkesville, which was true. Inside, she kicked herself for making the match. Did she unwittingly doom Beth? Her friend would be stuck here now, growing into adulthood the way their parents had, isolated from the world outside. But Beth seemed happy. To each his own, Hank always said, unless, of course, he was talking about his only daughter.

Beth's mom had heard that Victorian bed and breakfast on the route from school to Elbert Farm was in urgent need of help to ready the place for the grand opening three weeks from now, so Catherine gave them a call.

Her meeting was with Mrs. Mitchell—Kendra, please,

she had said on the phone—on Friday at four o'clock. After much begging, pleading, and overall groveling, she was able to obtain use of the godforsaken shitmobile, instead of having Peter or Russell drive her. This was a surprising victory, seeing as it interfered with the brothers' liquid appetizers before the Friday Night Quartersfest at Skip Nagurski's. But even Clara had to concede a job interview trumped a pre-party party. The boys would have to settle with only Quartersfest, poor babies.

When Catherine pulled up, two Joe Ritter and Sons Landscaping vans were blocking the Mitchell House's driveway. Men in gray jumpsuits swarmed, erecting trellises and arbors, planting roses and ivies on one side, and Lilies of the Valley and hostas in the shade of two enormous elm trees. Another crew assembled a children's playground atop black rubber mats. This was much different from the playground they had all grown up with at James A. Garfield Grade School. Every time Catherine took the jump off the middle swing too wide, she landed hard, right in the asphalt, tiny shards of gravel burying themselves into her wounded knee. That place was cursed. Who would name a school after a man who was assassinated after serving only six months as president of the United States?

A woman descended the Victorian's front steps. "You must be Catherine. Watch yourself over there. It's a little treacherous." Kendra Mitchell looked to be about thirty-ish, mid-thirties at the oldest. Most of her honey-blonde hair was pulled back into a ponytail, a renegade strand curving over one hazel eye.

"It's nice to meet you, Mrs. Mitchell. I've watched your renovations during my bus rides to and from school. It looks beautiful."

"Why, thank you." Kendra sighed. "It's been crazy. Poor Maddie. Oh, that's my daughter. She's around here somewhere.

She hasn't had a day without construction noise since we've moved here. Anyhow, why don't you come in?"

The three-story foyer was awash with light courtesy of a stained glass skylight. "Is that a Tiffany?" Paying attention in Miss Keller's class had finally paid off.

Kendra nodded. "Good eye. It's pretty awesome, isn't it? I think that's what sold us on the house."

Yeah, that and pretty much *everything*. A hand-carved banister floated upward to greet the skylight. There was a built-in window seat on the second-floor landing, where Catherine could only imagine spending countless hours tucked in, reading. This house was every bit as magnificent as the Pabst Mansion, maybe even better.

"Let me take you on a tour, and then we can sit down and discuss the job." Kendra ushered her into the formal living room that held a fireplace with cherry mantle and black granite inlay. Next was the dining room, featuring mahogany wainscoting and a lovely chandelier—Tiffany, of course. Must have been a twofer sale that day.

The kitchen was half-completed, newly gutted and updated to make it functional in this century. Cherry cabinets sat awaiting their countertops and hosted large gaps that eventually would hold the refrigerator/freezer, stove, microwave, and double ovens. The octagonal breakfast nook had stained-glass transoms atop each full-length window, which repeated the skylight's design of green ivy leaves with a red rose in the center.

Intricate black wrought ironwork held up the conservatory's glass walls, which housed only two mangy plants that also looked tired of the construction. "We will get to this when we can. What can I say? Someday it will be fabulous, and we will serve tea in here." Kendra laughed. "On to the next level."

The second floor held five bedrooms, all updated to

include their own bathrooms. Two were already furnished, the family's presumably, while the other three had the basics in place—bed, chest of drawers, side tables, mirrors—and were awaiting their final touches.

They climbed the stairs to the third floor. "It's a little smelly up here. The crew is putting on the last coat of paint. This is where we would like to hold weddings or parties someday."

Two sets of French doors opened up to reveal a magnificent ballroom. Catherine imagined gentlemen with handlebar mustaches and mutton-chop sideburns escorting women in fine silk ball gowns, then waltzing to the latest Strauss melody, whirls of sapphire, emerald, and scarlet gliding across the black and white marble floor.

"Let's head down to the dining room." The owner's words startled her back into the present.

"Have a seat. Well now." Kendra Mitchell folded her hands. "I read about you in *The Burkesville Gazette*. Number three, right? Congratulations. That's quite an achievement."

Not really. You're obviously new to the area.

"Where will you be going to college? I presume you're looking only for summer work?"

The idea of telling Mrs. Kendra Mitchell she would be attending Muskegee County Community College while sitting on a real Chippendale chair under a Tiffany chandelier was not appealing. Catherine silently cursed her upbringing and searched for a more acceptable answer. Failing, the response would have to be the truth, God help her. She winced and sputtered, "Muskegee County," then stared at the table.

"What? Well."

"It's all my parents can afford."

"I see. So why is it you want to work here?"

"To be honest, I've always been kind of fascinated by your house. I can do anything you need. Housekeeping, serving, answering phones."

Kendra sat back, gazing directly into the girl's eyes.

Catherine got nervous and began spewing. "Please, I can't work another day on my family's farm. I know how to bake. I can clean. I'll even mow your lawn. Whatever you need."

"How about this? We'll try you out on housekeeping, but the job might change from day to day, depending what we need. Adam, my husband, and I have never owned a bed and breakfast before. We are making this up as we go along, even though Adam did just finish his master's in hotel and restaurant management before he quit the bank. I told him, my God, you'd better study this industry before we make a move like this. Anyhow, what if we try you out on weekends until school gets out, then we'll add more hours during the week? Can you start tomorrow? How's eight o'clock sound?"

Early. "That will be great. Thank you very much, Mrs. Mitchell."

"Kendra, please."

"Hey, Hank, did ya hear? The missy's going be a housekeeper over at that bed and breakfast. Can't remember how to keep her room clean, yet she'll high-tail it over to the mansion to scrub their toilets."

Clara, Russell, and Peter got a good laugh out of that one. Only Hank seemed not to enjoy the humor. "I wish you were workin' here with us, Cat."

"I'm sorry, Pop. I need to save up as much money as possible for school. College textbooks are expensive."

Catherine's stupid gold tassel kept biffing her cheek from the breeze. Albert Schneider droned on about "a time for new opportunities" and "our future lies before us" in his valedictory address. Then Mary Frankenfurter, Frankenstein, Frankenwhatever delivered her salutatorian remarks. At least all "number three" had to do was show up and tack a Top Ten pin to her graduation gown, like being first runner-up in the Miss America pageant without having to fake a smile, all the while knowing you would much rather pluck the winner's eyes out and eat them on toast.

Mr. Gusselman waved his hand, a cue for the seniors to join the rest for the ceremonial song. The choir choked out "The Halls of Ivy," which, of course, would have been more appropriate in England, where they actually had ivy-covered walls, but whatever, as if anything made sense in Burkesville.

Finally, the diplomas were handed out, and mortarboards went flying, except for a few kids who wanted to keep their tassels with the honors society charm as evidence they really were intelligent at one point in their lives in case they ever developed Alzheimer's or had teenagers or something.

"Congratulations, Cat. We're proud of you." A pat on the back from Hank. Clara flung a bouquet of pale pink carnations sprinkled with baby's breath at her daughter.

"We did it!" Beth and Catherine hugged.

"How 'bout a picture, ladies? Why don't you pose right there?" Russell took the photo, while Peter made his way toward a dumped-after-prom Rose Slattery.

There they stood, Beth, red-faced and teary-eyed, barely visible over the enormous bouquet of roses from her parents, and Catherine, sporting something no one in her family had seen for a very long time—a genuine smile.

CHAPTER SIX

Burkesville, Wisconsin
Two Years Later

THE REFLECTION IN THE MIRROR made Catherine shudder. Kendra was into the preppie look and insisted all Mitchell House employees wear kelly green polo shirts and khakis.

"But they make my butt look huge!"

"Don't be silly, Catherine. You couldn't look fat if you tried."

"As long as the shirt won't have one of those alligators on it."

"Actually, it'll be the Mitchell House logo instead. Oh, and could you buy some matching socks and white Keds? Don't worry, I'll give you a check for uniform expenses tomorrow."

Kendra Mitchell was nice that way, slipping her a few extra dollars here and there. She said it was for her excellent performance, but Catherine suspected Kendra thought her husband's offer of two hundred dollars a week was a bit low.

"Wish you'd put the same time into your chores here as you do at that bed and breakfast," Clara groused. "Your dad could use more help."

"That's what Russell and Peter are for. I'm making money for college, remember?"

Catherine plopped on the bed and kicked off her shoes.

Her feet ached. It had been a long day. Business was starting to pick up, and two of the suites were booked this weekend. Tony and Gina Belmonti from Chicago were celebrating their first wedding anniversary, and an elderly couple from Rhinelander, Patrick and Greta Hagen, were attending their granddaughter's wedding in Sleepy Hollow. Twice as many beds to change, linens to wash, bathrooms to clean, muffins to bake. The work was compounded by having to pre-empt housekeeping duties for the Keats suite until the shouts of "Ah, ah, ah, OH YEAH!" ceased. Poor Kendra had to keep Maddie occupied outdoors for almost the entire day, creating projects and games until the lovers left, exhausted, for dinner.

Adam Mitchell, however, only heard the sweet sound of cash register bells ringing in his head. This was the first weekend the Mitchell House would make a profit, and the only time Catherine had ever seen Mr. Mitchell jovial. Usually, he darted around the mansion, twisting his right eyebrow between stubby fingers. But today, he managed to relax ever so slightly, one less crinkle creasing his brow.

Catherine did not feel comfortable calling him "Adam," seeing as he was so much older, older than Kendra, too. How did those two ever get together? Of course, it was a good thing they did, otherwise little Maddie would not exist. Maddie Mitchell was a great kid. Sometimes she and Catherine played on the swings during a break. Catherine had always wanted a little sister, especially when stuck playing tackle football with Russell and Peter, who seemed to forget she was not the ball.

Catherine fluffed up a pillow, leaned against the wall, and turned on her very own, twelve-inch color television, the one luxury purchased with a combination of Mitchell House earnings and some graduation money from Aunt Ida. Here Catherine would sit, blissfully alone, away from the morons battling for television viewer supremacy downstairs, a fight she lost one hundred percent of the time.

Flipping through the stations, she settled on a PBS travelogue. Red brick buildings held funky shops and restaurants. Lobsters streamed from fishermen's giant nets. A lighthouse majestically stood, its pristine white with a trace of black a stark contrast to the jagged rocks and foamy surf below. The beckoning light. The voracity of the ocean.

This would be her escape.

———————⁓⁓⁓———————

"Hey, Josh. What do you know about Portland, Maine?"

Josh Prescott straightened up and wiped away a dirt smudge from the tip of his nose with a gloved hand. Adam had hired him as a groundskeeper, an extra pair of hands, and overall Mr. Fix It. He was somewhere in his twenties and from Sleepy Hollow, which immediately elevated his status in Catherine's eyes. That and he had a brain, something she had not yet experienced with certain other males of his age. Before the Mitchell House had any guests, which was most of the summer, she and Josh had worked on miscellaneous projects—seasonal gardening, painting the gazebo, and organizing the kitchen.

"Portland? Let's see." Josh moved a flat of yellow chrysanthemums from the bench to the picnic table and sat down. "Not much."

Catherine slid next to him. "Have you ever been there?"

"Nope. We went to Boston once on a family road trip, but never made it up to Maine. Why?"

"I saw it on a show last night. The ocean looked so amazing."

"It's like you're at the end of the world, but you know you're really not. Little different from Lake Sikapu, huh?"

"No kidding."

"Good day, Catherine, Josh." Adam Mitchell was partaking in his morning ritual. After breakfast, he motored around the property, checking if the roses were growing, if the pond was free of algae, if the playground equipment was clean. Then he would walk out to the mailbox and face the mansion, hands on his hips, and survey his land with all the manly gusto he could muster.

"Excuse me, Lord of the Manor? You have a phone call. Hi, kids. Josh, the flower bed looks great. Catherine, would you come in with me? I'd like to go over this month's schedule."

"Sure, Kendra." Cat sprang from the bench. "Later, Josh."

"Coffee?"

"No, thanks."

Kendra poured herself a cup and joined Catherine at the table. "Listen, I know school starts next week. I'm not sure how many hours you are taking, but would it be possible to stay on with us? The Shelley suite is almost ready, and I've got four weekends booked up starting in mid-September. We're completely packed during Johansen's Pumpkinfest or whatever it's called. Then I was thinking of maybe expanding the business to include Christmas parties in the ballroom. What do you think?"

"Wow, Kendra. Ambitious."

"I can't do it without you and Josh. You're my dynamic duo. The only problem is that most of the work would be on the weekends." She grimaced, knowing weekends were sacred for college students.

"That's no problem." The more time spent here, the more time away from the farm. Besides, there were so many crappy jobs around Burkesville, being surrounded by the luxury of the Mitchell House was a great gig.

"Wonderful. Okay, here are my plans for the ballroom."

"Maine? While you're dreamin', why not go somewhere warm, like Hawaii? Hey! How 'bout Tahiti?" Russell laughed and reached for the TV remote.

"Give me that. I'm trying to talk to all of you."

"How 'bout some place farther, like New Zealand? Can I have her room? I'm sick of this butt-hole." Peter biffed his brother.

"Hush. Cat, what on earth would make you want to move to Maine?"

Take a deep breath. Do not get emotional. Present a rational, logical case. "Well, Pop, I believe it is time for me to get out and see the world. Many of my classmates have moved out."

"Yeah, to Sleepy Hollow or Milwaukee or somethin', not to Maine."

Catherine shot Russell a look. Where was a poison dart when you needed one?

"Where will you stay?"

"I'm not sure, Pop. I'll figure it out when I get there. Don't worry."

"No Elbert has ever..."

"You're right, Ma. I want to be the first."

"You'll come crawling back, mark my words. Won't she, boys?"

"Won't last a week."

"Shut up, Peter. As if you've ever done anything better than Quartersfest." *Calm. Rational. Non-emotional.*

"At least your brother knows his place. Knows his duty."

"Duty? What duty?"

"To his family and this farm. Why do you think we even sent you to college in the first place? You wasted our hard-earned money, now you're leaving."

"I worked my butt off at the Mitchell House to help pay expenses."

"Oh, there you go. The Mitchell House. Some sort of God's gift. We raised you, clothed you, fed you, and this is the thanks we get?"

"Isn't that what parents are supposed to do?"

"Watch your mouth, young lady. That's your mother, and she deserves respect."

"Why? She's never shown me any." *Screw it.* Catherine turned to Clara. "You have never once told me I did a good job on anything. You are constantly criticizing me and siding with them." The brothers sat like vultures, smelling their sister's blood about to spill. "I brought home six awards in eighth grade. Six! What did I get from you? Nothing. Peter brings home a "C" on his report card, and you'd think he'd cured cancer."

"Tommyrot. You're making this up."

"I'm number three in our graduating class, you buy Russell a car."

"Wait a minute," Hank interjected. "We needed it for the farm. That was different."

"You are such an ungrateful child. I would have given my eye teeth to go to college."

"Yeah, I got to go to a school you that picked out for me, with classes you chose. You never even asked me if I was going to work on the farm. Do you know that? You just assumed I'd follow blindly like my moron brothers."

"Every Elbert from the last three generations…"

"You don't get it, do you?"

"Oh, please enlighten me, missy smarty pants. Or do you think I'm so stupid, I don't know what that word means?"

"I never said…"

"That's enough!" Hank stood up. "You both better stop before something's said that can't be taken back."

"Just know this. If you leave, you're not welcome back here again."

"Clara!"

She put her hand up. "That's my final word." She rose and went upstairs, with Hank following at her heels.

Catherine ran out to the front porch for some air. What the hell? Clara was going to disown her for moving away? Isn't that something adult children are supposed to do? It was impossible to wrap her head around it all. She expected a fight, but for Clara to throw down the gauntlet like that completely blindsided her. Her mother was forcing her hand, daring her to leave.

Catherine wished she could call Beth, but her baby was only three months old, still not sleeping through the night, and colicky. Josh! He would know what to do. Catherine ran back into the house and dialed the phone.

———*(21\\)*———

Though Catherine's back ached, she felt a smug sense of satisfaction knowing Clara would have to weed the cooking garden herself after she was gone. God knows she would not trouble the morons with it. *I'm going to burn these denim overalls.* Standing up, she stretched her back. Hank climbed off the enormous John Deere tractor a bit more slowly than usual. Farming was a younger man's profession, even with all of the machinery supposed to make things easier. Red-faced and sweaty, he pulled a handkerchief from his back pocket and wiped his head.

"Pop, may I talk with you?"

"This must be important, usin' 'May I' and all. Guess the mansion is rubbin' off on you."

"Please? This is serious."

"Okay, just give me a second." He took off his gloves and rinsed his hands under the hose. "It's a hot one today, isn't it?"

"Pop, you have to talk to Ma for me."

"Oh, Cat. Come on. I'm not gettin' in the middle of this."

"She is trying to disown me. It's a little important, don't you think?"

"Watch your tone, young lady. You and your Ma are two different people. It'll work itself out. Always has."

"You don't get it, do you? I'm leaving whether she likes it or not."

"Don't be so melodramatic. You both have always had these problems, even when you were a tiny baby. She would try to read you a nursery rhyme, you would kick the book out of her hands. Ma would start singin' you a lullaby, you would wail twice as loud and punch the sky."

"Please."

"One year, let's see, you must have been five or six. Ma brought home some clothes for school. You refused to wear them. One week, you hated yellow. The next, blue. And God help us if anyone tried to get you to wear purple."

"She should have known I hated those colors. She's my mother."

Hank sighed. "You changed your mind so much, who could keep up with you? And now you are doin' it again, don't you see?"

"See what?"

"You don't like college now, so you're gonna to traipse halfway across the country. What do you know about Maine anyhow?"

"There's the ocean. And lobsters. A great shopping area in downtown Portland."

"Well, there you have it! What did you do, watch some travel show on PBS?"

"I've done some research," she lied.

"Cat, you are barely twenty. You're not even old enough to know what you don't know yet."

"I'm not a complete idiot, Father. I was number three in my class. I can't be that stupid."

"That's not what I am talkin' about, and you know it."

"I'm going to Maine period. You're not going to stop me."

"That is no way to plan a move, Catherine. I wish you'd calm down and listen to me."

"I've had enough of this farm, enough of fucking Burkesville to last me a lifetime."

"Catherine Elbert!"

Stalking out of the barn, Catherine kicked the bucket filled with weeds and trampled through Ma's vegetable garden. "You want traipsing? I'll show you traipsing."

Up in her room, she activated the escape plan. "Hello, American Airlines? I'd like to purchase a one-way ticket to Maine."

She had about two thousand dollars in her bank account. The rest would take care of itself when she got there.

Josh lowered the suitcase into the trunk of his car. Hank, Clara, Russell, and Peter stood on the front porch, the brothers' eyes shooting back and forth between mother and sister.

"I guess this is it. Good-bye, Russell, Peter." Catherine stopped in front of Hank. "Pop?"

He hugged his little girl tight. "Here's somethin' to help you out," he whispered. "Don't let your mother see," he said, slipping a wad of money into her jacket pocket.

"Thanks."

"Please be careful. God watch over ya."

Clara stood, arms crossed, stone-faced.

"Good-bye, Ma."

Silence.

"Okay, well, time to go."

The men on the porch waved haphazardly as the car pulled away. Catherine turned to face forward, having no desire to see Elbert Farm ever again.

CHAPTER SEVEN

Portland, Maine

ERRY RIDES FOR THREE DOLLARS. Monthly Passes Available. Peaks Island. Great Diamond Island. Little Diamond Island. *Eenie, meanie, miney, moe.*

"One ticket to Peaks Island, please."

"Yes, miss. The next ferry leaves in fifteen minutes."

There was a little furnished studio apartment for rent above the people who owned the ferry line's house. Apparently, their daughter had moved into town with some friends just last week. It was a blessing to let the place so quickly, Catherine's new landlord said.

The island had a small grocery store, which was two blocks from the apartment, where she picked up some cleaning supplies, toilet paper, hot dogs, buns, soda, and milk. That would do for now. Time to clean.

Catherine unfolded the drawing Maddie had made of everyone in front of the Mitchell House as a going-away present and propped it up against the kitchen wall, making a mental note to pick up some tape next time she ran to the store. Kendra and Maddie were sad to see her go. Mr. Mitchell gave her a bonus check "to cover incidentals," which was very generous. Kendra had a tear in her eye as she hugged Catherine tight.

She plopped down, hot dog in hand, on the denim sofa that came with the place. There also was a coffee table and an entertainment center. Across the bay, Portland glistened against the night sky. The sound of waves hitting the docks rushed through her open windows, along with fresh, manure-free air.

Thanks to seagulls and blaring sunshine, Catherine rose at godforsaken five thirty in the morning. *Must get blinds today.* She slogged to the kitchen and chugged some milk. *What the hell was this watered-down white concoction?* Her tongue darted in and out, a desperate attempt to rid itself of that god-awful taste. "Vitamin A and D. Grade A Pasteurized. Homogenized." At home milk was rich, flavorful, creamy goodness that slid down your throat. Straight from the cow's teat. Peter said it as much as he could, like he was getting away something blatantly sexual right in front of the whole family. *Idiot.*

It was Tuesday morning, so the ferry was filled with commuters readying themselves for another day. Catherine found a seat next to an older lady carrying an L.L. Bean tote bag and a traveler's mug. In the row ahead, a thirty-ish woman sat wrapped in a trench coat tied snuggly around her slim waist. Thick black tights ended in chunky Doc Marten boots. Silver chains slithered up her ankles. Blood-red fingernails clutched a well-worn book, *Women Who Kill.* Her aquamarine eyes darted from book to ferry riders back to book, before settling upon Catherine.

"What?"

"Um, nothing."

Scoffing, her raccoon eyes resumed reading.

"Passengers, take your seats," a voice boomed over the speaker. "The ferry will depart in one minute."

"Hold on! We're coming!" A man and boy toting a

humungous cooler ran up the plank, stomachs flapping, followed closely by a woman bogged down with jackets, hats, and a beach bag. They dropped the cooler on the floor and slid onto the bench across the aisle, thighs squeaking across the cedar.

"We made it." The man smiled, resting his feet on the cooler.

The woman dabbed her brow with a folded up tissue. "No thanks to you, Herb."

"I'm sorry. I had to, you know."

The boy rolled his eyes. Guess it didn't matter what age you were, your parents always manage to embarrass you. Catherine felt a sort of kinship with the boy until he reached up his nose and pulled out a clear, crusty booger.

"I'm hungry," he said, wiping his hand on his mother's thigh.

"Georgie, for goodness sake. Breakfast was less than an hour ago."

"But I'm hungry."

"Oh, all right. Herb! Get something for Georgie from the cooler."

Round and pink, the three sat, anticipating their day's adventure.

The buildings of Portland grew larger as the ferry approached and docked at Maine State Pier. Georgie and his parents headed left, toward a string of four restaurants. Shocking. Catherine headed to the coffeehouse across the street.

Sea Dogs was an odd mix: half nautical, half hippie. Ship ropes enswathed the windows instead of drapes. A faded deep sea diving suit, its large, bulbous head slumped over in perpetual need of caffeine, sat to the left of the entrance. The right arm was draped over some huge gray metal thing. An air tank, maybe?

Corporate types buzzed in and out, each time slamming

the red-paned door. The menu was written on the chalkboard behind the counter. "Mild: New England Breakfast Blend. Medium: Sumatran Sunrise. Bold: French Roast. Coffee of the Day: Hazelnut. Specialty Items: Espresso, Cappuccino, Latte. For the coffee-averse (though why you'd even step foot in this establishment is beyond management's feeble mind): Strawberry-kiwi juice with a wheat germ boost."

"What'll it be, honey?" A pair of owl-like brown eyes stared out from behind the counter.

"Can I have a small New England breakfast blend, please?"

"Small New England Breakfast Blend Isaiah!" she bellowed. "Two bucks, please. Here's your change, hon. You can pick up your drink over there." She gestured to her left.

Clang! Isaiah rang the ship bell on the counter and called out, "Small hazelnut! Annabelle, what's next?"

The pick-up counter afforded a better view of the Sea Dog owners. Annabelle was short and squat, probably somewhere in her sixties. Isaiah, about six foot two and as thin as a rail, was knocking on seventy. They both had tanned, creased faces.

"Double espresso stat! Mike, here had a rough night," Annabelle shouted over her shoulder with a wink to the customer at the counter.

"I'm on it, Annabelle, dear."

Clang!

Portland was larger than Catherine had expected. She was so caught up in the whole island thing, she had forgotten about the city part and was definitely not used to this many people, much less all this chaos, this early.

A portrait of a stern man gazing off in the direction of the docks hung on the wall flanked by two Grateful Dead posters: one from a concert at RFK stadium in 1973; the other from their appearance at Woodstock. Had Jack Sprat and his wife behind the counter followed them around the country like the other deadheads?

"It's Longfellow, you know." He took a sip from a gigantic cup, a bit of froth remaining on his upper lip.

"You have a little something, um, foam is on your..."

Deflated, he wiped it off with his jacket sleeve. Ugh, some irritating male habits must come along with the testosterone. However, Catherine was willing to ignore it, since this preppie guy was way cute. "Now what were you saying?"

"Well, it's difficult to sound educated after that."

"Try."

"All right. Identification of said portrait. Take two. It's Longfellow, the poet. Have you read any?"

"I've heard of him, but I can't remember why."

He jumped into his best tourist guide voice. "Longfellow is Portland's favorite son. His boyhood home is here, too. There is a tour, if you're interested."

"I'll have to see."

"He wrote 'Paul Revere's Ride,' you know. *Listen, my children, and you shall hear. Of the midnight ride of Paul Revere.*'"

"Nope, don't remember."

"He also wrote 'The Lighthouse' about Portland Head Light."

No response.

"The most famous lighthouse in New England? The one you see in all the pictures?"

"I just got here yesterday. This is my first time."

"How long are you staying?"

"Indefinitely."

"What?"

"I moved here."

"Without ever coming here before?"

When he said it, it sounded ridiculous. "Yup."

"Really?"

"Really." Okay, this was getting annoying. "What about you? Have you lived here long?"

"All my life. My parents are islanders. I go to the University of Southern Maine and work giving walking tours part-time at the Visitor Center. Oh, shit. What time is it?"

"Ten after nine. Why?"

"I'm late. Gotta go. Good luck." He dashed off.

Great, the first guy she meets in Portland thinks she's nuts. Catherine finished the last bit of coffee and headed out, past red-bricked buildings accented with black and white trim, down cobblestone streets lined with shops. Cashmere capes in one window, colorful blown glass in another. Replicas of maritime artifacts mingled among oil paintings and bronze sculptures. Scrimshaw next to Rolexes.

"Morning." A man who looked like the Gorton's fisherman, yellow slicker and all, nodded as he passed. She relaxed and blended in with the crowd, anonymous for the first time in her life, not "that Elbert girl" at the Quickie Mart or "Smellbert" in the Burkesville High School hallways.

Twinkling lights caught her eye on Exchange Street, not blinking in an obnoxious, overpowering "It's Christmas! It's Christmas!" way like the ones at Padowski's Tavern every December, but rather like flickering, glistening, little snowflakes magically falling from the sky. A sign was suspended from curled black wrought iron, "Christmas Bells" in gold letters across a burgundy background, the "C" and "S" accented with holly leaves.

A life-sized Santa Claus stood in the window, plush toy woodland creatures hiding amid his flowing, forest green robes. A black bear cub. Two squirrels. A bunny. He held a small Christmas tree and a strand of berries and pine cones, no doubt for his furry friends. The other window featured a majestic tree, dressed in gold ribbons and balls, with deep red poinsettias tucked in the branches. A huge present wrapped in gold paper lay underneath, its tag reading "Merry Christmas to All" in calligraphy script.

So caught up in the beauty of it, Catherine decided to forgo her usual cynicism about the commercialization of the holiday season and went in. The smell of cinnamon and apples danced around her nose, as sleigh bells heralded her arrival.

"Well, hello, my dear. Is there anything I can help you find?" The woman had perfectly white hair. Gold-rimmed glasses framed sparkling blue eyes. She was wearing an emerald green dress, over which she was tying a red plaid apron. My God, it was Mrs. Claus! Exactly the one she used to color at age five. "Oh no, just looking."

"All right then. Take your time. Enjoy Let me know if you need anything." She smiled and went into the stockroom behind the register counter.

There was a gorgeous fireplace on the right wall, over which was a portrait of St. Nick, his head adorned with a holly-leaf crown. Jewel-toned velvet stockings hung from the mantle. Several trees created a path to guide visitors through the store. The flocked one glistened white and silver, snowflakes and icicles dangling from its limbs. A patriotic tree hosted red, white, and blue folded art Santas and snowmen, while mini-flags wound around outer branches. A Maine tree was stuffed with boats, mariners, lighthouses, kayaks, life preservers, and even lobsters.

"Try not to hold it against me. The tourists love that crap." The shopkeeper had reappeared.

Did she look like a local already?

"I wouldn't be caught dead with any of that Christmas kitsch on my tree, but don't quote me on it." She stuck out her hand. "Katie McLellan. Hope you didn't come here with your heart set on a Christmas lobster. You don't look the type. Great boots, by the way. I'd much rather have my jeans and boots on too today." She flounced her skirt uncomfortably. "Can't wait to change. I was getting some pictures taken for an ad. This thing gets warm."

"I bet. The Santa in the window is beautiful. I've never seen anything like it."

"Yeah, got him in Frankenmuth, Michigan, at the World's Largest Christmas Store, or so they say. My whole shop could fit into the entrance of that place. It was gargantuan."

"I can't even imagine."

"Overwhelming, actually. I prefer this little place. No light-up plastic Jesus. No atrocious blinking flamingo lights."

"And here I was, hoping to buy some illuminated chili peppers for my new apartment."

"Can't help you. But if you were going to hang them for an end of summer margarita bash, I could be persuaded to order them if you promise to invite me."

"Need some friends first. You are only the third person I have spoken with since I arrived."

"Where are you from?"

"Wisconsin."

"You're not a Packer fan, are you? My husband hates them."

"No way. My brothers are, therefore, I'm not."

"Good girl. So what brings you here?"

"Escape."

"I see. Did you find a place yet?"

"Yeah, on Peaks Island."

"Good Lord, I didn't think anyone from the Midwest would even know Peaks Island existed."

"I saw it on a travel show."

Katie McLellan smirked. "So, what are you doing about a job?"

"Not sure. This is my explore Portland day. I haven't given it much thought."

"Fall's just around the corner, and we're heading into the fall color tourist season. I could use some extra help, if you're interested. We are re-decorating the entire upstairs. People love those Department 56 villages. I need someone else besides Patsy, my full-time girl who is home sick today. Has a touch of the flu, or so she says." Katie winked.

This could quite possibly be the coolest old lady in the universe.

"C'mon. Let me show you the rest of the place." They walked through a hallway of shelves filled with nutcrackers of every sort, from golfers to fishermen, past nativity sets on tables and ornate wreaths on the walls.

"This is the kids' room."

A ten-foot tree with multicolored lifesaver garland stood in the center, decked out with cupcakes, lollipops, candy pieces, and marshmallow snowmen. Three mechanical elves wearing kitchen hats "stacked" presents underneath. A sports tree was on its left, and a small tabletop "Baby's First Christmas" tree on the right. Rocking horses and Radio Flyer wagons cluttered the floors, while a train chugged high above on a pint-sized track that ran the room's perimeter, about a foot from the ceiling.

Now, this was Christmas! Not the raggedy tree with its next-to-nothing decorations the Elberts had every year. "Why waste good money on something you only use for a week or so once a year?" Clara had told little Catherine when she had asked for a box of Shiny Brite ornaments of magenta, green, and silver. Every December 24, her mother purchased two lousy boxes of candy canes half-priced for two bucks from the Quickie Mart and hung them on a small evergreen Hank had cut down earlier that day. They were gone by Christmas morning, thanks to the moron brothers, leaving nothing but a few strands of red bubble lights burping up supposed Christmas merriment like Jonesy's acid reflux disease.

"So, Mrs. McLellan, when would you like me to start?"

CHAPTER EIGHT

"WOULD YOU HAND ME THAT box over there? Scrooge? No. No. To the right. Yeah, that one. Thanks." Patsy Allen teetered on top of the two-step step-stool. "He needs to go right...about...there."

"Okay, great. Let's go."

"Catherine! We still have to make it snow. That's the best part."

They had been creating displays for two weeks now. Christmas in the City. New England Village. Dickens Village. And Catherine's new favorite, Halloweentown, whose starter set came with a witch's house, a gnarled tree, and small graveyard. Dracula's castle was "wicked," a phrase she had picked up from Patsy and her friends. Everything was "wicked" this, "wicked cold," or "wicked something."

Patsy was a meaty girl, not fat necessarily, but certainly not thin. Solid, Clara would have described her, like she was an ox from a farming era gone by, one that even Clara herself was not a part of. Maybe Patsy was farming folk? Catherine bristled at the phrase. Sometimes one cannot escape the vernacular, no matter how valiant the effort. Perhaps her family farmed in a New England-y sort of way, pumpkins and such, apples probably. How would she know? Catherine's only exposure to New England agriculture was through folk art paintings.

Ill-conceived a thought as it was, Catherine was pretty sure Patsy has some sort of farming or rural background. Kind of like how artists can spot other artists, or bankers can sniff out people with money. Leave it the rural ex-patriot. What were the odds?

"You ladies look like you need a break." Katie McLellan tossed cans of soda to the girls. In an attempt to catch hers, Patsy nearly crushed Dickensian England, but managed to gain her balance at the last second.

"You all right there, Patsy? Good. It's about lunchtime. Who wants sushi? It's on me." Sleigh bells jingled. "I'll take care of whoever that is. You girls grab your coats."

"Hi, Mrs. McLellan. Here are those fliers from the Convention and Visitors Bureau. Would you mind if I put them somewhere people would notice them?"

"Put them by the register." Katie McLellan was uncharacteristically cold.

Patsy and Catherine came out of the stockroom. The guy from Sea Dogs her first day in Portland was here was putting some papers next to the jars stuffed with green and red stick candies, the old-fashioned kind like in Oleson's Mercantile on *Little House on the Prairie*. He glanced at Catherine, and then spied the other girl.

"Um, hi, Patsy."

"Scott, what are you doing here?"

"Dropping off some hand-outs, that's all."

"Oh, well, we were just going out to lunch. Gotta go. Bye." Patsy pulled Catherine through the door and whispered, "Just pretend I said something hilarious. Please."

"That's hilarious!" She fake-laughed loudly.

The Scott guy glanced in their direction, like he wanted to say something, but thought it best not and merely muttered "Good-bye, ladies."

Mrs. McLellan joined Catherine and Patsy outside. "Come on girls, let's go down Middle Street. I'm starving and no Scott Dithersby is going to keep me from getting my lunch."

"What was that all about?" Catherine was struggling to keep up with Patsy and Katie as they bolted down the street.

"I don't want to talk about it."

"Patsy."

"No! I can't go there."

"But..."

"Suffice to say, just stay away. So what's your favorite sushi? I'm in the mood for yellowfin tuna. Mrs. McLellan, don't you like Alaskan rolls?"

Lobster boils. Steamed two-pound lobsters. Wild blueberry cake. Lobster rolls. Sushi. Catherine could not get enough of it. And the chowder! She'd never tasted seafood before she moved to Maine. Deemed too expensive for the midwestern Elberts, here in the land of lobster plenty, it was reasonably priced. Beef? Who could remember it with all of this delicious seafood around? Only one thing was a staple in both diets—corn—but that was okay. Hank did not grow any and, although Burkesville was surrounded by it, the Elberts did not eat it much since Russell hated the sight of it.

Katie and Catherine closed Christmas Bells at exactly five o'clock and headed out for a Sunday dinner featuring Marty's famous lobster stew.

"It is really nice of you to invite me over again, Mrs. McLellan."

"We are glad to have the company, Catherine. Besides, all of Marty's recipes serve twelve or more people. Apparently, his mother never learned fractions. Marty either, come to think of it." Katie chuckled.

"Do you both come from large families?"

"Not me. I'm an only child. But Marty? Oh yeah, he had four brothers and two sisters. Quite a bunch. All four boys played football, so you can imagine the size of the spread for Thanksgiving. The poor sisters had to be quick if they were going to get any turkey. How about you?"

"Two brothers." Catherine stared out the car window, hoping for no more questions. Her days were passing pleasantly. No need to mess them up with thoughts of the morons.

Mrs. McLellan sensed this and changed the topic. "So, what's your favorite thing about Portland so far?"

"The freedom."

It was a chilly morning. Summer's warmth seemed to have faded with each lost minute of sunlight. Pop used to keep track of those kinds of things, like there was anything anyone could do about it. Catherine lit the fireplace at Christmas Bells, then began straightening the nutcracker case.

"Katie! It's unbelievable! Katie!" Velma Dithersby burst through the door, almost tripping over the threshold. Her white-blonde hair had the look of a wind-blown day. Spindly and fussy, her lightly wrinkled face bore the look of urgency. A body perpetually on a deadline. An unforgiving soul.

"Calm down. What's all this about?"

"This." Velma banged a piece of orange paper on the counter. "A scarecrow festival! What are they trying to do? Take all of our money from Merry Madness, that's what! People only have so much money to spend."

"Take it easy." Katie picked up the offensive literature. "The Portland Scarecrow Festival, huh? Seems to me it could be another way to get people in the shops. Kick-start the holidays. Halloween is getting more popular, you know."

"A pagan ritual, that's what it is. Why don't we just invite all the freaks from Salem up here?"

"Don't get your undies in a bunch. People will buy your

over-priced, quote-unquote gourmet food items no matter what the season."

"'Gourmet' implies expensive," Velma Dithersby huffed. "I give the people what they expect."

Patsy came through the door, unzipping her fleece jacket. "Whew! It's wicked cold." Velma glared at her, and she took off for the stockroom.

"Good Lord, pagan festivals, now *her*. The world's going to hell in a hand basket."

"I'd appreciate you keeping your opinions about my employees to yourself. Perhaps your son is the one with his head up his ass."

"Katie McLellan! I try to warn you to protect your business, and this is the thanks I get?"

"Don't let the door hit you on the way out, you old Sea Hag."

Patsy peeked out. "Is she gone?"

"Coast is clear, honey."

"Isn't that the lady from Casco Bay Gourmet Foods?"

"I wouldn't call her a lady, Catherine." Katie poured some hot cider. "Velma Dithersby has been plaguing us for twenty years or more, ever since she and her husband sold their original business and decided to open a store down the block."

"What did they do before?"

"Funeral directors. Good old Velma was the reason everyone preferred Pettibone Brothers. Was probably better for the Sea Hag, closing up that funeral parlor. People kept confusing her with the stiffs and trying to shove her in a coffin. Anyhow, this Scarecrow Festival sounds like a good place for us to publicize our new Halloween village. Maybe we should do a window with lots of black and skulls. Catherine, you seem to gravitate toward that sort of stuff. How about a lesson on window decorating?"

Pasty held the black tulle, while Catherine draped it around the side and top of what was to be Christmas Bells' first-ever Halloween window. Velma Dithersby walked by, pretending to ignore them, but the next day, pumpkins and Indian corn magically appeared on the Casco Bay Gourmet Foods front stoop.

"Go on, get out of here!"

"But, Mrs. McLellan."

"No buts, Catherine. You need to go out and experience autumn in Portland before the snow comes and doesn't leave us until March. And that's if we're lucky. You can't do it locked up in here, no matter how wonderful Patsy and I might be to work with. Go and have some fun while the weather is still bearable."

A brisk but beautiful day, the sun cast gold highlights on tree tops and white church spires. Orange leaves clung to their branches in the light breeze.

"Here's your change, miss. Enjoy the tour." A zit-faced boy with braces and glasses handed Catherine a ticket. Poor kid. This, too, shall pass, she wanted to tell him, but didn't want to make him feel worse than she was sure he already did, so she smiled, thanked him, and tucked the ticket and change in her purse. She had enough time for a quick trip to the ladies' room before her walk to Long Wharf, where the tour began.

Catherine had not taken more than two steps before coming face to face with Scott Dithersby.

"Looking for me?" He smirked, eyes dancing.

"No. Why would I be?"

"Good morning to you, too, Catherine, is it?"

"How do you know my name?"

"I make it my business to collect information on all lovely ladies new to the area."

"Bet you do."

"No, actually, my mother found out somehow, probably through Katie McLellan."

"Yeah, because they are such great friends."

"Have you come to take one of my famous walking tours?"

"Nope. Trolley tour." Catherine checked her watch. "Which I will be late for if I don't leave now, so bye."

Scott held his chest and hung his head, one strand of black hair falling over a grayish-green eye. "You're breaking my heart."

"Alrighty then." Catherine turned and walked away.

Alrighty then?

This Dithersby guy was proving to be an interesting character, a *gorgeous*, interesting character. Clearly, he and Patsy had dated at some point, which struck Catherine as odd considering the look Velma had given Patsy when she came into Christmas Bells huffing and puffing about the Portland Scarecrow Festival. Catherine needed to find out the whole story, but how?

Exhaling, she sat back against the trolley's seat. Tourists filled in around her, armed with cameras and sightseeing maps. It was their fault she had been working so hard. Mrs. McLellan kept Christmas Bells open seven days a week during the fall foliage tour season to capitalize on all the foot traffic. Catherine squelched the urge to give them death stares. Besides, Mrs. McLellan had given her a surprise day off. How great was she? Someone Catherine had met only, what, two months ago was more in tune with her than her own mother. Big shock there.

The trolley headed toward Eastern Promenade, by Casco Bay, its bright blue waters dotted with white sailboats, through town past the Wadsworth-Longfellow House, which would have been impressive if not for its association with

Scott Dithersby in Sea Dogs on Catherine's first day here. And past the Victoria Mansion, which made her think of Kendra and Maddie. Wonder what they were doing today? Probably getting the Mitchell House ready for visitors from Johansen's Pumpkin Farm. Her stomach leapt in anticipation of a northeastern Halloween. Salem was not that far away. Maybe she could talk Patsy into a road trip.

Making its way across Casco Bay Bridge, the trolley stopped at the most iconic thing in all of Maine—Portland Head Light in Cape Elizabeth. There it was, a sentinel over foamy shores, the very thing from that PBS travelogue! According to the sign, it was one of four colonial lighthouses authorized by George Washington. So cool. So old. All Burkesville had was a lame log cabin, practically the size of a dog house, built by some no-name fur trader who probably ran Native Americans off their own land. While he was struggling with Lincoln Logs, England already had castles for more than six hundred years. Whatever. But George Washington? Here was some *real* history.

A plaque marked the spot where Longfellow was inspired to write "The Lighthouse." Seems he was friends with the light keepers and visited here often. Catherine sat on the flat-topped rock in front of the sign, eager to experience the same view as the poet.

The ocean—the craggy, rough Atlantic —was barred from visitors by a waist-high thick white chain link fence upon which was perched one lonely yellow flower. A remnant of a bridal bouquet, perhaps, or something more sinister? How many tortured souls had flung themselves onto the jagged rocks below before the fence? How many trapped, hopeless people did not have the good fortune to escape as she had? Catherine said a silent prayer and boarded the trolley, ready to get home.

Columbus Day brought a flurry of activity to Portland, with the usual long-weekenders up for nature's brilliant display. The Scarecrow Festival was officially kicking off "Peak Week," a term used to denote peak autumnal color in southern and coastal Maine, but which the good people of Peaks Island embraced whole-heartedly as their own personal holiday. The islanders were walking a little taller, with a little extra spring in their step. Many of the eight hundred or so could be spotted wearing various sweatshirts with "I'm at my Peak" scrawled upon them. This was not the case for Long Island, which sounded "too New York" for Maine inhabitants, Cousins Island (too cheeky), or Chebeague Island, which no one could pronounce and had the dubious distinction as the home of the Dithersbys. Its population numbers were dwindling. The Sea Hag alone was known to have run off at least ten families over the years, Katie McLellan had heard from Francis Flannagin.

The Portland Scarecrow Festival was set up about two blocks away from Christmas Bells, in one of the larger squares. Patsy and Catherine walked across the grassy area where the entries were set up.

"Ah, there you are, girls. Ta-da! Edgar Allan Crow!" He stood six feet tall, appropriately dressed in a black suit and holding a quill pen. A large blackbird sat atop his shoulder.

"Mrs. McLellan, he's fabulous."

"Wicked cool."

There were traditional scarecrows, a choir of scarecrows made by the First Congregational Church, Franken-Crow, and...what was that? A Christmas tree with carved mini-pumpkins as ornaments?

The three scrambled to see its sponsor.

"Casco Bay Gourmet Foods."

"Unbelievable! She really is something." Patsy was furious.

"No skin off my nose." Katie shrugged. "Ours is cooler. Well, I think one of us should stay around here and look after Edgar. Persuade the voters. Winning 'Favorite Scarecrow' would really put a bee in old Velma's bonnet, wouldn't it? Catherine, why don't you stick around, and Patsy and I will head back to Christmas Bells."

"Okay. I'll pass out our Halloweentown brochures. Drum up some business and, hopefully, some votes." Catherine watched Mrs. McLellan and Patsy walk off. Patsy was pretty great, a little slow on the uptake sometimes, but she was okay. Mrs. McLellan was warm, funny, kind, the anti-Clara. Wonder why she never had kids? Of course, if Hank and Clara hadn't... ick, never mind.

People began milling around, checking out each scarecrow. A group of boy scouts dragged their parents to see Troop 625's entry. So that was who was responsible for Franken-Crow.

The Visitor's Center had provided a Longfellow scarecrow, big shock, seeing as they used his face everywhere to promote Portland. Do dead writers and artists know they are still popular on earth? So many of them died unappreciated or in obscurity, Catherine hoped there was some sort of message system to let Jane Austen know her books were still studied and that movies based on them are total blockbusters. Maybe that was part of Hermes' job. Upon closer inspection, Hermes might want to keep this Longfellow thing quiet. It was more like a blob with a cotton-ball beard. Who would make a scarecrow head only? Creepy. Catherine sent a telepathic signal to Hermes inviting him to check out Edgar Allan Crow, because, of course, it was totally the sort of thing Poe would go for.

"Why is it that I keep running into you by Longfellow artwork?" Scott Dithersby took her by surprise.

"I would hardly call this thing 'artwork.'"

"We tried the best we could."

"My apologies, but you failed."

"Cold. Very cold. I'm wounded." He grabbed his chest.

"Too bad, so sad. Gotta run." Catherine passed out fliers as she walked. Scott followed.

"What's up with the attitude?"

"I heard you were someone to stay away from. Besides, your mother's a nut job. You couldn't possibly be normal."

"My moth...Jesus, you're rude."

"Stop following me so I can do my job."

"What has Patsy told you about me?"

"Nothing."

"You expect me to believe that?"

"Really. All she said was stay away. You must have done something horrible. Patsy usually would spill her life story to everyone who comes into the store if she could."

"I'm a nice guy, ask anyone. Well, almost anyone. And I can't help who my mother is."

Scott did have a point there. God forbid anyone judged her because she was born of Clara Elbert. "What do you want?"

"I was only coming over to say hello. That's all. No spying for Casco Bay Gourmet Foods or anything, just hi."

Their luck, Sea Hag would add a Christmas section to steal away their customers. "Thanks for the head's up. I'm glad you don't work for the CIA."

"If I was spying on you, do you think I would tell you?"

"Maybe that's what you want me to think."

"I didn't realize saying hello to an attractive woman would ignite a debate."

Catherine paused and absorbed the words "attractive woman." Scott Dithersby was cute, there was no denying it, more than cute. Way cuter than Bill Davies. His eyes seemed to look right through her. It was unnerving and exciting at the same time. "Um, yeah, okay, so I guess I'll be on my way now. Have to pass out fliers, you know, very busy."

Scott smiled. "Clearly busy. Very important flier-passing-out business."

She managed to blurt out "bye" and scooted off, determined to find out what had happened between Patsy and Scott.

———— ✺ ————

Waiting in line to buy tickets for *Top Gun*, Patsy would not shut up about Tom Cruise. "Remember his dance in *Risky Business*? Oh baby."

"Get ahold of yourself." Catherine caught her tongue before the word "missy" came out. "He kinda looks like Scott Dithersby."

That stopped Patsy cold. "Why would you say that? He doesn't look anything like him."

"Sure he does. Same greenish-gray eyes."

"When have you gotten close enough to notice his eyes?"

"Well, I ran into him at the Scarecrow Festival."

"Why didn't you tell me?"

"I didn't want to upset you, and I was clearly right. What's the deal between you and him?"

"I told you before, I don't want to talk about it." The line began moving. "Two tickets for the eight o'clock *Top Gun*, please. Thanks." She pulled Catherine through the doors. "If you are my friend, you won't push me. It was a very painful time in my life, which I've moved on from and do not care to rehash now, especially when we are supposed to be having fun. It's Friday night. Come on. Let's get some popcorn."

CHAPTER NINE

S LEIGH BELLS. CASH REGISTER BELLS. Everything was ringing at Christmas Bells on Merry Madness Night. Customers jammed the shop. Patsy served eggnog, while Catherine worked the register.

"Excuse me, do you have any more of those darling lobster ornaments?"

Mrs. McLellan and Catherine exchanged looks. *Tourist.*

"Let me see if I have some in the back." Katie yelled into the stockroom. "Marty, dear, would you see if we have any lobster ornaments back there?"

"Sure thing, hon." It was so busy, the reserves were brought in. Marty McLellan had played football with the Chicago Bears in the early 1960s. He was still large today, which surprised Catherine who was under the impression old people shrank over time. If this was him old, he must have been a wall on the line.

Mr. McLellan emerged triumphant. "Here you are, ma'am. It's the last one," he said with a large grin.

Catherine smirked. Everyone seemed to be getting the very last one of something or another tonight.

Marty McLellan shrugged his shoulders. "Eh, if it makes 'em happy, why the hell not? It's an extra benefit to their purchase."

Katie punched him in the arm as she walked by.

"She loves me, see?" A rough-and-tumble guy, Mr.

McLellan was athletic director of Portland High School until he retired last year. Now every morning, he met a bunch of other old guys at Sea Dogs. Catherine had run into them a couple of times while grabbing a latte on the way to work. The entire group yelled "Hi, Catherine!" when she walked by. Once, Mr. McLellan shouted out "Say hello to my bride." How cute was that after all those years of marriage?

Mrs. McLellan joined them occasionally, but preferred to let her husband have his time with the guys. After all, she did not want him nosing around Christmas Bells, giving his two cents about how to run her business, so she opted to give him some personal space. Merry Madness was the only time Marty McLellan stepped foot inside the shop.

"That will be nineteen eighty-nine, please." Out of the corner of her eye, Catherine saw somebody peering in through the Santa Claus window. "Out of twenty. Eleven cents is your change. Thank you and have a great holiday." When she looked outside again, no one was there.

———— ❧ ————

Ten o'clock could not have come soon enough for the weary Christmas Bells team.

"A toast to the most successful Merry Madness yet. Cheers!" Mrs. McLellan had added some brandy to the eggnog, this being Friday night. "Thanks, ladies. And you, too, Marty, dear." She put her glass down. "Well, let's hit the road. I'm bushed. Enjoy yourselves tonight, but not *too* much, if you get my drift. You can come in a little late tomorrow. How about eleven?" December meant all hands on deck for Christmas Bells, including weekends.

"Good night, Mrs. McLellan." Catherine buttoned her coat and headed out with Patsy. It was a tradition among the younger retail employees to do a Pub Crawl after Merry Madness. This year's point of origin was O'Malley's.

"Hey, Catherine, do you mind if we start at Parallel instead? I'm supposed to meet Susan and Mary there. We can catch up with the others right after we pick them up."

———— ⁘ ————

Catherine found a few seats by the Parallel bar. "Do you mind if I sit for a while? My feet are killing me. I'll hold these."

"Sure. I'll go look for them," Patsy said.

Should be a thrilling evening. Last time, all Susan and Mary did was sit there with the same dull expressions on their dumb faces, while Catherine grasped at tidbits of conversation. Across the bar, a group of black-leathered, pierced punks sported multicolored spikes protruding from their heads. One's hair was magenta, the other's jet black with electric blue tips. A guy in a tight Ramones t-shirt and black jeans slid past her, green mohawk undulating the same tempo as his hips. On the other side, frat boys in polo shirts and jeans discussed the Patriots game. Across from them, a group of skank chicks in micro-miniskirts, tight tank tops, and huge over-permed hair teetered on their six-inch heels trying to get the frat boys' attention. One sauntered past them. Nothing. The next bent over, providing a full view of her red push-up bra as she retrieved her dropped napkin. Nothing. The third tripped and hobbled back to her friends in shame.

Smiths music began, signaling it was time for dancing, followed by Alison Moyet, the Talking Heads, Depeche Mode, and Echo and the Bunnymen. Catherine pondered what to do for fun with Tweedle Dee and Tweedle Dum? *Great, here they come.* Ding! She signaled to the bartender and waved them over. "Hello. Good to see you. Grab some seats, ladies. I've ordered us some peppermint schnapps shots."

Three rounds and many choruses of "Deck the Halls" later, each time sung more loudly than the next, as if volume improved pitch quality. By the looks they were getting, maybe it was time to wrap up that gig and move onto something else less annoying.

"Ah, ladies. Our Susan here has yet to purchase. Fork it up, baby. Bartender Joe, another round, please." Was it hot in here? Catherine got up and stumbled slightly. "I'm going to the little girls' room," She tried to whisper to Patsy, but since the music was so loud, ended up announcing that she needed to pee to pretty much the entire bar area. It was a very proud moment, which Catherine tried to cover up with a deep bow and headed through the crowd with a flourish amid much laughter.

She did a quick face cheek in the mirror, enjoying this new role as court jester, reapplied some red lipstick, and emerged ready to face her public.

"Hello." He materialized from out of nowhere. "I was hoping I'd run into you. I've been thinking about you all day. Ever since I saw you your first day here at Sea Dogs, actually." Scott Dithersby's eyes were glistening, his cheeks slightly flushed. The combination brought a blush to her own cheeks. "Would you like to dance?"

Before Catherine could answer, Scott took her hand and led her to the dance floor. He pulled her towards him, slow dancing despite New Order blaring around them. He bent his head down and brushed her lips with his as they swayed. Catherine's head tingled.

"Let's get out of here," he whispered in her ear.

"I have to tell Patsy I'm leaving." *Omigod, Patsy.*

Scott saw her panic and whispered again, "Patsy doesn't need to know. Tell her you're tired and need to go home."

"But I was supposed to stay at her house tonight."

"Tell her you decided to catch the last ferry. They are running later because of Merry Madness, remember?"

No, she did not. Her brain was all mixed up.

Scott kissed her again, this time with more intensity. "Go on, say your good-byes."

Catherine repeated everything Scott had made up and met him outside, around the corner. They practically ran to his car, hurling themselves into the back seat. He unzipped her coat and slid it off, then flung his own over the front seat. Pulling Catherine on top of him, they resumed their unison movements from the dance floor. Catherine raised her sweater up over her head, wanting nothing more than his hands on her body.

Fog enveloped the pier as the ferry approached. Catherine ambled up the slope, past the row of evergreen bushes with their omnipresent flies. At first, she thought the bugs congregated there because of some spilled garbage or the effect of summer's heat on dog shit. But when December came, she altered the theory. They were, no doubt, guardians of a decaying corpse, some missing homeless person buried on the island to keep it all quiet.

Her mouth felt like she had eaten a box of mothballs. At least five gallons of Gatorade (Patsy's remedy. She kept yelling her cure to everyone she ran into last night from about midnight on) *and* a full pot of coffee (Catherine's inclination was more toward massive doses of caffeine) would be required. What time was it? Eight thirty. Ugh, work at eleven.

A small light was on in Mrs. Marabelle's window. The faded blue wood siding and chipped white window boxes with fake pink and yellow tulips stuck inside were a sure sign a senior citizen inhabited the premises. To her credit, Mrs. Marabelle did hand out the best Halloween candy on Peaks Island—full-sized Hershey bars. Catherine had overheard some kids talking on the ferry. Made her want to put on a costume and ring her doorbell. Candy was not in her budget. Mrs. McLellan paid okay, but it was not like Catherine was rolling in dough, and she refused to phone home for money. They had not called her, not one of them, not even Hank, even though she had sent a change-of-address card. She could do without candy.

Her head killed as she climbed the stairs to her apartment, each step bringing a new throb to her temples. Details were fuzzy from last night's Pub Crawl, which was really just a Pub Stay-Put. The Pub Crawl partiers eventually came to them, since Parallel was stop three.

Images flashed through Catherine's aching head. Schnapps shots. "Deck the Halls." Scott Dithersby. The way he looked at her when he took her face into his hands. If she were a sigher, this would have definitely been the time for it.

They had ended up crashing at Scott's friend Phil's apartment, where they spent the entire night talking and etc. Okay, more et cetera than discussing current events. Catherine mentally replayed the evening in the shower, while she applied makeup to her exceedingly pale face and concealer to her puffy, dark-circled, lack-of-sleep eyes, as she ate toast to combat the nausea.

"Morning, Catherine. Don't you look a little worse for wear?"

"Thanks a lot, Mrs. McLellan. Is Patsy here?"

"No, not yet. Good time last night, I presume." She winked. "I've heard about those Pub Crawls. That's why old folks like me high-tail it home after Merry Madness."

"Oh, yeah, like you've never seen your share of debauchery."

"Why, Catherine Elbert! I'm shocked you would say such things about your beloved boss."

"You couldn't even get the words out without smirking."

"Hello." Patsy jumped as the door slammed behind her. "Ouch. That's wicked loud."

"And here's the other one. Catherine, she looks even worse than you. Poor Patsy, come here, dear. I'll get you some coffee."

Patsy took a seat behind the counter. "They do not make a pain reliever big enough for this headache."

"I hear ya."

"This is all your fault, you know."

"Me? Why?"

"Peppermint schnapps shots? I vomited up my innards at about two thirty. And where were you? Nowhere to be found."

"I told you I wanted to catch the last ferry," Catherine lied.

"I know. I know." Then Patsy said, in a hushed tone, "I saw Scott Dithersby there last night when you were in the bathroom. It was a good thing you left when you did. He was on the prowl."

"Did you see him with anyone?"

"Nope. He probably went onto the next bar. There was a big group calling themselves 'the diehards' that were determined to make it to all four stops. One of them was Phil Bannerman, so I assume Scott went with him."

"Oh yeah, probably." That explained why the apartment was empty. Not possessing the brain power to continue deceiving Patsy anymore, Catherine psychically willed her to stop talking. Miraculously, it worked. Her night with Scott had left her with super powers! She concentrated on having Mrs. McLellan bring her coffee too, but Katie emerged from the stockroom with only one cup. Alas, she was not a telepath. "You're a woman now" flashed into her head from those stupid pamphlets Clara gave her when she got her first period. The car, the apartment, Scott's touch on her...

"Catherine! I'm talking to you."

"Sorry, Mrs. McLellan. What did you say?"

"Would you go upstairs and straighten up? Make sure the villages are tidy, and organize and re-stock the kids' room. I'm sure it could use it after last night."

The Dickens Village looked how Catherine felt—askew. She half expected to see Scrooge and the Ghost of Christmas Present passed out in front of the little Melancholy Tavern. Was Scott just on the prowl last night, like Patsy said? He didn't say he would call when she left this morning. A one-night stand? The phrase made her squirm. Great, now she would be struck down by lightening as soon as she stepped foot outside Christmas Bells.

There was hours of work in the kids' room. One of the present-stacking elves was broken, rocking horses and wagons were thrown all over the floor, and the large sports tree was missing well over half of its ornaments. Catherine brought up boxes of new decorations and got to work, happy to be hiding up here, away from Patsy.

Feel cheap, don't ya, missy? I told you to wait until you found the right one, but did you bother to listen? Clara Elbert's omnipresence could not be silenced a mere one thousand miles away. She was wrong, of course, well, okay, partly wrong. A good portion of Catherine was glad it happened. For years she had hoped it would be with Bill Davies, until the VFW fish fry put an end to that silliness. They were engaged, Bill and Denise. He had proposed to her on Thanksgiving, according to Beth's Christmas card.

Enough of that. How did a Baby's First Christmas ornament get on a sports tree? The powder-blue bear, with wide eyes and pinned diaper, smiled up at Catherine. Too cute. Then it hit her.

They did not use protection.

CHAPTER TEN

*T*HIS YEAR, CATHERINE ELBERT WOULD be celebrating her first Christmas as a free woman, far away from the farm. Since her only experiences were in Burkesville, Catherine had no idea what normal people did for the holidays. Did Mainers stuff lobsters? She chuckled to herself. She would find out soon enough at Patsy's house tomorrow.

Fresh Christmas Trees. The lot was almost empty now except for a few half-dead scrawny pines.

"I'll take the wreath, please."

"Sure, miss. Merry Christmas to you."

Catherine trudged toward the ferry in the slush from last night's snowfall. She was beginning to understand what Mrs. McLellan had tried to explain a few weeks ago. Snow just kept piling up here, not like in Wisconsin, where it snowed then melted, snowed then melted. Her left leg slid right out from under her, almost causing her to wipe out right on the dock. So that's the wicked dangerous ice Patsy had warned her about. She took a seat and closed her eyes, glad to have made it on in one piece. The ferry's bell jolted Catherine out of her slumber, disoriented and disturbed. The large multicolored Christmas lights adorning Mrs. Marabelle's cottage brought her back into the present, calming her pulse.

Walking up the stairs to her apartment, Catherine noticed a box in front of her door postmarked "Burkesville, WI." Maybe they had not forgotten about her after all. But when she opened it, there were no Christmas presents, not even a card, just four high school yearbooks, her graduation tassel, and the picture of her and Beth on graduation day.

"Thought you might want these." Hank's scrawling penmanship wrote. "Hope you are okay. Pop."

That was it?

Catherine threw the box on the floor and rummaged through her drawer for a small nail so she could hang her wreath on her door. Merry Christmas to you, assholes, she thought, wondering how she had survived the Burkesville years with any shred of sanity.

Christmas morning, Catherine was treated to a scene worthy of a postcard. All it needed was the words "Greetings from Maine" splashed along the top. A few inches of snow had fallen overnight, dusting the trees in fresh, white, sparkly splendor. Outside her kitchen window, two deer chomped a breakfast of twigs, while a red cardinal watched from a nearby evergreen.

Ready for her own meal, she loaded up a plate with cookies from the assortment Mrs. McLellan had sent home with her yesterday, all but the chocolate whiskey balls, which were a little too potent for this time of day. Almond macaroons, gingersnaps, almond brittle, fudge, and butter cookies with red and green sprinkles—delicious!

In a little bit, she would get dressed and make her way to the Allen's house, but first she needed to finish wrapping their presents. Patsy had coveted this bracelet every time they walked by LaFemme. She was going to flip out when she opened it. For Mr. and Mrs. Allen, Catherine chose a sweet-faced Santa dressed in green carrying a walking stick from Christmas Bells, of course. She bunched four *Little House on the Prairie* candy sticks and tied them together with red ribbon for Patsy's brothers. She had been warned about their potential for rowdiness, which was almost a deal breaker. Who wanted to spend Christmas with some snot-nosed kids? It had to be better than Elbert Farm, though. Right about now, Clara would be lugging in ten pounds of potatoes that needed to be peeled, cut, boiled, and mashed, while the men took up residence on the sofa watching football, then basketball on TV.

"They work hard every day. Deserve a holiday, that's fer sure," her mother would say every year. "Now, get to it, Catherine. Those potatoes aren't gonna peel themselves."

Not this year, suckers! Make your own goddamned potatoes. She popped the last gingersnap into her mouth and licked her fingers.

Patsy had talked more about Tom Cruise than her family, so Catherine was curious to see what kind of people lived in this modern Victorian, more streamlined than most, and free of all the frilly gingerbread. Every window was outlined with multicolored Italian lights and had matching wreaths hanging from red ribbons in the center. A gigantic Maine balsam pine wreath adorned the door. She rang the bell.

"Oh, hi. You must be Catherine. Come on in." Dark hair, spiked. Echo and the Bunnymen t-shirt. Black jeans. Black converse gym shoes. A cousin, perhaps?

The Allen home was large and inviting, with dark walnut moldings and trim throughout. An ornate fireplace in the living room, or *parlor* since it was a Victorian, was draped in more fresh greenery with red tea lights interspersed among the branches, while stockings labeled Steven, Andrew, Jim, Robert, and Patsy hung below. No farming family she knew had a house like this. Clearly her barnyard radar was faltering. Good! One step further away from Burkesville.

"Here, let me take your coat." He helped her off with her parka. "Merry Christmas, by the way. I'm Steven."

Pasty bounded in. "Hey, Cat! I see you've already met my brother."

"I thought you said all of your brothers were younger than us," Catherine whispered.

"No, silly. I said older. I'm the youngest. Come in and meet the rest." Patsy led her past the kitchen, where the smell of roasting turkey enticed her nostrils, to the family room. Three male heads on the sofa turned to see who was at the door. "Cat, these are my brothers."

"Andrew." Light brown hair. Ralph Lauren polo sweater. Jeans. Boat shoes.

"Jim." Blond. Red-checkered flannel shirt. Jeans. No shoes.

"Robert." Brown hair. New England Patriots football jersey. Gray sweatpants. Socks.

Patsy pointed to the kitchen. "And my parents are over there." She grabbed Catherine's hand, tugging at her until she moved.

Each one of the Allen brothers was more gorgeous than the next. It was like a buffet. "Huh? Oh, sorry."

Mrs. Allen wiped her hands on her apron. "Catherine, so nice to meet you." She hugged her. "We've heard so much about you, I feel I know you already."

"Hello, dear." Mr. Allen was the spitting image of Patsy, or vice versa. "Want some eggnog?"

"Yes, Mr. Allen. Thank you. I brought some...wait, where did they go?" *Oh shit!* The gorgeous brothers would think she was crazy giving them candy sticks like little kids. To her horror, Steven was lifting his parents' present from Catherine's L.L. Bean tote. "Mom, do you want me to put the gifts Catherine brought under the tree with the rest?" The pile was so high, presents touched the bottom branch.

"Sure, honey." She turned toward Catherine. "I have to put the finishing touches on this chestnut stuffing, if you'd excuse me for one second."

Mr. Allen carried a tray filled with glasses. "Toast time! Everyone grab some eggnog. Come on, Mona. Okay, to my beautiful wife, my amazing sons, my sweet daughter, and our new friend, Catherine. Good health, joy, and prosperity to us all. Cheers!"

Shouts of "Merry Christmas!" filled the room. Catherine watched as the Allen family took turns hugging each other, smiling and laughing as they went from person to person. Suddenly, Steven's arms wrapped around her.

"Don't want you to feel left out. Watch the eggnog. Dad tends to get a little heavy-handed with the brandy."

She could feel the muscles in his back through the t-shirt. "Thanks for the heads up." He smelled like a heavenly mixture of pine and oranges.

"Get off her. It's my turn." Robert gave Steven a little shove and slid into his place. Taller than his brother, beefier too, his arms totally engulfed Catherine. Very cozy.

Mrs. Allen clapped her hands. "Okay, okay. Don't crush the poor girl. Andrew, put on the Christmas music. Let's open presents!"

It was a free-for-all. Paper ripping. Shouting. Wrappings flying everywhere. She was having such a great time watching all of them, she almost forgot to open her own.

"Catherine! I can't believe you bought it. Omigod!" Patsy made her way through the chaos, flinging her wrist. "Here. Here. Open mine."

Catherine tore at the red-and-green plaid paper. *The Complete Works of Edgar Allan Poe.* "Thanks! This is massively cool."

"I remember how much you loved our Christmas Bells scarecrow."

"Catherine!" Mrs. Allen shouted from across the room. "He's beautiful! I know just the place for him." She ran off to the parlor with the green Santa.

Andrew held up a beer stein. "Hey, Jim. Very nice. Thanks!"

"Robert, love the tape," Steven yelled to his brother. "You like Depeche Mode?" He passed it to Catherine.

"Love 'em. This is the new one, right? Cool. They play them a lot at Parallel."

"Best dance club in Portland. How come I have never seen you there?"

"Only been there once. After Merry Madness." Cloudy visions of Scott Dithersby invaded her mind. Asshole had never called. Whatever.

"What's up, Doc?" Steven chuckled and socked his brother in the arm as he walked by.

"You do know it doesn't get funnier repeating it over and over until my head's going to explode, right?" He punched him back.

Seeing Catherine's confusion, Steven told her Andrew was in pre-med at Johns Hopkins.

"And this turd thinks equating it with Looney Tunes is hilarious."

"Have you broken your funny bone, doctor?" Jim interjected.

Andrew biffed Jim's head. "Don't think so, nature boy."

"He's all about the great outdoors. A virtual poster boy for L.L. Bean," Steven explained. "Loves camping, hiking, fishing, kayaking, cross-country skiing. All that shit. Oh, hey, I put those candy sticks on the counter over there. Thought they were probably for our cousins. That was sweet of you."

Whew! Thank goodness for younger cousins.

"Cat! You haven't opened up your other present yet." Patsy plunked down on the chair next to her. "C'mon, before the rest get here."

"Who's all coming?"

"Aunt Ginny, Uncle John, and their kids. Oh, and the McLellans."

"Our McLellans?"

"Yeah, sorry, thought you knew. My grandmother and Mrs. McLellan were college roommates.

Small world. Catherine unwrapped a comfy scarf and pair of sherpa-lined gloves.

"Everyone needs those to survive a Maine winter." Mr. Allen chuckled. "Well, I'd better go see if the missus needs help in the kitchen. Boys, let's get this room cleaned up."

Catherine followed him. "Can I help with anything?"

"Ask the boss."

Mrs. Allen eyed the contents of the refrigerator. "Howard? Grab these for me, will you?" She tossed lettuce, red peppers, some sort of cheese, and a bottle of dressing at her husband, all of which he caught with surprising ease, then shut the appliance's door with his butt. "I think Howard and I have everything under control, so go relax and enjoy yourself. Would you mind putting this artichoke and spinach dip out? Oh, sassafras. I forgot to make the bread bowl. Okay, Catherine. Looks like I have something for you to do after all. Carve a hole in the middle of this and arrange bite-sized pieces of bread around it. The other loaf over there needs to be cut for dipping."

Steven swooped in. "I'll do that one."

"Show Catherine where the knives are. Thanks. We only have a half an hour until the others arrive."

"Aye, aye Captain!" Steven saluted his mother and got to work. "How does someone from the Midwest decide to move here?"

Catherine told him the story of the PBS travelogue and a two-minute synopsis of the hell that was Burkesville.

"Well, it's a good thing you're so adventurous. Otherwise, my Christmas would not be half as merry. Come on, let's put these by the other appetizers."

Catherine set the bread bowl in the middle of a large glass platter. Steven filled it with the dip, then they both arranged the bread pieces around it.

"Touchdown!" roared from the family room. Robert ran, high-fiving everyone down the line of the sofa.

"Hope we're not too loud for you," Steven said. "It can get a bit crazy."

"No, I love it actually."

"Good. Want to watch the game?"

Whenever Robert got up to high five his brothers when the Patriots did something good (which was often), Steven's leg would brush against hers. Catherine could not tell if this was intentional, or if it was because so many people were squished together on the sofa. Either way, it was good for her.

"Hey, she's my friend, bug." Patsy sat on the sofa's arm next to Catherine. "This is just like when we were kids. Steven was always poaching my friends, luring them into playing with his Easy-Bake Oven."

"What can I say? Easy-Bake Ovens rocked. The first time I pulled one of those tiny cakes out, I knew I wanted to be a pastry chef."

Clara had refused to buy Catherine one, saying she should learn something useful, like how to bake a real cake, so she frosted the little creations at Beth's house. "Which was your favorite—yellow or chocolate?"

"Yellow. Has to be yellow. For some reason, the chocolate one never tasted right."

Catherine clapped. "I always thought so, too."

Robert looked at her crestfallen. "Are you a Jets fan? That might be a deal breaker, you know."

Oops, something must have happened in the game they were supposed to be watching. "Oh, no. Sorry, we were talking about Easy-Bake Ovens." The three burst into laughter at his incomprehension.

"Ding. Dong. I let myself in, Mona. Didn't think you would mind."

"Katie McLellan, I thought you already had your own key anyhow." Mrs. Allen drew Mrs. McLellan into a hug. "Merry Christmas."

Mr. McLellan followed behind carrying a large pot.

"Here, Marty. Let me take that for you. Smells delicious. Nothing better than your lobster stew." Mrs. Allen set the pot on the stove.

"There they are, my girls!" Mrs. McLellan embraced Patsy and Catherine, then whispered to Cat, "Enjoying the view?"

Marty McLellan took a seat next to Robert. "How are my Pats doing?"

"Great, Coach. They're up by fourteen." Robert was Mr. McLellan's star middle linebacker three years ago at Portland High School.

The doorbell rang again. This time, it was Mrs. Allen's sister, Ginny, her husband, John, and their children, Jackie, age nine, and Gregor, age six.

"Ho! Ho! Ho!" Ginny kissed her big sister. "Deck the Halls and all that shit." She lowered her voice. "My genius husband decided that to save some money, we would assemble the kids' new bikes ourselves. We were up 'til four! Then the kids jump on us screaming 'Santa was here!' at seven. It's gonna be a long day."

"You couldn't pay me to go back to those days. I'll put some coffee on for you." Mrs. Allen rummaged through a cabinet. "Howard, where's that Christmas Blend I bought the other day at Sea Dogs?"

"Pantry. Top shelf."

"Thanks, hon." Mrs. Allen turned to Ginny. "Sit. Sit. I'll take care of everything."

"Excuse me, can I grab some dip? It's excellent, Mrs. Allen."

"Thanks, Catherine. Have you met my sister?"

Ginny smiled and piled spinach-artichoke dip onto her plate. "Oh, this feels good. Haven't sat all morning. And that includes church," Ginny said. "Never run late for church on Christmas morning. Easter either. That's when all the half-assers like me go, like it's going to make any difference. When I meet St. Peter up at the Pearly Gates, he'll probably be able to tell I'm a half-ass churchgoer just by looking at me."

Mrs. Allen squeezed her sister's shoulders. "Face it, you're damned."

Ginny finished a last bite of bread and wiped her mouth. "Well, if hell comes with three square meals that I don't have to cook and an occasional bath, count me in!"

A cheer went up in the family room. The end of the Patriots' game signaled it was almost time for dinner. Mona Allen knew better than to interfere with football, even on Christmas Day. Why put all of that time into cooking if all they do is shovel it into their mouths as fast as possible so they can get back to the game?

Patsy, Robert, Steven, and Catherine had volunteered to sit at the kids' table so Aunt Ginny could help Gregor cut his meal and so Jackie could join the rest of her family.

"Steven is the best cook. Wait until dessert," Patsy said. "He made all of them—pecan pie, pumpkin cheesecake, and individual apple tarts drizzled with caramel."

Robert agreed. "No doubt about it. You're in for a treat."

"Really, you are too kind. Keep going. But seriously, while I'll be slaving away for a pittance, Robert here will be raking in the big bucks."

"We'll see about that." The ex-football player blushed.

"He's already got a job lined up after graduation." Steven was clearly happy for his brother.

"Icon Systems. At the San Jose branch," Patsy added. "He interned there this summer, and they offered him a position.

"That's wicked good! Congratulations!"

Steven nudged his sister. "See that? She already sounds like a local."

CHAPTER ELEVEN

A FRIGID LATE-JANUARY MORNING FOUND CATHERINE wishing she had dried her hair completely instead of running out the door, semi-dripping, to catch the ferry. When she caught her reflection in Sea Dogs' window, the Bride of Frankenstein stared back. Bangs standing almost straight up highlighted a large pimple in the middle of her forehead. Lovely. All hail Zit Queen of the Universe. Frozen hair. Large zit. Raging cramps. It was going to be a great day.

At least she was wearing her new coat, purchased at a seventy-five-percent off, after-Christmas sale. While everyone else roamed Portland in black, gray, and an occasional red, Catherine strutted down Exchange Street in a robin's egg blue, wearing all black underneath, of course, as to not shock her own system, as well as those of her co-workers.

"Psst."

The street was crowded with people en route to their various places of employment. Maybe one of them had farted too loudly.

"Psst. Psst."

There it was again, conjuring up made-for-TV-movie images of men wearing large trench coats trying to sell watches and drugs on dark city streets. But, please, this was Portland.

"Jesus, Catherine, would you wait up?" An irritated Scott Dithersby showed up behind her. "I've been trying to catch up with you for blocks."

"Walk faster then."

"Same old Catherine."

She tried in vain to smooth her bangs down. "What's that supposed to mean?" Like he knew her after one night of unbelievable sex? Or maybe it wasn't that great? After all, she had nothing to compare it to.

"You're always so happy to see me when we bump into each other."

"Bump into? You said you were following me."

"You are mad I haven't called you."

"What? Do you usually pick fights this early in the morning? You must be very popular with the ladies."

"*Are* you mad I haven't called you?"

Unsure what to say or where to look, Catherine began shifting her weight from one foot to the other, while she watched other pedestrians pass, people whose souls were not being bored into by Scott Dithersby. All she could come up with was a lame "you wish."

The last month had been spent pretending the night with Patsy and her daft friends never occurred and anything that happened afterward was only a dream, a really hot dream. This denial was working quite well. Who needed virginity anyhow? Unfortunately, only half of Catherine's brain complied with the avoidance plan. The other side waited, a mixture of fear and panic striking the closer her due date came. You hear about it all of the time. Girl's first time and bam! God's little karma joke. She was never so happy to have her period in her life.

"Most girls would have freaked."

"Really, Dithersby, that is so cliché."

"Disassociation by usage of last name. Interesting."

"What are you? A psych major?"

"Actually, yes."

"Goodie for you."

"Hostility, too. I can only come to the conclusion you wanted me to call, and when I did not because I was in Colorado over Christmas break, you denied our tryst and are now refusing to admit your true feelings."

"Which are?"

"You want me, of course."

"Yup, that must be it. Well, now that you have that all straightened out, I need to get to work."

Scott grabbed her arm, his breath warm in her ear. "I thought about you every day. Us in the car. Us at Phil's apartment." His proximity shattered Catherine's protective sardonic shield. "Can I see you tonight?"

The thought made her tingle, but she did not want to appear too willing. "I guess."

"You're on Peaks, right?"

Catherine gave him the address and hurried off to Christmas Bells, unsure of what had just happened.

———※———

Scott had phoned again asking if he could see her tonight, and now here she was, schlepping flowers, wine, and pasta carbonara ingredients home on the ferry. Catherine had started exploring the culinary arts after realizing that several months take out was heavy on the wallet, as well as the waistline. Carbonara was her most sophisticated meal thus far. Besides, this was a night to celebrate.

She did not get to see Scott very often, what with all of the hours she put in at Christmas Bells. And Scott was taking a full course load at University of Southern Maine and working at the Visitor Center. Catherine intended to make the most out of this Wednesday evening.

The doorbell rang. She tugged at the bottom of the teddy hidden under her blouse and skirt and then buzzed him up.

Carbonara scent permeating her apartment, Catherine stood eagerly at the door.

Scott Dithersby took one look at her and hurled himself on her, mouth ready to explore.

She pushed him away slightly. "Wait. What about dinner?"

"Who needs dinner when something so appetizing is before me now?" He pulled her toward him. "Come here."

"But, I made pasta carbonara from scratch." She gestured to the kitchen, where the table was set with all the new things Catherine had purchased for just such an occasion.

Scott did not seem to notice. She was the only thing in his focus. He pulled her down on the sofa and began unbuttoning her blouse.

One hour later, Catherine was scrapping burnt carbonara sauce from her brand new stainless steel pan, while Scott sat on the sofa, drinking wine.

"I love the view from here."

"The city does look pretty, doesn't it?"

"That is not what I'm talking about."

Catherine smirked at him. Blushing, she turned back to the pan. "This is never going to come off."

"Don't worry about it. We had more important things to do. It was worth it. What's one pan?"

Fifty bucks of my hard-earned money, Catherine thought, but did not want to break the mood. Just then, Scott sauntered up behind her and began kissing her neck lightly. She sighed, abandoning the pan, and wiped her hands on his lovely backside.

Catherine entered Christmas Bells unusually chipper for a Thursday morning. This Dithersby dalliance had been going on for many months now, a secret to all but the two of them, which made it even more exciting.

"Good morning, Mrs. McLellan."

"Morning, dear. You are looking spry this fine day. You must have had some fun last night."

Catherine choked on her coffee. "Um, no, not really. I mean, nothing better than usual."

"Are you okay? Do you need some water?"

Before Catherine could answer, Patsy bounded through the door. "Hello, everyone. Well, all two of you," she giggled.

Mrs. McLellan looked at Patsy, then back at Catherine. "What's up, Patsy?"

"Oh, nothing." She giggled again and began straightening the candy sticks in front of the register, but could not contain herself. "Well, okay, so here's the thing. I've got a date tomorrow." There it was again. That giggle.

"That's great. With whom?"

"Well, I, um...I really don't want to say."

"Why?"

"Things have been going so well, I don't want to jinx it. We have been seeing each other for about a month or so. He wants to take me to Bar Harbor for the weekend." Giggle. "By the way Catherine, would you cover my Saturday shift for me? Pl-eee-ase?"

"Sure. I don't have anything else to do anyhow." Scott had told her he needed to study for midterms all weekend.

Thankfully, Patsy's giggles subsided when Mrs. McLellan began outlining the day's activities. The announcement of spring cleaning at Christmas Bells managed to drive away the morning's excessive joy.

"Okay, ladies. Let's get to work!" Katie said in her best task master voice, while Catherine and Patsy followed behind.

CHAPTER TWELVE

S PRING PASSED QUICKLY IN PORTLAND. Warmer temperatures and melting snow heralded maple syrup season, and the trees were usually tapped once the thaw began. After Maine Maple Sunday—the last weekend in March—little sugar shacks began popping up along the highways.

"Taking my business away, that's all they do," complained Velma Dithersby to an unsympathetic Katie McLellan in front of Christmas Bells. "Tourists think it's 'cute' to get their maple syrup from one of those damned shacks, all the while my shop is losing revenue."

"Well, Velma, I'm sure you will sleep better tonight knowing good Portland visitors are paying what they should for syrup instead of twice as much at your place." Katie turned and went inside. "Hey, girls. The Sea Hag is at it again. Moaning about losing money to the sugar shack owners. Can you believe it? She's a piece of work."

"Well, it is sort of true, isn't it?" Patsy piped up from the storeroom.

"Patsy, what are you smokin'? The prices she charges for her 'gourmet' syrup could feed a farmer's family for a week. Not to mention all of the other over-priced crap she sells. Velma Dithersby is doing just fine. No need to worry about her." Katie stomped upstairs, grumbling.

"Since when are you a fan of the Sea Hag?"

"I'm not...I just...I guess I could see what she was saying, that's all. You know, she might not be as bad as Mrs. McLellan says."

"What? Isn't she the one who blatantly insulted you the first week I started working here?"

"Maybe she had a bad day."

Catherine shook her head and started working on the new candy cane tree.

"Let's hop the ferry and go to Parallel." Excited, Catherine popped out of bed, reaching for her panties.

"Wait." Scott pulled her back down and wrapped his legs around her. "Why do we need to go anywhere? I'm pretty comfy right here."

"Come on. We never go out together. Let's have some fun."

"I am now officially insulted. I think I will slink home now, mortified and ashamed." He pantomimed a half-assed attempt at getting out of the bed.

This time, it was Catherine who pulled him down on top of her. "That's not what I meant. Of course you are fun. Wicked fun." She stroked his face and said softly, "I cannot imagine anything better than being here with you."

"Of course you can't." Scott rolled over on top of her and nuzzled her neck.

Catherine could barely sit still during the cab ride to the McLellans. Tonight they would finally meet Patsy's mystery man. She wished Scott could have been there with her, but seeing as they had not gone public yet, that was impossible. Soon, though. They had discussed it a few nights ago. Patsy and Mrs. McLellan would just have to get used to it, wouldn't they? Would Katie and Marty throw a dinner party for them?

Two white Adirondack chairs sat on the front lawn of the McLellan house. Pots filled with various coleus and sweet potato vines cluttered the front porch. Rosa Rugosa bloomed fragrant white splendor. The vocal strains of Tony Bennett traveled out the open windows and down the street carried by the cove's gentle breezes. Catherine rang the doorbell.

"Hello, sweetie." Marty McLellan smiled. "Come on in." He gave her a hug, careful not to smash the flowers the girl had brought for Katie. "Everyone is out on the patio. I'll get a vase for these."

Catherine made her way to the lit gazebo, then stopped dead in her tracks. She would recognize those shoulders anywhere.

"Cat!" Patsy ran to her friend, gesturing for the man to join her. "Surprise! We are back together. Can you believe it?"

"But I thought you hated him," was all she could spit out.

"That's all in the past, isn't it, honey?" Patsy rubbed Scott Dithersby's back. He smiled back at her. Catherine shot Mrs. McLellan a look.

Katie crossed the yard to give her a hug. "Good to see you, sweetheart. Come, let me get you a drink." She ushered her into the kitchen. "I know. I cannot believe it, either. But, I suppose it is her life, and we have to support her."

Catherine glanced out the window at the two of them, trying to catch Scott's eye. *Look at me.* But he and Patsy were in their own little world. Scott whispered to her. She playfully tickled him.

"Ssh. Not yet." Patsy giggled.

"Oh, come on. Everyone is here." Scott set down his drink and clapped his hands. "May I have your attention, please? Patsy and I have an announcement."

Catherine and Mrs. McLellan exchanged worried looks.

"We're engaged!" Patsy beamed. "We wanted you to be the first to know since you all are like family."

The McLellans and Catherine stood like statues until Marty broke the silence. "Well, I hope your years together will be as blessed as mine have been with my darling Katie."

"Cat? Aren't you going to say anything?" Patsy appeared distraught.

Scott took over immediately. "I understand your shock, but Patsy and I were together for two years before you moved here. We have a lot of history together. When I saw her at Parallel one night, I realized how much I missed her." He kissed a blushing Patsy's hand.

Parallel? "You know what? I need to grab something from my purse. I'll be right back."

"Hey, Catherine," Scott said loudly enough for everyone to hear as he followed her into the living room. "I hope we can put aside any past animosity and be friends." He lowered his voice. "And you are going to play along, aren't you? After all, what would poor Patsy do if she found out her best friend was fucking her fiancé? You would not want to be responsible for that devastation, would you? So be a good Kitty Cat and scamper back into the kitchen with a smile on your face and congratulations on your lips as I stare at your hot ass in that skirt." He pushed her toward the kitchen.

Patsy ran to her friend. "Are you okay, Cat?"

"Of course she is, my darling. She's just overwhelmed with joy for us, aren't you, Catherine?"

Patsy hugged her. "I am so happy. I know this is early, but would you be my maid of honor?"

All of the color rushed out from Catherine's face.

"There is plenty of time for that later, Patsy. Why don't you get the champagne we brought out of the refrigerator."

Catherine turned to Scott. "Why Patsy?"

"I think what you really mean is why not you? My dear Cat, you are a delicious mid-week snack. Nothing more." He turned away from her and joined his fiancée. "Patsy, darling. Let me help you with that."

Catherine's red eyes were obviously from tears of happiness. How touching she cared so much for Patsy! Her silence was not even noticed, as Scott Dithersby monopolized most of the dinner conversation, ingratiating himself to the McLellans. What a wonderful meal! This dessert is fantastic! He played the perfect fiancé, never more than a minute going by without a touch, a loving glance, or a wink to his beloved.

Whether or not this was believed by Katie McLellan, no one knew, but for Patsy's sake, their hostess attempted to be pleasant. Still, Katie could not shake the notion that something was not quite right.

CHAPTER THIRTEEN

"Hey, Kitty Cat. Where you goin'?" a fifteen-year-old Skip Nagurski yelled.

"Out." Catherine jumped on her bike. Skip nodded to Sammy, and they both took off after her.

"Come back, Kitty Cat. Skippy wants to play."

They sped up, overtaking her at the gate.

"Get out of my way."

"Oh, poor Kitty Cat. My, my you are certainly fillin' out that shirt well."

Sammy came up behind her and snapped her bra strap.

"Cut it out. Leave me alone."

"But I want to play with the kitty." Skip pushed her against the gate.

"Get off me."

"I like 'em feisty. Ain't that right, Sammy?"

"You're pathetic. You know that? What? No one will go out with you so you have to try to feel up your friend's little sister?"

"You know you want it. Look at you, with your tight little shirt and short shorts. C'mon, kitty."

Skip grabbed her left breast. Catherine kicked him square in the crotch. He buckled over. "What the hell, Catherine? I'm just tryin' to have some fun."

"Don't ever touch me again." She got on her bike and pedaled as fast as she could.

"I'll get you for this, Kitty Cat," Skip yelled, mounting his bike, but the pain in his groin made it impossible to ride off after her. "Oh, shit. Do somethin', Sammy."

"What the hell am I supposed to do?"

Catherine hid behind the World's Largest Christmas Trees, praying they did not follow her, then after a bit, took off for the house.

She biffed Russell's head as she walked past him, slouched on the couch per usual, hands in his pants, watching *Wheel of Fortune*. "Tell your asshole friends to leave me alone."

"What the hell? What are you talkin' about?"

His sister recanted the details.

"Probably asked for it." Russell stood up and headed for the door.

Catherine punched him with all she had, right in the solar plexus. Her brother doubled over.

"What happened to you?" Peter laughed as he grabbed the remote. He turned to his sister. "You do this to him?"

"So what if I did? You want to be next?" Catherine bolted up the stairs and slammed her bedroom door. Curling up on her bed, she drew Pookie Dog tight.

CHAPTER FOURTEEN

ATHERINE LAID IN BED, THE same bed she and Scott had made love in on so many Wednesdays. But there was no love involved in their "fucking," as he had so bluntly called it.

That's why they call it hump day, right?

A plaything. Some asshole's toy; that was all she was. No wonder he had never wanted to go out. He couldn't risk being seen with her. Those supposed mid-terms? He was in Bar Harbor with Patsy. She was such a fool. And now they shared a dirty little secret that would kill Patsy if it ever got out. She felt nauseous.

But why would he propose to Patsy so quickly? No matter how much she tried to deny it, Catherine kept coming back to the one question Scott Dithersby knew she would ask.

Why not me?

The week before Memorial Day, the Christmas Bells crew double-checked the inventory and stocked up the shelves, readying the store for the summer tourist season. Patsy was unusually quiet, but Catherine did not have the strength to ask why. Thankfully, the bride-to-be had not once asked her to check out a picture of a bridesmaid's dress today or nagged her about which flowers she preferred—roses or Sweet Williams?

In fact, for most of the afternoon, Patsy had been upstairs

in the children's rooms, putting the final touches on the new Baby's First Christmas tree, this year filled with ornaments shaped like bottles, booties, and diapers.

"Would you mind getting Patsy? I need her to start stocking, well, the stockings." Mrs. McLellan disappeared into the back room.

Catherine found her staring out the window, a box of Baby's First Christmas brag book photo albums on her lap.

"I'm pregnant, you know. That's why he asked me to marry him. His mother made sure I knew that today at lunch. Told me there was no way her son would ever marry someone like me unless I was carrying his child."

"Oh, honey." Catherine turned Patsy around and removed the box from her lap. Huge tears streaked Patsy's face.

"I thought I was the luckiest girl in the world. My parents were so happy I had found such a great guy until I told them about the baby."

Catherine folded Patsy into her arms, rocking her in the same way her friend would soon be rocking her own baby.

———————

It all made sense now. Once Scott found out about the pregnancy, he had no choice but to propose and probably assumed he could fool around on the side, while Patsy stayed at home playing the unsuspecting dutiful wife and mother. The whole thing would be a slight road bump, a minor inconvenience in his life.

Velma Dithersby would force the newlyweds to move in with her, where she would control every move Patsy made, every mothering decision, every ridiculous detail. Patsy's baby would end up ninety percent Dithersby with just a trace of its mother's normal family.

This was not right. Patsy deserved to be loved for her sweet soul, not to be chewed up and spat out by the Dithersbys. No, they would not do this to her Patsy.

But how could Catherine stop it without incriminating herself?

———⟨𝒰⟩———

"I have an idea that will get you out of all of this." Catherine set a glass of water before a befuddled Patsy.

"There isn't one. I've been over this in my head a hundred times."

"You could have an abortion."

"My parents would kill me. Scott would go ballistic. And God only knows what his parents would do to me."

"It's your body, Patsy. Your life. No one else's."

"Not anymore," she said, rubbing her stomach.

"Your parents would get over it. They love you."

"What about Scott?

"What about him?"

"Catherine, I love him!"

"Does he love you, Patsy? Really love you the way every man loves his fiancée? Did you talk about marriage before you told him you were pregnant?"

"Well, no."

Catherine shook her head. "Didn't think so. You are going to end up an indentured servant, taking care of his child all by yourself, and putting up with his mother's shit."

"But it's my baby, too."

"You are young and healthy. You could have plenty of kids when the time is right."

"I don't know."

"Do you really want to be the stay-at-home prisoner, I mean, wife of Scott Dithersby? How many times a week, hell, a day, do you think the Sea Hag will stop by to visit her grandchild? Actually, since neither of you have any money, you'll probably have to move in with them. How would you enjoy that, Patsy? The Sea Hag and her spindly hellishness constantly criticizing your parenting, breathing down your neck, watching everything you do. 'Don't burp the baby that way. Do it like this.' 'How do you expect to raise my grandchild in this filthy room? You should clean it while the baby takes his nap. That's what I always did.' You think she is a pain in the ass now? Just wait."

Catherine leaned back in her chair, allowing her friend to digest everything she had said. Patsy started to cry. It was working.

"One little procedure, and all of this disappears."

"Would you come with me?"

"Absolutely."

The appointment was for ten o'clock at Dr. Mulrooney's office. Catherine squeezed Patsy's cold hand before her friend was led into the examination room.

Mrs. McLellan had given both of them the day off after Catherine told her Patsy needed a change of scenery and suggested a day trip to Augusta might do her some good. The whole thing was over very quickly. Patsy was sitting up, drinking some juice, and eating a graham cracker when the nurse brought Catherine in. "Hey, Cat. There's snacks. Do you want something?"

This was not the reaction Catherine had anticipated. She had expected to play the dutiful friend, while Patsy choked back the tears, unable to speak, not to see some overgrown nine-year-old who still delighted in snack time. "How do you feel?"

"Pretty good, actually."

A nurse handed Patsy a small piece of paper. "Here is your prescription for Tylenol with codeine for pain. Take one every four to six hours today and as needed tomorrow. You might feel a little cramping."

That explained it. Patsy must have the same reaction Russell did to codeine when he had that concussion from Peter throwing the pumpkin at his head, Catherine thought he would have been crying for hours, but when he was wheeled out of the emergency room, Russell had a big grin on his face and would not shut up about the stitches in his head. "Catherine, you won't believe it. They actually took a needle and some hospital thread and sewed my head, just like Ma does with our socks. Cool!"

Catherine drove Patsy's car to the docks. From there, they took the ferry to Peaks and hung out at Catherine's apartment, so Patsy could take it easy for the rest of the day. After chicken soup and a Tom Cruise movie marathon, it was time to get Patsy home to her unsuspecting family. She would break the news to them in a day or two, after she was feeling ready.

———ᘓᘜ———

Mrs. McLellan was starting to worry. Patsy had not shown up for work in three days. "Did she get sick in Augusta?"

"Where?"

"Your day trip to Augusta. Did Patsy seem ill?"

"Oh, yeah, sorry. I spaced for a second. No, she definitely was not sick."

"If I hear damn Velma Dithersby did something to our Patsy, I'll wring her skinny neck."

———ᘓᘜ———

Summer hours were in full swing at Christmas Bells, which meant the store stayed open until nine o'clock again for any tourists eager to spend money on after-dinner strolls. Catherine hurried down Exchange Street. It was twelve forty-five, and her shift started at one o'clock.

Weird that Patsy had never returned any of her calls. The secret must be out, and her friend was dealing with the ramifications. What Catherine really wanted to know was whether or not Scott Dithersby was with her when Pasty told her family about the abortion. How Catherine wished she could have seen his face!

Not wanting to be accosted by the Sea Hag, Catherine walked quickly past Casco Bay Gourmet Foods. The store was dark, and a closed sign hung on the door.

Catherine rounded the corner and was just about to reach for the Christmas Bells door when, from out of nowhere, someone grabbed her, twisted her arm behind her back, and pushed her into the alley. Catherine tried to break free, but he was too strong. He smashed her face against the wall, holding her head tight.

"It was you, wasn't it?"

"I don't know what you are talking about. Let me go." She struggled to free her arm, red brick scraping her cheek.

"Don't play dumb with me, Kitty Cat. I know it was you."

"Scott?" Catherine kicked backwards at his leg, each time getting closer to his crotch. "I swear to God, if you don't let me go, I'll..."

He lost his grip. Catherine stumbled.

"Admit it!" His eyes were wide and maniacal.

Catherine felt her check. It was bleeding.

"Patsy told me last night. Ah ha! See! You do know what I'm talking about."

"No, I really don't."

Red-faced and seething, Scott threw the words into her face. "You killed my child!"

"I did no such thing."

"You talked Patsy into getting that abortion. There's no way it was her idea."

"Are you insane?"

"You bitch," he hissed raising his fist, then hesitated, remembering he was in downtown Portland.

"That's the thing about karma, Scott. One never knows when it will strike." Catherine began walking out of the alley. "Have a nice day."

"You're not going anywhere, Kitty Cat." Scott grabbed her hair, yanking her backward. Then he dragged her around the building, up the Christmas Bells stairs, and pushed her through the door.

"No need to slam. How can I help you?" Katie McLellan froze. "Scott, what are you doing? Let her go, son."

Katie's pleas only incensed him. He yanked Catherine's head further down and threw her to the floor, where she sat, the salt from her tears stinging her bloody cheek.

Patsy tromped down the stairs. "Scott! Stop!"

Turning on Patsy now he demanded, "How could you have listened to her? I was the father!"

"Scott, calm down now." Katie tried to maneuver her way to the telephone next to the cash register.

"Tell her, Catherine. Tell stupid bitch McLellan how her sweet, darling Cat killed my child. Tell her!" Scott kicked Catherine hard in the left side.

Patsy screamed. Katie picked up the phone and began dialing.

"Tell...her...Catherine!" Scott punctuated each word with a kick.

"It's my fault. Not Catherine's." Patsy turned to Mrs. McLellan. "I had an abortion a few days ago, when Catherine and I were supposed to be on a day trip."

Katie dropped the phone and brought Patsy into her arms.

"Dumb, misguided cow that you are, the blame lies with only one person in this room. The puppet master herself." Scott mockingly bowed toward Catherine. "Bravo."

Catherine inched herself off the floor, propping up against the Christmas Bells fireplace, certain Scott had broken at least one of her ribs. "Scott, stop."

"That's not what you said all of our Wednesday nights together. Let's see, almost every week since, when was it? Oh, yes, Merry Madness. I bet our dear little Kitty Cat never told either of you about our Wednesday night hump days, did she?"

"Catherine?"

"That's right, Patsy. Your best friend was my mid-week booty call."

Catherine tried to talk, but it hurt to breathe. "I didn't know he was seeing you, Pasty, I swear!"

"And now, ladies, I bid you adieu." Scott looked down at Catherine. "You were right. Karma *is* a bitch," he whispered, slamming the door.

"I'll call an ambulance." Katie McLellan dialed 9-1-1. "Patsy, honey, come on into the stockroom. Let's get you some water."

They disappeared, leaving Catherine to wait for the ambulance alone.

Catherine pushed the nurse's buzzer. Unlike Patsy and Russell, codeine did not send her to a happy place. She needed something stronger. It hurt every time she moved, every time she took a breath. All she wanted was something to take her away from this place, far away, where the Dithersbys did not exist.

She lay in her hospital bed with a cracked rib and stitched-up face, badly bruised and broken-hearted. At least that crazy asshole could not get to her in here.

Katie McLellan had come to check on Catherine yesterday. Her face wore incomprehension and disappointment. Was this the same Mrs. McLellan who had once helped a fly escape from a spider web? Where was the compassion?

"This is Scott's fault, Mrs. McLellan, not mine."

"I do not excuse what he did to you. What I want to know is why you felt the need to talk Patsy into having an abortion. Whether you like it or not, Scott Dithersby was the father and had the right to be involved."

"Seems to me he gave up any rights when he two-timed Patsy with her best friend."

"It takes two to tango, my dear. You knew he was trouble, though, apparently none of us knew just how much. You should have never gotten involved with him."

"I loved him."

"Please, Catherine, you can't be that naive. A red flag never went up when he only saw you on Wednesdays?"

"We had to keep it secret so we wouldn't hurt Patsy."

"Now you blame Patsy? Good Lord, girl, have you no shame?" Mrs. McLellan shook her head.

"I provided Patsy with a better option."

"You used Patsy just as much as Scott used you! She has not left her house for the past two days. She can't eat. Can't sleep. Her mother told me she wakes up in the middle of the night screaming for her baby. You did that to her!"

Catherine rolled her eyes.

Mrs. McLellan continued, "They were going to work something out, Patsy and Scott. Who knows? Maybe Scott would have settled down after the baby came? Now, Patsy's a mess, and Scott is sitting in jail charged with assault and battery."

"Look at me! Look what he did to me!"

"Catherine, obviously I'm sad to see you this way, and I do not condone what Scott did to you, but you have to be willing to admit your share of the blame."

"I can't believe this! Patsy made her own choice. Scott sure as hell made his. I'm not the devil on either of their shoulders."

"Aren't you?" Katie McLellan stood stone-faced, arms crossed over her chest, fingering her necklace.

The image of Clara Elbert from the night her parents told her she was forbidden to play Ado Annie flashed into Catherine's head. "Get out of here! I don't need you. I don't need anybody. Fuck you all."

Katie McLellan sighed and left the hospital room.

CHAPTER FIFTEEN

San Diego, California

CATHERINE TRUDGED THROUGH THE FINE, deceptively heavy sand. Tide had not yet come in, and the shoreline was dotted with people. A little girl scampered after a seagull until the annoyed bird spread its wings and took flight, leaving behind giggles of glee. A teenage couple embraced, waves encircling their feet. A father and his two sons bravely faced the foaming waves. Wait...wait...wait...run! They retreated inland to avoid total submersion.

She traced a "C" in the soft sand, which was flecked with gold dust. Catherine had never seen anything like this before. The Maine shore had been rocky, white, and harsh. This ocean seemed more tame, more friendly. Definitely warmer.

A curly-haired blond boy scooped up two crabs and ran to show his mother, while two others staged their own D-Day invasion on the beach. Preteens boogie boarded on small waves, trying not to crash into the Japanese family walking by them.

The Hotel del Coronado sat just over her shoulder, a mere thirty minutes away from her tiny apartment, famous as the location where *Some Like It Hot* was filmed. Of course, Clara Elbert had chastised her for watching a movie highlighting cross-dressing comedians and ample views of Marilyn Monroe's bosom. Catherine adjusted her swimsuit strap, suddenly conscious of her own breasts peeking out from purple fabric.

Except for two ocean liners far from shore, nothing was on the horizon. A red dragon kite hung on the gentle breeze, a "kid" in his sixties tugging at its tail.

A football flew over her head. "Got it!"

"Nice catch," Catherine found herself commenting to the receiver.

"Thanks." Football man ran toward the huddle, glancing back at her with a grin.

A bit further down the beach, about forty white chairs were set up near some huge rocks. Malibu Barbie and her equally perfect fiancé were conceptualizing their dream beach wedding. Catherine checked out their potential view. Spectacular. Sure beat St. Agatha's and a reception at the VFW hall, which was customary in Burkesville.

She supposed she should call home and tell them about the move. Maybe this weekend. Her rib was almost healed. The bruises on her face were gone. She was an entire continent away from Scott Dithersby. He could never hurt her again.

People started to pack up now, ready to go to their hotel rooms to freshen up for dinner. Cat checked her watch. Six thirty. She gathered her things and headed home.

———— ⌀⟍ ————

Catherine had passed training and was now a full-time employee of the San Diego Zoo. She hung out at a different animal habitat each day during lunch hour. It made her feel "out and about," a term forever etched into her cerebellum courtesy of her mother who had insisted upon using it every time Catherine or her siblings left the house.

"Out and about, eh? Where ya goin'?" Clara's neck would crane, looking up momentarily from peeling potatoes for that evening's dinner. When she received the usual response of "nowhere" or "Beth's house," Clara barked, "be back for dinner" and went on peeling. Did her mother not realize there were alternative starch forms like rice? The Elberts were strictly meat and potatoes. Clara would have none of those foreign side dishes, as if serving her family plain white rice would get them run out of Wisconsin.

Catherine picked up a cheeseburger and soda, eating on her way to Gorilla Tropics. The zoo was crowded today, more so than the last few days. Maybe it was a school holiday.

Frail and frumpy, leading a parade of children destined to be labeled dorks, a short woman trekked through the crowd, her final destination the ice cream cart. Her face, ashen. Her eyes, small and without visible lashes. Over permed, fuzzy blonde hair framed her perspiring face. Her children chirped their demands, baby birds twittering, waiting for their sustenance. Catherine shook her head. She could never see herself as a parent. Placating to the demands of others every waking moment was not her idea of life. She had had enough of that in Burkesville and had no intention of running the risk her child would end up being a mini-Clara. Family traits were passed down, whether people like to admit it or not. The thought made her shudder. At least she had saved Patsy.

She joined the crowd wandering through Gorilla Tropics, the only dark-haired female within fifty feet, not counting the new mother gorilla nursing her baby. Were there really that many blondes in the world? Maybe out here, blond men only marry blonde women, some sort of genetic inbreeding thing. Catherine tried to feel exotic with her brunette tete, until four Asian women glided past, shimmering straight black tresses complementing latte skin.

Oh shit! It's one o'clock! She took off running for the Ituri Forest Outpost.

"Hey, Catherine! How's it going? Omigod, I did not sleep at all last night. Probably shouldn't have watched *Dracula* at ten, but I really like Gary Oldman. He's so creepy, yet so cool in that gray Edwardian suit, gazing intensely over those awesome John Lennon sunglasses. If I were Mina, I'm not sure I could resist him either, but then I would become Dracula's undead vampire wife and have to dump Keanu Reeves, who has his own merits and has come quite a way from Bill and Ted, don't you think?"

So it went. Every morning, Brooke Bentley's great oration on film criticism and/or pop culture. No one was exempt. She read all the tabloids, watched every award show, and never missed *Entertainment Tonight*. Brooke even made a yearly pilgrimage to Hollywood to view whatever television show she could get tickets for, tour Universal Studios, and lovingly caress Clark Gable's star on Vine Avenue, even though he had died a full decade before she was born. Brooke also educated Catherine on other Gable facts, such as how he made women swoon and had received five thousand marriage proposals from adoring fans.

"Vivian Leigh supposedly complained about his bad breath on the set of *Gone with the Wind*." Brooke shook her head, jamming her purse into the locker next to Catherine's. "I think I could have dealt with it."

Brooke worked in the Kid Store near the zoo's exit, where she could often be seen making rubber snakes slither around unsuspecting mothers' necks while their children agonized over which stuffed animal to purchase. Panda or tiger? Koala or lynx?

"Wanna meet for lunch today? I'll call you on the walkie-talkie."

"Sure. Sounds good." Catherine was assigned to Express

Bus Stop Number Three in Horn and Hoof Mesa, filling in for Phil something or another who was out sick. The morning passed quickly, directing zoo visitors to wait in line until the next bus came, which was about every fifteen minutes. It was a popular stop. People loved the Sichuan takins across the walkway. The goat antelope's babies had begun wobbling around, head butting each other, and cavorting on the rocks.

"Catherine Elbert. Paging Catherine Elbert. Do you copy?"

Catherine turned down her walkie-talkie. "Hey, Brooke."

"Lunch time, fun time. Meet you at Skyfari East."

Initially, the Skyfari Aerial Tram had freaked Catherine out, especially when the flying bucket thumped and rocked while passing under the immense white towers that held the wires up. But, now, at least she could marvel at the view as she crossed the zoo. Balboa Park's magnificent Museum of Man's tower rising over the the palm trees. The giant pandas lying on their backs, chomping bamboo. The Scripps Aviary's gentle waterfall.

Her gondola pulled into Skyfari East station.

"There you go, Catherine. Please watch your step." Some guy she remembered from training offered his hand and a smile. Catherine sped down the ramp toward Brooke.

————

People buzzed around Catherine, darting from store to store, errand to errand, each with a purpose she was void of.

"Excuse me, dear." A petite lady whizzed past her, white wispy poofs of cotton candy crowning her head. "It's a bit crowded today, isn't it?"

Catherine nodded and let the lady enter before her through the automatic doors. Milk, half-gallon. Strawberries. Two frozen meals. Her groceries were simple. A large detergent lasted more than two months. Same for multipacks of toilet paper and tissues. She ate most of her meals at the zoo. The novelty of cooking for one had worn off some time ago.

"Cut it out. God, you are such a brat," an exasperated preteen bellowed, while the perpetrator, wearing a Mickey Mouse t-shirt and huge grin, continued ramming her brother's ankles with the grocery cart.

Twin girls toting blonde-haired, blue-eyed baby dolls swaddled in pink blankets entered, following their mother's footsteps so closely, it was amazing the elder did not end up face first on the black plastic mat, well-timed automatic door thuds besieging her head while oblivious shoppers stepped around her.

"Cookies! Ice cream! Pizza!"

Did all twins speak in unison? Jane Bauer and Johanna Reichman were about as close as Burkesville had to twins, but they were merely unimaginative girls who dressed alike, did their hair identically every day, and talked in the same mock-Valley Girl accents, which was like totally out of place in Wisconsin, fer sure.

"Fancy meeting you here, Catherine." Bill Wolfe worked in the shop by the koalas. Catherine glanced down at his cart, piled high with Corona beer, light and regular. Three bags of limes sat where toddlers were usually strapped in. "Oh, yeah, this. A few friends of mine are having a party at the beach tonight. Hey! You should come. Brooke will be there. At about sevenish, after the tourists leave. In Carlsbad. South Carlsbad Beach. You take 101, Pacific Coast Highway, north."

Catherine had not yet ventured past La Jolla. Negatives? Probably filled with Kens and Barbies. Positives?

"Just wear shorts and bring a light sweater or something for when the sun sets." Bill bent over his cart. "Wait, what's that I hear? Oh, si, Señor Corona wants you to go." He picked up the limes. "Señorita Elbert. Come play with us."

"Okay. South Carlsbad Beach. Seven o'cock. Got it. See you then."

"Great! It's gonna be a blast."

Driving up 101, Catherine turned off the radio to hear the waves ebb and flow. She hadn't had much social activity since she moved. Her life consisted of working at the zoo, lunch with Brooke, walking around various parts of San Diego, and spending as much time on the beach as possible, digging her feet into the warm sand.

The sign said "Carlsbad," so she slowed down and searched for Bill and Brooke. It was impossible to see from here. Before she knew it, she was in Oceanside. *Shit.* It would be dark soon. There were smatterings of cars and trucks parked up the road. What did Brooke drive again? Nissan? Honda? Some Japanese car. *Shit.*

Large orange and gold flames shot up, about a quarter mile up. "Carlsbad South Beach." This must be the place. Catherine parked her car, adjusted her bra, fluffed her hair as best as she could, and went to find Brooke.

By now, it was pitch-black. All she had to do was get through the rocky descending embankment without tripping flat on her face. Catherine moved in slow motion, it seemed, plodding through the sand toward the bonfire.

"Hey, Allie. How's it going?" A blond guy wearing a bright Hawaiian shirt and yellow shorts hugged her, rubbing her back. "It's been a long time." He pressed his face into her hair.

"That was very nice, but I'm not Allie." Catherine pulled away.

The mystery guy held her at arm's length. "I'm sorry. You look just like her. It's dark."

"It's okay." She held out her hand. "I'm Catherine."

He took it, puzzled. "Chuck."

"Do you know where Brooke Bentley is?"

"Brooke?" Chuck scratched his head. "I don't know any Brooke."

Oh great. Wrong party.

"Are you Allie's sister?" He was not letting this go.

"No, I have two brothers. No sisters."

"It's just that you look so much like her."

"Well, I'm not." Awkward in so many ways, Catherine was frozen there with Chuck and his confusion.

"What did you say your name was?"

"Catherine."

"Well, Catherine, who looks exactly like Allie, can I get you a drink? Aw, c'mon. It's a great party."

There was something endearing about this Chuck. Maybe it was the way he held her when he thought she was Allie, the way he nuzzled into her hair.

"Why not?"

———⁂———

"Catherine! Omigod!" There was a perpetual state of urgency in Brooke's voice, no matter if the next sentence was "What do you feel like eating?" or "Did you hear some psycho tried to land a plane on the White House front lawn?" She continued. "I'm so hungry, like I could die. My mother always told me not to skip the most important meal of the day, but I ran out of time this morning and only had coffee."

Catherine need never utter another syllable. There was comfort in that. Her mother would hate Brooke Bentley, which made walking with her under this cloud-free azure sky so wonderful, amid plant and animal species that could never survive a Wisconsin winter.

Brooke was *dying* for the baked vegetarian pasta at the

Treehouse Cafe. "So, where were you on Saturday? Bill said he ran into you at Ralph's and invited you to the beach party."

"I drove around trying to find it, but gave up." It was partly true. "Did you have fun?" Catherine put an iced tea on her tray next to the Cobb salad.

"Awesome. Hey, do you think Ross and Rachel on *Friends* will ever get together?" Brooke handed money to the cashier.

"You know, I really don't watch it." Catherine searched for an open table.

"Brooke, over here!" Morgan Jones waved. He was sitting with that other guy from Skyfari East, Will Overman.

"Hi, guys. Mind if we join you?"

"Sure. Plenty of room." Morgan scooted his chair over.

"Remember Catherine, right?"

"Yup. She and I had training together." Will smiled.

Cat took a seat, finding their silly, sheepish grins amusing, grins that appeared on every male's face when a woman like Brooke Bentley acknowledged his presence.

Sitting on the deck surrounded by palm trees brought Catherine back to the first day of training with that goof Archibald Angsley. "Did you know, ladies and gentlemen, the San Diego Zoo is also a world-class botanical garden? Of course you didn't." He had puffed out his chest like a frigate bird, pleased he could impart even a minute amount of his zoo knowledge upon the poor newbies. Catherine chuckled.

"What's so funny?" Morgan inquired, a spot of marinara sauce from his chicken parmesan dotting his check.

"You might want to wipe." Catherine indicated the red stain.

"Oh, thanks," he snapped, clearly thinking her snickers were directed at him.

Catherine did not bother to let him think otherwise.

"Has anyone seen *Jerry Maguire* yet?" Brooke asked. "I went Friday night."

No doubt Patsy had, Tom Cruise lover that she was. Last Catherine had heard, Scott was out of jail with a warning and a huge fine gladly paid for by the Sea Hag to free her beloved son.

"What do you think, Catherine?" Will turned toward her.

"What? Oh, sorry, I haven't seen it."

Morgan Jones rolled his eyes. "Of course not."

"God, I'm stuffed." Brooke sat back, rubbing her flat belly.

"Sit down here girls," a woman balancing a large tray and Louis Vuitton bag barked at two identical girls (again?) with yellow pigtails, pink capris, and flowered t-shirts. The mother had a perfectly coiffed blonde (of course) blunt cut with lighter blonde highlights. Her lipstick and nail polish matched the polka dots on her otherwise all-white t-shirt and shorts.

"I wanted a hot dog!"

"You said a chicken sandwich."

"I wanted pizza!"

"They don't have any here. How many times do I have to tell you?"

"Mom!" They shouted in unison, causing everyone in the immediate area to stare.

"Eat your lunches, or we are going home," the mother hissed through gritted teeth.

"I could never have kids," Morgan groused. "I don't have it in me."

"I want four. Of course, mine would not be brats like those kids." Brooke sucked up the last sip of her drink.

"I love my nephews."

"That's because they are boys, Will, not bratty, bitchy girls." Morgan looked straight at Catherine, who gave no reply.

"Well, gentlemen." Brooke got up. "It's been a slice, but time to get back to work."

"Bye, Brooke. Bye, Catherine." Will crumpled up his napkin and threw it on his plate.

"Later, Brooke," Morgan added.

"Why do you hate Catherine so much?"

"Oh, please. She doesn't exactly give off a warm, fuzzy vibe, now does she? The girl is a bitch. I can spot them a mile away. Come on, let's go."

Will disagreed, but arguing about it would be useless. She was an enigma, Catherine Elbert, unwilling to offer anything more than "thank you" when he helped her out of the Skyfari. Joe Miller had nicknamed her "The Ice Princess," but Will sensed something else was going on behind those steely eyes. But what?

CHAPTER SIXTEEN

"*H*EY! THAT ALASKAN BROWN BEAR looks like Mike Ditka!"

People say the silliest things while viewing animals. The mix-ups are understandable, like a father not remembering the name of a turacos bird or a tragopan. After all, how many bird species are there in the world? But when the sign was right in front of their faces, it's difficult not to laugh. Part of the delight was not knowing when these little gems would drop, like tiny gifts from the zoological gods, bestowing enough humor to carry on for another day. There should be some sort of zoo employee conference where everyone could get together and share stories. Oh, wait a minute. It's called "lunch."

Brooke, Catherine, Morgan, Will, and to everyone's surprise, Callie, gathered around the table, careful to keep their voices down so none of the visitors could hear. Callie managed the gift shop next to the koala exhibit. She was notoriously antisocial. Why she chose to join them for lunch today, Catherine could not even begin to guess.

"I was grabbing a cigarette over by African Kopje," Callie began. "There was this woman with I'd say maybe a seven-year-old and a teenager dressed all in black, eyeliner, the works. Anyhow, the little kid yells out 'Mommy! Look how small that deer is!' The Klipspringer antelope, right? So the mom responds 'I see, Jimmy. Actually, I saw one in the backyard last week while you were at school.'"

Everyone at the table roars with laughter.

"But wait, it gets better. The teenager says 'Really? You saw an animal that is almost extinct from the wild, *African* wild, mind you, munching away on our bushes?' Then the mom goes 'Shut the hell up, you good-for-nothing know-it-all.' The teenager scoffs. 'Yes, a mind is a terrible thing to waste.' Priceless!"

"Okay, okay, I got one." Morgan quieted them. "I'm at the snack cart near Gorilla Tropics, grabbing a pretzel, minding my own business on break, when this lady comes running toward me. 'You've got to stop them! Two gorillas are fighting. It's horrible!' I try to calm her down and tell her not to worry about it, that they are probably playing around. She grabs my arm and starts pulling me saying over and over 'But you have to stop them!' I look at her like get the hell off of me, but calmly say 'Ma'am, sometimes they like to wrestle. Boys will be boys and all that.' She looks me square in the face and says 'Well, that's unacceptable. They are setting a bad example for my children.' So I say to her 'Ma'am, I would love nothing more than to climb into their habitat and stop a fight between two western lowland gorillas who could kick my butt with one hit. What do you want me to do, put 'em in time out?'"

"Shush. We'd better keep it down." Brooke tried to remind everyone amid the laughter.

"I saw this last week. Same place. Gorilla Tropics," Will began. "There are these two guys, jeans, t-shirts, big pot bellies, both holding humungous sodas. They start banging on the window to get the gorilla's attention. One turns around and just looks at them. They keep banging on the window, but he stays still, staring at them. The one guy yells 'stupid animal' at it. The gorilla fakes like it is going to leave. The guys lean on the glass. The gorilla turns around, charges toward them and bangs full force on the glass with both hands. The sodas shoot up in the air, then spill all over them."

"You're shitin' me." Morgan is practically hyperventilating.

Will put his left hand over his heart and raised his right. "I swear to God, I saw that gorilla laugh before it ran away!"

Morgan high-fived Will. "Classic!"

"Serves them right," Catherine said.

Brooke chimed in. "I think that deserves a toast." The five raised their cups. "To the more evolved species."

Callie checked her watch. "Well, I have to hit the road."

"Yeah, me, too." Will rose. "Bye, guys." They headed off in the same direction, still laughing about the gorillas.

"Are they together?" Brooke's eyes followed them down the path. "Has he said anything to you, Morgan?"

"Nope. Will and Callie? That don't feel right."

Catherine stacked her dishes on her tray. "Maybe she just didn't feel like eating alone today."

"Nah, this was too much of a coinkydink."

"Coinkydink?" Morgan mouthed.

Catherine translated for him. "A Brooke-ism for coincidence."

On the way back to her post, Catherine stopped briefly by the hippos. What was it about seeing Will Overman with Callie that made her so on edge? Will was a part of the lunch bunch, that was all. Brooke kept saying he had a crush on her, but clearly she was wrong. But, Callie? What a minute! What did any of this matter? She had sworn off men to avoid this kind of stupidity. She was her own woman who did not need anyone to be happy. She lived in San Diego, for goodness sake, with the best weather on earth.

She scanned the zoo visitors around her. A family. An old couple holding hands. Little kids and a frazzled teacher all wearing Bayside Day Camp shirts. Most of the time, people referred to the various animals as "he," which she always thought was rather sexist. This time, Catherine could not believe her ears.

"She's a big one, isn't she?"

"Wow! She's some animal!"

"Look at her swim! I'm surprised she can even move."

The only animal in the entire zoo referred to as a *she* was a hippopotamus? Why didn't they all burst into a rousing rendition of the "She's Too Fat for Me" polka? Where was Frankie Dubrowski when you needed him?

She hated people.

Catherine popped the bottle cap off the Corona and smashed a lime wedge inside. The last time she drank one of these was at the beach party in Carlsbad. Sweet, amusing, dumb Chuck had left message after message on her answering machine wanting to get together for dinner sometime. They would never be returned. She had no desire to lead him on or play with him knowing she had no intention of a relationship. He deserved better than that. So had she.

Catherine was well aware of all the names that swirled in her wake at the zoo, but she did not care. This time, she was in charge. Brooke Bentley was too wrapped up in the movie of her life for any real friendship, which suited Catherine just fine. No probing questions. No fake intimacies. Just pop culture and lunch. Perfect. This was her life now. "Good girl" did not work well for her in Wisconsin. "Friendly" only brought trouble in Maine. Maybe "bitch" would play in California. The Corona's bitter liquid stung Catherine's throat.

Gone were the days of sweetness.

Islands have a rhythm. Motor boats pulling into the harbor. Sails clicking against their masts. Peepers in the early summer; crickets in the fall. Waves lapping against the shore. Nature's metronome.

When she closed her eyes, Catherine was back at Christmas Bells, setting up the Halloween village with Patsy or eating lobster stew in the McLellan's kitchen, laughing at one of Marty's old "When I was teaching" stories. Mr. and Mrs. McLellan. Patsy. They are her family. *Were* her family.

Lobster was crazy expensive in San Diego. It was hard to imagine anyone eating it every day here, like Patsy's uncle and his family did because it was all they could afford. Lots of lobstermen did. Now, it was back to being an unobtainable luxury item. Guess it was better that way. Reminded her too much of Portland anyhow.

She could never go back. The disappointment on Katie McLellan's face had cut through her more than Clara's words ever did, more than any rude remark from the moron brothers, more than, well, anything.

Catherine wiped her eyes.

Cities sound like traffic. Perpetual vibrations of cars rolling over sewer grates, grinding on concrete drowning out the gentle waves of the bay, not that she could afford to be on the water here anyhow. The peach stucco walls of her apartment building did nothing to shield the expressway hum behind the complex, a constant static which left no room for the voices in Catherine's head.

"*My dear Cat, you are a delicious mid-week snack. Nothing more.*"

"*She wakes up in the middle of the night screaming for her baby. You did that to her!*"

After several beers, she fell asleep on the sofa, not bothering to move to the bedroom. Tomorrow was Saturday. No zoo. No errands. No plans with friends. Just time.

CHAPTER SEVENTEEN

San Diego, California
Five Years Later

S AN DIEGO'S MODERATE DECEMBER TEMPERATURES, a full thirty degrees warmer than either Burkesville or Portland, invigorated Catherine. She was free today, free from the constraints of "the family Christmas" and all that phrase connoted, much as she had been every Christmas for the past five years. Once again, she strolled down the snow-free streets, only a light sweater protecting her from the non-existent elements. Sixty-five degrees and sunny.

Maybe she would go to a movie. Maybe get some Asian food, like that scene in *A Christmas Story* after the Bumpus' dogs eat the family's turkey. Catherine chuckled to herself. Who was she, Brooke?

What she really had a taste for was some good curry.

"Chopsticks?"

"Yes, please."

"Here you go, miss. Thank you." Mr. Wu handed her a bag.

"Merry Christmas" automatically came out of her mouth. "Oops, I mean, have a good day."

The man behind the counter smiled.

It was hard to remember everyone was not Christian here. Song Li downstairs was Buddhist. Brooke's roommate was Hindu. In Burkesville, everyone was either Lutheran or Catholic. Not much diversity there.

For some reason, "Good King Wenceslas" popped into her head, which she began humming, holding her curry chicken tight as she walked home.

"Catherine? Is that you?" Will Overman waved and crossed the street.

Her humming ceased. "Hello, Will."

"Merry Christmas!"

"Same to you."

"What are you up to on this festive day?"

"Picked up some curry. Going to watch *A Christmas Story* or some other nonsense on TV."

"Don't you have anywhere to go?"

"Excuse me? Are you insulting my Christmas plans? What are you doing around here anyhow?"

"My brother lives around the corner. I was on my way to dinner with his family."

"Jolly."

"It is. Hey, do you want to come? I'm sure Tom wouldn't mind setting another place at the table."

"No, I'm fine. Don't let me keep you."

"But…"

"My curry is getting cold. Have fun, Will."

He had never met anyone like her, wanting to be alone on Christmas. Who does that? "Are you sure?"

"Yes. Run along now."

"Well, then, Merry Christmas, Catherine."

Unable to shake the feeling someone was following her, Catherine's heart raced. Determined never to be a victim again after the Scott Dithersby incident, Catherine's hand slid to the omnipresent mace in her purse, fingers ready to spray. Whipping around, she found herself pointing the can directly in Will Overman's face.

"Catherine, it's me. Stop!"

"You scared the shit out of me. What the hell are you doing?" Not letting her guard down, she stood firm. "Why are you following me?"

"Easy please. I felt bad you were spending Christmas alone, so I called Tom and told him I wasn't coming. He has a houseful today anyhow with all of Rebecca's family there, so no biggie. I was following you to see if you wanted to hang out or something."

Giving up his family Christmas so she wouldn't be alone? The Overmans must really suck. Still, the offer melted Catherine's ice slightly. Keeping one eye on him, she put away the mace. "Why would you do that?"

Will shrugged. "It's Christmas. You're not a Scrooge, are you? You don't look like a Dickensian curmudgeon."

"I do make a mean porridge." Catherine laughed. "I guess we'll need more curry."

They sat together on her sofa, eating curry chicken with chopsticks, next to the twinkling lights of Catherine's Christmas tree, a full-sized one this year, decked with pandas, tigers, zebras, koalas, and various other animal ornaments not found in Christmas Bells' inventory.

Will popped open the bottle of champagne intended for his brother. Catherine found two glasses.

"Merry Christmas, Catherine." He clinked her glass.

"Merry Christmas to you, Will."

He leaned in and gently kissed her. Five years she had lasted. Five long, lonely years. Flustered, Catherine drained her glass. "So, would you like to watch *It's a Wonderful Life* for the twentieth time? There's a marathon on Channel Four."

Will smirked. "Sounds great."

The brochure stated the Star of India was an 1863 merchant sailing ship, but that hardly mattered to the two boys sword fighting as they climbed the lower rigging. To them, it was a pirate ship and anyone who told them differently could walk the plank.

Will chuckled. "My brother and I used to play like that for hours on end in our backyard."

"So, where are you from?" Catherine could hear a trace of midwestern accent, but never wanted to bring it up for fear of revealing her own Burkesville background.

"Chicago. My brother went to San Diego State, married his college sweetheart, and got a job here after graduation. He made California sound so good, I had to see it for myself. Came here for my gap year and never went back."

"Gap year?"

"When you take a year off after high school graduation to travel before college."

"Very nice. Back home, we call it unemployment."

"Don't kid yourself. I kept getting phone calls from my parents like 'If you don't wrap this up and go to school full-time, working at the Gap is all you will be good for.' How about you? Give me the basics. Hometown. College. All that stuff."

"You know what? I'm getting hungry. Wanna grab something at Anthony's patio over there?"

The thing about living in a tourist destination is one never wants for entertainment, all of which can drain a bank account pretty quickly. Although he worked at the zoo, Will Overman seemed to have an unlimited budget and insisted on paying for every date. Catherine tried to grab the check at Guadalajara, but Will was too fast, distracting her by pointing out the Mariachi band serenading the embarrassed couple at the table next to them.

"Will, please let me pay next time." Catherine had no desire to be beholden to anyone.

"Don't worry about it. I'm old fashioned. What can I say? Senorita? How about a moonlight stroll on the beach?"

"Muchas gracias, señor. Sorry, that's all the Spanish I know."

———*ଅ*\⅄———

Towering at least forty feet in the air, the bamboo's ethereal leaves cast shadows in the morning sun. They were short a person at Sydney's Grill today. Would she mind coming straight over?

Humming while walking through Sun Bear forest, Catherine was drowned out by the Gabriella's Crested Gibbons, little alarm clocks that they were, who seemed intent on waking every living creature nearby.

Just outside of Bear Canyon, a little past the lions, the terrain changed. Large Australian Cycads rose from either side of the path. Bushes with palm-like leaves and huge red flowers filled the spaces below. Orange blooms snaked up bougainvillea trees. The smell of eucalyptus filled the air. Catherine's stomach leapt a little. Koalas had been her favorite animal since the fourth grade continent project. She and Beth were lucky enough to draw Australia and had made a larger-than-life replica on butcher paper, which they covered in spray-painted cotton balls.

Time for a dose of cuteness before her shift began. The little fur balls were up in the eucalyptus trees, dozing as usual. Only one was up, Maloo, who was quickly spotted by the early-entrance visitors who gathered around his tree.

A short, chubby woman pointed her camera his direction. Right as her finger pushed down to take a picture, Maloo turned away. She tried again. Right before the click, Maloo ventured to the other side of the tree.

Clever boy.

"Why look! It's the only creature cuter than these koalas in the entire zoo!"

Catherine turned to see Will striding toward her. "Good morning. What are you doing in Australia?"

"Working the Dippin' Dots cart outside of Sydney's Grill."

"What a coincidence! I'm working Sydney's Grill." She eyed him suspiciously.

"Is that so? I don't know how zoo patrons are going to handle all of this cuteness in one area. Come here." He pulled her behind the koala store. "I asked to be transferred here today so we could work together. I needed a Catherine fix."

"Very sweet."

"Yes, yes I am."

The morning passed by pleasantly, each of them stealing glances and exchanging smirks. They were besieged by the lunch rush and before either knew it, three hours had passed.

Catherine scraped at some ketchup caked on the white table. People could be such pigs. Next to her, a woman sat gobbling Chex Mix straight out of the bag, feet up on the chair in front of her, reading *People* magazine. Every handful was followed by a lick of each finger, a grand snort, then a sniff, presumably to dislodge some clog deep within her sinus cavities. Grab. Chew. Lick. Snort. Sniff. Grab. Chew. Lick. Snort. Sniff. The blonde hair, perfectly manicured nails, and designer clothes could not conceal the truck driver within.

Will served ice cream to a family of four. "Here you go, sir," he said, handing the dad his change. "Greetings, milady."

"Crazy today, huh? What are you doing tonight?"

"Well," he cocked his head. "I was thinking of decanting a fine single-malted scotch and reading *Beowulf* in Middle English."

Catherine hit him with her towel. "Wanna watch a movie at my place?"

"Hmmm. Let's see. Me thinks the lady doth invite me to her quarters for a repast and some tomfoolery."

"Who are you all of a sudden, Shakespeare?"

"Why yes, fair maiden upon whom I have cast a lustful eye many a time from behind this cart of flavored creams."

"You're crazy." Catherine chuckled and got back to work.

"The Ice Princess melt-eth." Morgan Jones laughed and high-fived Will. "No wonder you weren't at Skyfari today."

"I'm going to her place tonight," Will replied, huge grin on his face.

"What are you smiling about, Master Overman?"

"See ya, Morgan." Will bowed. "My lady."

"So, I guess I will meet you at my place." Catherine rummaged for her keys at the bottom of her purse.

"I'll pick up a movie on the way. You call for the pizza."

"Cheese and sausage?"

"Perfect."

Catherine stood on her tippy toes and gave him a kiss. "See you there."

"Count on it." He winked and got into his car.

They never made it through the movie. A blank screen lit up the family room, while a trail of his and hers tropical-print shirts and black shorts led to the bedroom.

Afterward, he kissed the top of her head. "I love you, Catherine."

She hesitated to answer the phone, knowing it was Will. "Hey, where have you been all day?"

"Sorry, I got called to work at the bus stop by the Birds of Prey this morning."

"Okay, well, what about lunch?"

"Can't. Have to work through it. Call you later. Bye."

Brooke was busy, so Catherine ate a solitary lunch at the Canyon Cafe, which was half the zoo away from Skyfari East, a safe distance from Will. The place was big enough to not have to run into him every day. In fact, there were plenty of co-workers Catherine had never met. The giant pandas next to Canyon Cafe were almost as cute as the koalas. The Express Bus Stop Number Five was close. Yes, this could all be done very easily. Besides, she hadn't had fish tacos in a while.

He would never understand how their wonderful night together had opened a portal through which the feelings she had worked so hard to suppress for more than five years came storming her psyche like soldiers on Omaha Beach. Every kick. Every snide remark. Every amused look Scott shot her during the engagement dinner at the McLellans.

No, it was better this way. Her months with Will were a temporary oasis.

Back to reality.

———⁖⁘⁖———

The red light was blinking on Catherine's answering machine. "Hi, Catherine. When you get this, call me, okay? Is something wrong?"

———⁖⁘⁖———

"A guy, maybe, but what girl sleeps with someone, then cuts him out of her life?" Will whispered then flashed a smile. "Watch your step, please. Thank you for riding the Skyfari, and enjoy your day."

"Right this way, thank you." Morgan guided a family of five into the basket and slammed the door. "I told you, man. She's a bitch. Forget her."

"I can't."

He waited until Brooke had veered toward the Kid Store before making his move. "Why won't you return my calls?"

Catherine screamed.

"It's okay, everyone. No worries. Enjoy your day at the San Diego Zoo." He pulled her into the locker area.

"Get your hands off me! Jesus, Will, you scared the shit out of me. Is that your big signature move or something? Startle them, then pounce?"

"Why are you being this way?"

"Believe me, it's not you, it's me."

"Unbelievable. Morgan was right."

"About what?"

Will shook his head. "I'm done."

There were only three things Catherine Elbert knew for sure. 1) Out of the three locations she had lived in the last seven years, Portland was the most real, even with the Dithersby incident. The Burkesville Wisconsinites had their heads up their asses, and most of the southern Californians were entirely too concerned about theirs. Maybe she should start thinking more about her own ass, which had to be getting bigger from all of this beer. But, her jeans still fit, so she grabbed another. 2) She possessed a stellar ability to massively screw everything up. 3) She missed Will Overman so much, sometimes it felt like her heart would be crushed under the weight of her stupidity.

She hadn't cleaned her apartment in weeks. Small dots of mold swam in her toilet bowl. The end tables were so thickly covered with dust that when she picked up the TV remote, it left a perfect outline. The only clean thing in the entire place was the one coaster upon which her ever-present Corona sat, dust-free from beer bottle condensation.

Work was the only thing keeping her sad situation from becoming totally pathetic. Once home, she existed on Coronas and cheap chocolate bars, having given up her beloved curry because it reminded her too much of Will and their little Christmas.

The doorbell rang.

"Go away," she yelled, not bothering to get up.

It rang again.

"I said go away."

"No. Come on, Catherine. Open up."

Oh shit, it was Will. "One second." She ran into her bedroom, checked her hair, rolled some deodorant under her arms, and unlocked the door, forgetting she was still in her pajamas even though it was three o'clock in the afternoon. "Hello."

"I need answers. Everything was going so well between us. I don't get it." Will scanned the room and noticed the garbage can overflowing with Corona bottles. "Are you okay?"

"Sure. I'm great. Never better."

"Goddammit, Catherine. What the hell is wrong with you?"

Catherine winced and braced herself. Seeing this, he lowered his voice. "Honey, what is it? What's so wrong?"

The events of her past came tumbling out of her. Scott Dithersby. The engagement party. Patsy's abortion. Christmas Bells. Burkesville. Hank. Clara. The moron brothers. *Oklahoma!* All of it. Throughout, Will listened, stopping her only once to retrieve some tissues for her. When she was finished, Catherine did not dare to look at him. What would good, honest Will think of the muddled mess that was her life?

He pulled her close, moving an errant strand of hair off her face. They sat for a long time, every once in a while, a shiver ran through Catherine's body, a cold, naked reminder that the facade was over. It was just her now. Not Catherine the farm girl. Or Catherine the friendly Mainer. Or Catherine the ice princess Californian. Just Catherine.

"You know what you need? Some soup. Soup always makes everything feel better. Wonton or egg drop?"

"Wonton."

Will tucked a blanket around her and smiled. "I'll be back in a jiffy."

Catherine merely nodded, wondering who said "jiffy" anymore, but thought it best to quell the bitch within who was all too used to being released. She closed her eyes and saw his sweet face, sandy hair, and honest blue eyes. Will Overman was genuine. He did not put on a show. He did not judge. He did not use. No one had ever comforted Catherine the way he had, not even her own mother.

"I'm back. Hope you like crab rangoon 'cause I got some of that, too." The two sat in silence, except for the occasional embarrassing soup slurp, after which each of them laughed nervously.

"Finished? Let me get that for you." Will rose to clear the dishes.

"Thank you." Catherine brought the covers up to her shoulders and snuggled into the blanket. She had never had an honest relationship with anyone. Maybe Katie McLellan, but that was obviously finished. Kendra Mitchell? Not really. She was more like Catherine's way out of Burkesville. Beth? Ended when she started dating Fred. God knows no one in her family.

"Kitchen's cleared up. Would you like more tea?"

"No, thank you."

Will crawled under the blanket and cuddled her close.

"You have got to be exhausted. You've really never talked about the attack with anyone since you left Portland?"

Catherine shook her head no.

"It must have been so difficult keeping that all bottled up inside. I'm a talker, if you haven't noticed," he said, grinning slightly. "If I can't get things out, I go crazy. I'm so sorry you had to go through that."

"Are you for real?"

"I don't see you like you do, Catherine. I see who you really are. And I love that person. It's getting late, though. Let's get you ready for bed. I'll tuck you in."

Catherine grabbed his arm. "Please don't leave."

"Never."

CHAPTER EIGHTEEN

CATHERINE DIALED THE PHONE, UNSURE of what would greet her on the other end. She had not talked to any of them for almost seven years. Maybe if she was lucky, Hank would answer.

"Hello?"

Shit, it was Clara. "Hi, Ma. It's me, Catherine."

"Well, I'll be. Where are you callin' from?"

"San Diego."

"Oh, I thought maybe you got bored there too and moved to Canada or something."

This was a mistake. "No, Ma. Still in California. How is everyone?"

"Your father and brothers are working their butts off in the fields. What are you doing in LaLa Land?"

"I'm not in Hollywood, Ma. San Diego."

"Same difference."

"I have a job at the zoo."

Clara snorted. "You're cleaning up animal crap now? First it was toilets at the Mitchell House, now animal cages? Really movin' up in the world. Must be all that education you got."

Breathe, Catherine, breathe. "I work in the restaurants and shops. It's a great job."

"Sure it is."

"Anyhow, I have some news. I'm getting married."

"You pregnant?"

"Oh my God, Ma! I'm happy for the first goddamned time in my life!"

"Watch your tongue, missy. What does this guy do for a living?"

"He works at the zoo, too. His name is Will Overman, and he's wonderful."

"Bet he is. Probably one of them surfer guys."

"He's not, but what if he was?"

"They're all crazy out there. Bunch of nuts and fruitcakes."

"Ma, if you would get out of Burkesville, you would see that there are all kinds of people in the world. That's what makes it interesting."

"Tommyrot. I don't need anything but my family and this farm, something you'll never understand. When's the wedding?"

"Don't know. He just proposed last night."

"Want me to call Father Wilhelm?"

"Um, no, probably not. We were thinking of getting married out here."

There was a long pause on the other end of the line. "Well, I guess I'd better be going. Lots of laundry to do. Best of luck to you then."

Click.

———— ⁓ ————

"My mother wanted to know if we would be getting married in Burkesville. Can you believe it? Why the hell would I want to go back there?"

"That's okay. My mother was ready to pack her bags and head west as soon as the word 'engaged' escaped my mouth."

The couple sat pretzel-style facing each other.

"She hung up on me."

"I'm sorry, sweetheart."

"Doesn't matter. What matters is our wedding."

"Absolutely." Will took Catherine's hand and kissed it. "So, what kind of wedding have you always dreamed of?"

"No idea. Never thought about it."

"Are you sure you are female?" He grabbed her crotch for affirmation. "Nope, no balls here." He pulled her on top of him and kissed her, lightly at first, then slowly building in intensity.

Her tongue traveled up his neck, stopping briefly at his earlobe for a lick. "Wedding plans can wait."

———*UW*———

Every time Catherine saw Will, her stomach flipped three hundred and sixty degrees then righted itself.

"Here's my bride-to-be now!" Will swept her up in his arms, twirling her twice. "I have something I need to discuss with you."

"You two are so cute," Brooke chimed in. "We have to go out and celebrate. How about Friday? Oh, wait, that's my dad's birthday. Saturday! Are you available Saturday?"

"Maybe. Can we get back to you?"

"Sure, Will. See ya!" Brooke trotted off toward the Kid Store.

Catherine and Will headed in the opposite direction toward Sydney's Grill. "What's up with that? We don't have anything going on Saturday."

"I was on the phone with my mother yesterday."

"I have yet to hear a positive statement ever follow that phrase."

Will coughed, then cleared his throat.

"Come on, out with it."

"My mother thought that since you did not want a traditional Burkesville wedding…"

"Honey, there is no such thing. The entire downtown of

Burkesville is smaller than the zoo. Besides, the VFW is not the stuff dreams are made of."

Will forged on. "How about getting married in my hometown instead?" He cringed and waited for her reply.

"So I guess San Diego City Hall and Chinese take-out isn't going to cut it, huh?"

"Is that what you really want?" He was clearly horrified.

Catherine chuckled and poked him in the belly.

Relieved, he continued. "My mom and I were talking about this beautiful old mansion-turned-tapas-restaurant and before I knew what was happening, she was off planning a guest list and booking a meeting with the manager."

"But we don't have a date yet."

"There's something else. My parents sent us tickets to Chicago for next weekend. They want to meet you."

"Oh, Christ. Here we go."

"Don't worry. Everything will be fine. You'll see."

Welcome to Naperville.

The limousine passed by schools, a train station, restaurants, banks, and stores. A bit outside of downtown, their drive began to parallel the river beside them, winding past an old cemetery, some office buildings, and, eventually, a forest preserve.

"Oh my God, Will, look at those houses!" Catherine was used to the massive beachfront estates that proliferated the Pacific coast, but not here in the Midwest. Well, at least not in her Midwest. "One, two, three, four stories with walk-out basements?"

"You have no idea," Will muttered under his breath.

Through blocks of mansions they rode. One resembled a mini-Hampton Court, Henry VIII's palace that Catherine had seen on another PBS travel show. Its neighbor seemed to have been plucked from the French countryside.

They pulled into a driveway and stopped next to a red-brick behemoth, a super-sized version of the northeastern homes outside of Portland.

"May I help you?" The voice came from a metal box. A surveillance camera scanned the car.

"Mr. Overman and Miss Elbert are here, sir."

"Catherine, there is something I need to tell you."

Intricate wrought iron gates with a large "O" wound with ivy through the center, opened to display rows of trees lining a mile-long driveway.

Surely this was not Will's house. Back in San Diego, he lived in a small, one-bedroom apartment not much bigger than her own. He drove a Honda Civic. Wore average clothes. Ate at McDonald's like everyone else.

"Catherine, I..."

The limo parked in front of a grand residence—the kind that should have its own name, like Pemberley or stately Wayne Manor—at least four times the size of the Mitchell House, more a castle than a Victorian. Dumbstruck, Catherine took Will's hand as he helped her out of the limo. Not letting go, they ascended the stairs.

"I've been wanting to tell you, but could never quite find the right moment."

Blythe Overman threw open the doors and leapt toward her son, hugging him tight.

"Mom, please. It is good to see you, too, but you are killing me here," Will was barely able to choke the words out.

"Oh, sorry honey." Blythe loosened her grip and turned to the young woman, extending a slim hand. "Hello. You must be Catherine. Lovely to meet you. Welcome to our home."

Benjamin Overman appeared over his wife's shoulder. He was tall and thin like his son, but with darker hair, graying at the temples. "Catherine, it is a pleasure to finally meet you." He shook her hand, smiling warmly.

"Likewise, Mr. Overman."

"Please, call me Benjamin."

"Hey, Dad." Will embraced his father.

"Good to see you, son. Let's get this luggage out of the way, shall we? Put Catherine's in the second guest room."

The men left Blythe and Catherine alone in a foyer the size of the farmhouse's entire first floor.

"You must be tired from your flight. I had the cook make you some sandwiches." Blythe ushered Catherine through the living room with its soaring two-story fireplace, to the kitchen, which was really three rooms in one: a sitting area by another fireplace, the cooking space, and a circular breakfast nook inside a turret, an actual turret. Had Mrs. Overman mentioned a cook?

"What can I get you to drink? Lemonade? Sparkling water?"

A shot of tequila. "Lemonade, please. Thank you."

Her betrothed took a seat at the kitchen table.

"Will, what would you like?"

"I'll have whatever Catherine is having."

Benjamin joined them, a Goose Island beer bottle in his hand.

"Here you go." Blythe set the lemonades before them, then retrieved a platter. "Roast beef with cheddar and horseradish sauce, turkey with avocado and alfalfa sprouts, and curried chicken salad. A little bird told me you were fond of curry."

"Well, that's more than he told me about you." Catherine glared at Will, then turned back to Blythe. "Thank you, Mrs. Overman. These look wonderful."

"Besides, I know how airline food is. Back in the day, you'd get a four-course meal and free drinks. Now, they throw peanuts at you and expect you to survive a four-hour flight."

"I flew to Singapore last week on one of those new business class things with your own...What would you call it?" Benjamin snapped his fingers. "It's like a sleep pod. A private cube with your own TV, headphones, reclining chair/bed. It was great."

"Do you fly to Singapore often?"

"I fly everywhere often, Catherine." Benjamin chuckled.

Catherine shot Will another look. What else had he not told her?

"No need to talk business now, of course. So what part of Wisconsin are you from?" Blythe asked.

"Burkesville. It's a little town not far from Lake Sikapu."

"Will, remember the Joneses? They used to go up there for a long weekend every fall for some kind of festival." His mother tapped the table, searching her memory for the name. "Stayed at a lovely B & B in an old Victorian."

"The Mitchell House?"

"Yes! That was it. Shannon said it was fantastic."

"I used to work there when it first opened, right after I graduated high school."

"Really?" Blythe replied flatly. She might as well have said "The help? How quaint."

This was too much to process. "Would you excuse me, please? I think I'm going to turn in for the night. Flying really wipes me out. Thank you very much for the sandwiches."

Benjamin and Blythe exchanged surprised glances. She was going to sleep at nine o'clock? But it was only six o'clock west coast time.

"I'll show you where your room is, sweetheart. Be back in a few minutes, Mom and Dad."

When they were upstairs, walking down a long hallway, a *really* long hallway, Will whispered, "What is wrong with you? It's still early."

"You tell me, Lord of the Manor Overman."

"I'm sorry I never told you. I just..."

"You just what? Thought I would go after you for your money?"

"It's not like it hasn't happened before. Like all through high school. Why do you think I left?"

"I don't know, Will. You did not relate that classified information to my money-grubbing self."

"Here's your room." Will ushered her in and quickly closed the door.

"I doubt they can hear anything so far away."

"Catherine, I wanted to be my own person, not international marketing genius Benjamin Overman's son."

"Your dad owns an international marketing company? No wonder he flies so much."

"Yeah. He has branches all over. London. Paris. Singapore. Tokyo. Sydney."

"Wow. Impressive."

"Yeah? Well, it's not that great when people pretend to be your friends to land internships."

"High school sucks no matter who you are. I'd rather be surrounded by this than livestock."

"You don't get it, do you? How do you compete with a father like that? It's too high of a bar. I thought you of all people would understand. Your parents wanted you to join the family business too. You ran away. It's the same thing."

"No, it isn't. Yours is 'My family is worth a fortune, and I'm slumming it here with you and the other yokels at the zoo.'"

"I never said that! I like my San Diego life. Besides, you can hardly call that area slumming it. It's not like Mississippi or something."

"Or Burkesville."

"I fell in love with you, not where you are from. Why can't you do me the same favor?"

"Because, Will, look around here. This guest room is the size of my entire apartment. Your family has a goddamn driver!"

"None of this is mine. It is all theirs. I never worked for it. My apartment in San Diego? That's mine."

"Why would you leave this? Most Americans would kill for this lifestyle."

"Five girls asked me to prom so they could show up with an Overman on their arm like an accessory and brag to their country club friends. In San Diego, Morgan and I hang out because we like to. Period."

"Morgan's an asshole."

"Yeah, but he's my asshole."

"Come here." Will patted the bed. "We fell in love because of who we are. None of this changes anything."

Catherine sat on his lap and put her arms around his neck. "Well, it does change one thing."

"What?"

"I know who is paying for the wedding now."

"He didn't tell her." Benjamin poured himself a scotch, ditching his beer as soon as Catherine left the kitchen.

"What do you mean he didn't tell her? Of course he told her."

"Did you see how wide her eyes were when she came through the front doors? How she was trying to catch his eye at the table? She had no idea."

Blythe poured herself a glass of cabernet. "Maybe you're right. She certainly did have a deer-caught-in-headlights look about her. What do we do now?"

"Get to know her. Let's get a feel for what kind of person she is. Will is a smart man. He wouldn't propose to just anyone."

"At least she's not some bleached-blonde boob job. And she did live in Maine for a few years. Perhaps she was sowing her wild oats, but that's not a very attractive trait in a young lady, is it? This estrangement from her family does not bode very well either. Well, my dear, I guess we shall see. Cheers." Benjamin and Blythe Overman clinked glasses and enjoyed their drinks until Will rejoined them, well over an hour later.

Catherine woke up in a mahogany sleigh bed surrounded by the softest sheets and the most gorgeous ecru comforter. A small drawing hung in an ornate frame on the wall opposite the bed. She got up to take a better look at it. A sketch of a horse done with an expert hand, she squinted to read the signature at the bottom right. *Renoir.*

She showered, making sure to put on a decent outfit and full makeup before forging out into the hallway. Who knew how Mrs. Overman showed up to the breakfast table? Probably not in baggy sweats and a Chargers sweatshirt.

Catherine ventured down the hallway, past another enormous room with a beautiful four-poster bed. Why did she feel like Jane Eyre all of a sudden? A tapestry of knights and maidens hung next to the floor-to-ceiling armoire. How did anyone reach the top shelf? Sure enough, in the corner sat a three-step mahogany stepping stool. Past the spiral staircase, where large windows looked out onto a balcony. Past the only room with its doors closed, which she assumed belonged to Will. Past yet another bedroom. Tom's? Past paintings of all genres from impressionists to surrealists to a huge game room with a pool table and another thing that looked exactly like a pool table, only a few feet longer. A dartboard hung on the wall, alongside a Chicago Bears jersey, number thirty-four, signed by Sweetness, Walter Payton. A game table was set up in the second story of what must be the breakfast nook turret.

Downstairs, Catherine bumped into the limo driver when she turned the wrong direction and almost headed into the master suite by mistake. He pointed her toward the kitchen with a haughty sniff.

Through another hallway/art gallery, where Catherine found herself in the library, which resembled every library in every classic movie she had ever seen, only this one was real. A glass case held a copy of *A Tale of Two Cities* opened to the title page, which was signed by Dickens himself. Catherine let out a little gasp, wondering what other treasures this house held.

A painting caught her eye as she was about to leave. A younger Will sat next to his mother, while presumably Tom stood to the left of his father's tufted leather chair. Both boys were dressed identically in khaki pants, navy blue blazers, white shirts, and yellow ties. They were a very attractive family, Catherine had to admit. What was hers doing around that same time this must have been painted? Oh, that's right. Disowning her. No wonder they never had the time to sit for a portrait.

Once out of the study, Catherine found herself in the foyer that led to the dining room with a table that could probably seat twenty and a cozy fireplace above which hung a coat of arms. She went through the butler's pantry into another hallway, which Catherine followed past the wine room, not a cellar really since it was not subterranean, but a climate-controlled vault.

Benjamin Overman sat at the kitchen table drinking coffee, newspapers fanned out around his laptop.

"Good morning, sir."

"Miss Elbert! Good morning. Did you sleep well?"

"I did, thank you. I'm sorry about last night. The flight, you know."

"Yes, traveling," he muttered, right eye peering over his reading glasses. "Coffee? It's on the counter."

Catherine poured some blessed caffeine and joined

Benjamin, who folded up *The Wall Street Journal* and tossed it to his left. "Will tells me you lived in Portland."

"Actually, on Peaks Island, just off the coast."

"Interesting. How did you decide on that? Family vacation spot?"

"I saw it on a PBS travel show."

"And..."

"And I knew that was where I wanted to live."

"What did your parents say? You had to be quite young."

Thankfully, Will appeared, ending the interrogation. "Morning, honey, Dad. Mom up yet?"

"Don't think so. I'll call the cook to start making breakfast."

How does having your own cook even work? Did he or she set the menu for the week, like in Jane Austen movies, or did everybody get to choose their own breakfast, like a diner?

A thirty-ish woman toting a bucket filled with cleaning supplies entered the kitchen. "Good morning, Grace. Mrs. Overman left instructions for you on the counter over there."

A cheery Blythe appeared in the doorway. "Hello, Grace. Would you mind working in the basement today? Thanks. So about this wedding." Blythe could not believe her good fortune that this Catherine did not want the wedding in some podunk Wisconsin town. Being the mother of boys, she had given up all hopes of ever planning a wedding long ago. Tommy's in-laws were lovely people, but they did not include them in any of the preparations. Blythe's job was to light some unity candle and smile for the photographs. That was it. No input or opinions required. Not many of their family had flown out to California for Tommy's wedding on the beach in front of the Hotel del Coronado either. It was spectacular, of course, but it was all Wolfe. Not a trace of Overman in sight.

"Mom, we haven't even had breakfast yet."

"I remember us discussing Meson Sabika on the phone,

but what about the club? It has more space for cocktails. Have you thought about where you would like the service?"

Service, not Mass? Catherine and Will had never discussed religious beliefs. "What are you?"

"I'm a man, Catherine. Did you skip sex-ed class in junior high?" Will smirked. "Oh, you mean, religion."

"Very funny."

"We don't follow a specific religion," Blythe chimed in. "We are more spiritual rather than dogmatic. How about you, Catherine?"

"Catholic."

"Oh, Christ," Blythe blurted before she could help herself.

"But I haven't been to church since I left Wisconsin."

"Whew! That's a relief. Otherwise you are stuck getting married in a Catholic Church. This gives us more options. Dates fill up quickly around here, sometimes one or two years ahead of time. Do you have a time frame in mind?"

"Not really."

"What kind of ceremony would you like?"

Catherine shrugged. "Don't know."

"Come on, every little girl dreams about her wedding day. How did you picture it?"

"Honestly, all I thought about was getting out of Burkesville and visiting all of the places I had seen on the TV."

Will placed a protective arm around Catherine. "Mom, please. Let's at least have breakfast before we dive into the wedding stuff any further."

"There's just a lot to do. Everything to do. And don't forget to call the jeweler."

"Yes, mom."

"Let them eat in peace, Blythe." Benjamin unplugged his laptop and gathered the newspapers.

Blythe left, only to return with her hands full. "Here. Look through these. They might help you get some ideas."

Benjamin could barely see Catherine anymore behind the enormous pile of bridal magazines. "Well, I'm off. I'll see you tonight for dinner. I heard Mom made reservations at Raffi's."

One by one, Catherine plowed her way through the bridal tower. "This one looks like she would rather eat her husband than marry him. Why do they all look so angry?"

Will chuckled. "Probably because they are getting nagged by well-intentioned, yet nonetheless annoying mothers. Want more coffee?"

The cook set a plate of strawberry crepes in front each of them. "Bon appetit."

"This is lovely. Thank you." Catherine placed a napkin on her lap.

"Geoffrey is the greatest. Been with my family since I was ten."

"Good to see you, young Mister Overman," the chef said and quickly disappeared.

"Mmm, delicious!" Catherine wiped her mouth with an off-white silky linen napkin, careful not to stain it with lipstick. "Okay, so clearly I have a job for today. Wanna look through these with me?"

"Not particularly. I'm going to smooth things over with my mom."

"What kind of wedding do you want?"

"The kind that includes marrying you." He kissed her and got out of there as fast as he could.

CHAPTER NINETEEN

"W
HO CARES? JUST ORDER FOR Christ's sake."
Russell, the oldest Elbert child, tore off his
Brewers hat off with exasperation.

"Watch your tongue." Clara could not condone cursing, especially when it concerned the Lord.

"Vanilla is good. But I love chocolate. And, some days, mixed. Oh, I don't know." Eight-year-old Catherine twirled in circles. She drove her family nuts each time they went to the Dairy Queen. There were only three soft serve flavors, but Catherine could never figure out what "mood" she was in.

"Do Eenie, Meanie, Minie, Moe." Peter, the middle child, spoke with authority. "Pop, I want chocolate."

Hank turned from the window. "Clara, how 'bout you?"

"Vanilla. In a cup." It was not ladylike to be seen in public licking away like some suckling pig.

"Okay, that's two chocolate cones, one vanilla in a cup, one mixed cone, and…"

"…and you are the one I am going to have…chocolate. But maybe…"

"Catherine!"

"Okay, chocolate."

The Elberts sat around a circular table, four out of five focused clearly on their desserts. The littlest sat staring, brown streaks snaking down her thin hands.

"What's wrong, Cat?"

"Nothing."

Hank wiped a dripped brown dot from the white table. "You look upset. No one's sad when there's ice cream."

"I wish I got mixed." She looked at her brothers devouring their cones with gusto. "You two are pigs."

Peter and Russell shrugged and shoved the last bits into their mouths.

"Here are some napkins. Go clean yourselves up." Clara turned toward her daughter, shaking her head. "I swear, does anything make you happy, little missy?"

Catherine's brown eyes emerged over the top of the ice cream cone. "I don't know."

CHAPTER TWENTY

"*Y*OUR WEDDING CHECKLIST: *A COMPLETE Guide for Your Big Day.*" The magazine made it seem so easy.

Bouquet choices

Romantic? Classic? Modern?

Glamorous? Rustic? Beach?

Bohemian? Traditional? Whimsical?

Cake choices

Chocolate? Yellow? Red velvet?

Checkerboard? A combination? Fondant?

Hand-painted? A four-tiered blush-pink cake somewhere between girlie and elegant?

Bridesmaid dresses

For friends I do not have, Catherine wrote next to the subhead. Brooke. Maybe the future sister-in-law she had never met? Would only two bridesmaids make her look like a loser?

All of the magazines made it very clear. This would be the single most important day of your life. No pressure.

"Practice signing your new name. It takes some getting used to," one publication advised.

Mrs. Catherine Overman.

It looked so odd, so foreign. Would Catherine Elbert disappear, swept away in a sea of wifely expectations? Maybe she should hyphenate.

Catherine Elbert-Overman.

Terrible. Why did women have to change their names anyway? Why couldn't the couple pick whose last name they liked the best?

Catherine Overman?

Since leaving the farm, Catherine had thought of herself as completely alone, unconnected to any ancestry or familial obligations. What did it mean to be an Overman? Who were these people? Did Catherine Elbert have to be replaced by Mrs. Catherine Overman, or worse, Mrs. Will Overman? How degrading to be known only as an adjunct of your husband! A by-product. An after-thought.

"Will!" Catherine tore through the house. "Will!"

"In the living room."

"Will, I cannot do this." She waved two bridal magazines in his face.

"Easy, honey. What's wrong?"

"Shower games? Stationery? Flowers or candles on the tables? Chicken or beef? White bridal runner? Two garters. One to throw, one to keep. This is fucking lunacy!" Catherine's voice rose higher with each word.

"Calm down."

"A special knife set to cut the cake with? Who gives a rat's ass?" She knelt down in front of his chair. "Please do not let your mother turn me into a cookie-cutter bride."

Blythe emerged from around the corner. "Don't worry, Catherine. I won't."

"I'm sorry you heard that."

"How could I not? Your 'fucking lunacy' comment echoed throughout the entire house. I hope Benjamin's client cannot speak English. He's on a conference call in the study, you know."

"Oh my God." Catherine's hand went immediately to her mouth. "I am so sorry. I thought he had gone in to his office, company, whatever, after breakfast."

"He works from home on Fridays," Blythe curtly informed her.

"Okay, let's take a break here," Will butted in. "In all fairness, Catherine was talking to me, Mom, before you walked in."

"Screaming at you, you mean?"

"I'm sorry for my volume and vulgarity, Mrs. Overman."

"It seems you have a vociferous voluptuousness." Will could barely get the words out through the chuckling.

Blythe Overman was not amused.

Day two. The shower's warmth was a welcomed reprieve. Catherine turned the knob until steam rose around her. Breathing it in, she tilted her head, allowing the warm blanket of water to flow over her hair and down her back. Will and his father were already gone, playing an early eighteen holes of golf before meeting up with Blythe and Catherine for lunch at the club. No joke. She had no idea what to expect. There weren't any country clubs near Burkesville (no shock there), and Catherine had never known anyone who belonged to one in either Portland or San Diego, or so she thought. Hell, she didn't even know Will golfed. Was this what they normally did, the Overmans, or was it a test to see how the country girl acted in that environment? What did they think she would do? Wear overalls and pick her teeth?

Still she was scared, knowing full well she was not of this place. *Come on, Catherine. You can do this. It's just another role, like doing the musical back home.* On stage, she was able to stash Catherine neatly away, emerging as whatever villager or dancer Mr. Gusselman wanted.

Rinsing the shampoo from her hair released an intoxicating scent of flowers and spices. Well, at least that is what it said on the bottle.

Here goes nothing, she thought, and began dressing for her Riverwood Country Club debut.

The limousine pulled into a circular driveway under a portico where valets stood at attention in front of a stately red-bricked Colonial revival, a white cupola crowning its green-gabled roof.

A teenager in a white shirt, black pants, black vest, and bow tie offered his hand to her future mother-in-law. To Catherine? Nope. She was forced to get out of the car herself, perish the thought. "Hello, Mrs. Overman. How lovely you look this afternoon."

"Catherine, this is Carter. His father plays golf with my husband. He is interning here. His family owns several hotels in downtown Chicago."

Carter eyed Catherine with questioning amusement. "Right this way, Mrs. Overman. I believe your table is waiting in the grill." He led them through two doors encased in massive, scrolling white molding. "The misters Overman are in the locker room and should be out shortly." Still evaluating Catherine, Carter helped Blythe into her chair, fluffed her napkin, and placed it on her lap.

When she was settled comfortably in her chair and busy reading the lunch menu, Carter shot Catherine one last glare. It was met with a mouthed "bite me," which managed to arouse a slight smirk on the little prick's country clubber puss.

"Catherine, another reason I wanted to bring you here was so you could see the facilities available for the wedding. There are three dining areas, but I knew the casual grill would be better suited for us today. Besides, the boys will be in golf attire. The main dining room has a dress code. Dinner jackets for men. Skirts or dresses for women."

"Well, there they are, Will, our beautiful ladies." Benjamin Overman greeted his wife with a light peck on the cheek and a broad smile for Catherine. Will tried to do the same, but instead got a mouthful of hair when his fiancée moved her head.

"Oops, sorry, Will. Wasn't sure which side you were coming from. Are you okay?"

"Fine. Wish my golf game was."

Immediately, a waiter appeared for drink orders. Since it was only noon, she opted for iced tea, while Blythe and Benjamin ordered Bloody Marys, and Will asked for something called an Arnold Palmer.

"Well, you've heard of the golfer, right?"

"No, Will. I was raised by wolves and lived in a cave for my first twenty-five years." Catherine chuckled. Blythe and Benjamin did not, and instead just stared at her, blank expressions on their normally animated faces.

"Anyhow," Will continued, "it's this drink of half iced tea and half lemonade that he invented."

"Sounds good."

"I don't know if I deserve to order one, though, the way I played today." Will rubbed his forehead. "Couldn't hit the fairway to save my life. My short game sucked, too."

"You haven't played for a while, and it showed. You just need a few lessons to tune up. Don't worry, it'll all come back when you start playing more," Benjamin said, scanning his lunch choices.

"Will, the scallops are still on the menu."

"I see, Mom, but I think I'm more in the mood for a burger."

"But you always like the scallops."

"Maybe for dinner, but not at lunch."

"It doesn't matter what time of day it is, if you want them, have them."

"Thank you, but I really have a taste for a burger."

"Of course, Will, I just meant..."

"I'm thinking about the salmon. Have you had it before?"

The three Overmans put their menus down and glared at Catherine, none uttering a word, as if she were speaking Portuguese. She might as well have been back on Elbert Farm. At least Russell would have actually responded, even if it was with something like "What do you care? It's fish. What do you think it tastes like? And you're the one they sent to Muskegee Community College?"

"Well...if you would excuse me for a moment, um, I need to use the...um..." Catherine darted off.

Where the hell was the bathroom? The huge, floor-to-ceiling mahogany door budged only slightly. What was it with all the mahogany in this place? She tried again, this time with more strength. The door flew open, crashing against the wall. Every single man in the room turned to see what all of the commotion was.

"Miss you cannot be in here," said the bartender.

"Excuse me, I was just looking for the restroom."

"You need to leave now. This is the gentlemen's lounge. Women are not allowed in here."

"Are you serious?"

"Yes. I am going to have to ask you to leave."

"What year is it, 1956?"

"Miss, please." He made a small hand gesture, and Carter came running. "Please escort the young lady back to her table."

He stared to take her arm, but Catherine wrangled free. "Hands off. I am perfectly capable of walking out myself."

The huge door slammed shut behind her.

"What were you doing in there?" Carter hissed.

"Actually, I was trying to find the washrooms. No one told me that area was off limits to females, which is so damn ridiculous, I cannot even process it."

"Well, Gloria Steinem, you are going to have to try, or they will throw you out of here."

"Heaven forbid."

"I get that you don't care, but I'm sure your future in-laws do, capice?"

"Come on, Carter. Even you have to admit that is infuriating in this day and age."

"Of course it is, but the men like it that way. Did you see those two standing at the bar? CEO of one of the largest oil companies in America. The other? Chief operating officer of a huge bank downtown. Are you going to tell them to change their rules? This club does not even allow women members."

"What? But there are women all around here. At the pool. On the course."

"Wives. They're different. A woman can use the facilities only if her husband is a member."

"Are you kidding me? What about female executives?"

"They are not welcome here unless they are a wife."

"That's discrimination."

Carter shrugged. "It's a private club. They can do what they please."

"Unbelievable."

"Catherine, there you are!" Will jogged down the hallway. "You were gone for such a long time, I was beginning to worry." He glanced curiously at Carter.

"This fine young gentleman was educating me on some of the club's policies."

Carter smiled and bowed his head. "Mr. Overman. And now if you will excuse me."

"Thank you, Carter. It has been enlightening."

"What were you doing in the Swynedale room?"

"Oh, you heard that, huh?"

"The entire club could hear it. My God, Catherine, are you determined to make my parents dislike you?"

"Okay, first of all, I was trying to find the bathroom.

Second, no one bothered to tell me there were areas in this place where women are not allowed. Third, the fact that it doesn't bother you blows my mind."

"I never really thought about it."

"Wow. Okay then. Do you think Daddy could fire up his jet and get us the hell out of here?"

"You know he doesn't have a plane."

"That's your answer. Not, 'I know, I hate it too?'"

"But I don't hate it."

Catherine closed her eyes and breathed in deeply. "Fine. I'll go back and play nice with your parents. But I'm telling you something right now, there is no way I am getting married in this sexist shithole."

They walked back to the table. By the look of things, Blythe and Benjamin had finished their second Bloody.

"Mr. and Mrs. Overman, I am very sorry to have caused you any trouble. I was looking for the ladies' room and walked into the Swynedale Room by mistake. I had no idea it was for men only."

"Of course you didn't, my dear. Sit down. Let me get you a drink." Benjamin gestured for the waiter. "Gimlet? Martini?"

"A glass of wine please. Thank you."

"Here's the wine list. Why don't you make a choice for the table to accompany lunch?" Blythe handed her a well-padded folder, eagerly anticipating Catherine's decision.

Cat put it aside, not taking the bait. "On second thought, may I have a Corona, please?"

"Absolutely, miss. Lime?"

"Definitely."

Blythe sipped champagne and perused wedding stationary ensembles—not invitations, but *ensembles*—of hand-calligraphied works of art upon the finest linen stock, "guaranteed to create a buzz for your event," as if Catherine and Will's wedding was a corporate launch.

"Here are the samples you requested, Mrs. Overman." Clarissa Derby of Clarissa Derby Designs proudly placed her work before Blythe without so much as a glance toward the bride-to-be.

"Catherine, what do you think?" Blythe handed sample number one to her as an afterthought.

Mr. and Mrs. Wilfred Overman

Yes, it was Wilfred, another thing the young Mister Overman, as he was known around his home, had neglected to mention. Catherine envisioned walking down the aisle toward a rotund, balding old man with a walrus mustache. C'mon, who else's name was Wilfred?

It made her queasy.

In fact, this whole weekend had. She didn't even know this Wilfred Overman. Where was the guy who would blow off Christmas Day with his brother to hang out with her? And who was this *Wilfred* who seemed to make pleasing his parents his life-long ambition?

After dinner that night, Catherine escaped into the garden, but not before Benjamin went through the full oration of its history. Modeled after the gardens at Hampton Court. Blah. Blah. Blah. She smiled weakly, feigning interest and awe, something Benjamin Overman seemed to enjoy immensely. His garden was as much a penis extension as his Porsche. It supposedly had its own boxwood maze, which was actually sort of cool. Visions of British costume dramas danced in her head.

Finally, he shut up, and Catherine set out to explore. She had to admit, the rose garden was lovely, especially the collection of red and white roses, an homage to the Tudors. Benjamin had beamed at the cleverness of it all. After the rose garden were some two-foot-tall boxwood plants. Nothing more. Was that it? She stepped back, trying to look at them from every angle. Guess they were planted in some sort of pattern. Catherine knew boxwood grew slowly from a PBS gardening show she watched once, but these must be the slowest growing plants ever. What were they? Part cactus? No wonder Blythe drank a lot.

And that she did, putting down three glasses of the bubbly during a forty-five minute wedding stationary consultation. So Blythe drank, and Benjamin golfed. Both of their lives centered around Riverwood Country Club for fun. "They serve the most magnificent foie gras," whatever that was.

How would she and Will ever survive this? The rich guy and the farm girl. She ached to be back in San Diego eating take out and watching a movie with Will. It would never be that simple again. Everything had changed.

Whether she liked it or not, the farm would always be there, the part of her from which she could never run away. And now, all of this would be right alongside it, polar opposites bound together in a level of hell she never knew existed. Imagine the moron brothers at Riverwood Country Club! What about Clara? The venom that would spew from her mouth would only be matched by the looks of horror Blythe Overman would try to unsuccessfully hide on a visit to Elbert Farm.

"Hey! I wondered where you'd gone off to." Will sat down next to her.

"Surprised you even noticed."

"Of course I did. I was trying to find the most opportune time to excuse myself from the table, but they would not stop talking."

"Getting up would have done the trick."

"That would not do, Catherine. Please."

"Did you just scoff at me?"

"What are you talking about?"

"Your condescending tone."

"You're crazy."

"Am I? You even talk differently here. You are the model of appeasement, *Wilfred*."

"I see no need to rock the boat. We are only here for one weekend. Besides, they mean well."

"Do they? Is it or is it not *our* wedding?"

"Yes, but my mother has always wanted to plan one. I told you that."

"Wouldn't want to upset dear mommy, would we?"

"No, actually."

"Maybe you should." Catherine began down the crushed limestone path.

Will did not follow.

CHAPTER TWENTY-ONE

*H*APPY TO BE BACK AT Sydney's Grill, Catherine filled the napkin containers then wiped off the counters. A new shipment of Animal Sippers cups needed stacking by the beverages. This time, instead of cute pandas or leopards sitting atop the huge green tumblers, pissed off lions bared their teeth. Kind of scary, really. What kid would want to drink out of that? Catherine shrugged. Things were less complicated here at the zoo. Do your tasks. Be pleasant to the guests. Eat Chinese for dinner. Repeat. But, how long would she be able to avoid the elephant in the room? Catherine giggled. Zoo pun.

Since their return to San Diego, Blythe Overman had become Catherine's email buddy, sending a wedding tidbit at least once a day, sometimes twice.

"What do you think of this cake?"

"So and so bridal website has the most darling favor ideas. You should check them out."

Over the weeks, Blythe's messages had become more persistent.

"You really need to try on some wedding dresses. They can take up to a year to get, you know."

"I can pull some strings at the club, but you must settle on a date ASAP!"

"MY GOD, DO BOTH OF YOU EVEN WANT TO GET MARRIED?"

"I don't know what to tell you, Will," Catherine said as they sat in the bistro known as échapper, strains of Edith Piaf's "La Vie en Rose" in the background. "I do know one thing. These fries are the best I have ever had."

"Pomme frites." Will corrected.

"Excuse me, *Wilfred*. Pomme frites."

"Sorry, I thought you would want to know the proper name. French fries don't exist in France. They are an American invention." He grabbed one from her plate. "See? Pomme frites are cut very thin. English chips are thick. Our french fries are somewhere in between."

"Not that I don't enjoy this little Henry Higgins/Eliza Doolittle thing going on here, but may I please eat my steak in peace?"

"Filet…"

Catherine delivered a death stare, challenging him to finish. Instead, he changed the subject. "So, how was your day?"

Smart man. "Pretty good, actually. A little slow. How about you?"

"The Skyfari is always busy. Oh, hey, Morgan's been dating someone. Met her a few weeks ago."

"I'm happy for him."

Will eyed her suspiciously. "Sure you are."

"I am. Just because he calls me a bitch doesn't mean I want him to mysteriously wake up one morning in the tiger exhibit."

"You are a nasty girl."

"I though that's how you like me."

Will blushed.

"On another note, what did you think about your mother's last email?"

"She does have a point about picking a date."

"It's not like I'm holding out for Valentine's Day or June or something. All I know is that we're not getting married in the sexist shithole country club. There. There's a decision for her."

"I don't know how we can avoid it."

Another Piaf song filled the air. This time "Non, Je Ne Regrette Rien."

Catherine reached for his hand. "Will, you are a grown man. I'm sure you can find a way to tell your mother we will not be married in a sexist shithole. Feel free to use those exact words, if you would like."

Will chuckled. "It'll be on the news that night. 'This just in. The entire Chicagoland area has been destroyed.' A huge mushroom cloud flashes on screen. 'We have confirmation now. The point of origin was Naperville, Illinois.'"

"Well, that would solve many things, now wouldn't it?"

"Catherine!"

———⚜———

Back in Catherine's apartment, they cuddled on the sofa, drank more wine, and watched *Four Weddings and a Funeral*.

"Now, that's a wedding. Big meringue dress. Terrible singers. Senile old people."

"The promise of sex as a bridesmaid."

"Will, if you would like to wear a bridesmaid's dress to our wedding, more power to you!" Catherine clinked his glass. "More wine?"

"Why not?"

By the end of the movie, both had cried profusely over Matthew's speech at Gareth's funeral.

"I love you so much," Will said, yet another tear welling up in his right eye. "I just want to spend the rest of my life with you. I don't care how we get married. Let's just do it."

"What? Are you serious, Will?"

"Well, I'm not sure the courthouse is open at this hour. We'd have to get a license."

"I know somewhere we could get married right now—

Vegas! Oh my God, it's perfect! We get married our way and forget the rest of the crap!"

"Yeah, but *Vegas*?"

"It's only a five-hour drive." Catherine cleared the wine glasses and smoothed her skirt. "Come on! We both look okay. Let's go!"

———— ❦ ————

Neon. Lots of neon. And colored fountains. By the time they reached the Las Vegas strip, it was two o'clock in the morning, but it could have been two in the afternoon. The place was packed.

"Which one?"

"I don't care. The first one we see."

Will pulled into Graceland Wedding Chapel. "I can't believe we are doing this."

They walked in, hand in hand. "We'd like to…" Catherine started.

"Sssshhh!" A plump lady waived them in. "He's just about to sing 'Viva Las Vegas.'"

Will and Catherine peeked into the chapel. Sure enough, an Elvis look-alike picked up his guitar.

"He can walk the bride down the aisle if you'd like."

Catherine smirked. "Oh, no thanks. We just want a regular thing."

"Okay. What package are you interested in?"

"No! Stop! We just want to get married. Nothing more. No packages. No extra frills."

"All right then, miss. Do you have a marriage license?"

"Um…no."

"Can't get married without a license, I'm afraid."

"Where do we get one?"

The plump woman, whose name was Priscilla, handed

Will a piece of paper and directions to the Las Vegas Marriage Bureau. "It's about a ten-minute walk, five blocks up. You can leave your car here, if you'd like. I'll put you down for a three thirty ceremony."

"Thank you," Will said, and they dashed off.

"Ah, you're back. Wonderful. Here's your boutonniere." Priscilla pinned it on Will's shirt.

"And your bouquet." She handed Catherine a tiny nosegay of three red roses.

"Here Comes the Bride" filled the room as Catherine walked down the little aisle toward the minister.

"Do you, Wilfred Overman, take this woman to be your wife? To love, honor, and cherish until death do you part?"

Will held Catherine's hands. With a smile, he replied, "I do."

"Do you, Catherine Elbert, take this man to be your husband? To love, honor, and cherish until death do you part?"

"I do."

They exchanged gold bands bought in the chapel's lobby.

"By the power vested in me by the State of Nevada, I now pronounce you husband and wife. You may kiss your bride."

"Elvis" barged in, strumming his guitar and began "Love Me Tender."

"Sometimes he can't help himself. Just joins in for fun. Congratulations!" Priscilla hugged the two of them.

Will kissed Catherine again. "I love you, Mrs. Overman."

Catherine bristled at hearing it for the first time, but tried not to ruin the moment. "I love you, too, Mr. Overman."

"You got married where?" Boom! There went Naperville. "Oh my God, Will, how could you?"

"It was all very easy." Will tried to sound nonchalant.

"But, I...the club...the..."

"Were all things you wanted. Catherine and I wanted to get married without all the fuss."

"What will the relatives think?"

"Who cares? Elvis even serenaded us with 'Love Me Tender' as we walked out."

"Delightful. Well, that's one thing Riverwood definitely does not offer."

"It was hilarious."

"I'm not laughing."

"I'm sorry you're disappointed by our decision, but it was you who wanted a large wedding, not us."

Blythe covered up the phone and yelled, "Benjamin! It's Will. Guess what he did this weekend? Go ahead, tell your father. I'm giving him the phone."

Will repeated their news. Benjamin, he was surprised to report, was happy for them. "Blythe was probably driving him crazy with wedding shit too since we left."

———————

The newlyweds began the practical matters of marriage, like breaking the lease on Will's apartment and choosing which furniture stayed and which went to charity.

One night, while they ate chicken chow fun and relaxed after work, Will asked Catherine if she was having as hard a time as he was getting the green off of his ring finger.

"Well, now that you mention it, I do have to scrub really hard. I thought those were supposed to be twenty-four-carat gold. Yeah, sure."

Her husband dropped to one knee and presented her with a two-carat, princess-cut diamond with a platinum band of smaller round diamonds and a matching wedding band. "Allow me, milady."

Catherine held out her left hand. "Oh, my God. It's so beautiful."

"Since I was jewelry shopping, I thought I would also get something for myself." Will produced a second small box. Inside was a platinum wedding band with two strips of tiny diamonds that echoed the design of his wife's ring. "Will you do the honors?"

"With this ring, I thee wed." Catherine slipped it on his finger. "I will always love you, Will Overman. You are my happy place."

———— ❦ ————

"Paging Catherine Elbert. Oops, I mean, Catherine Overman? Catherine, just Catherine, please report to Albert's Restaurant ASAP."

"I'll be right there, Brooke." Catherine tucked the walkie-talkie into her shorts' pocket. Chaotic. That was the best word to describe the day. Hordes of school groups. Senior citizen tours. Even the animals seemed to sense the insanity. The apes were unusually chatty. The aviary birds squawked louder. "Hey, honey." She gave Will a peck. "Do you know what this is about?"

"Nope. Morgan said to meet him here for a staff meeting."

"Shit. I'm exhausted."

When they opened the doors, shouts of "Surprise!" filled the air. A "Congratulations, Catherine and Will" banner hung across the restaurant's window.

"Hurray! It's my two favorite lovebirds." Brooke squeezed them tight.

"Congrats, man. Best of luck." Morgan hugged Will. "Catherine, be good to him, you hear?"

Everyone from their shift gathered around the couple. Bob from the Camera Den. Jeannie from membership. Even

Callie, the koala shop manager was there, each offering well wishes for the newlyweds. Atop a little wedding cake were two white doves.

"We weren't sure what to get you." An excited Brooke handed Catherine an envelope. "Go ahead, open it." Brooke jumped up and down, unable to wait. "It's a night at the Hotel del Coronado in the bungalow where Marilyn Monroe stayed! Isn't that awesome?"

"You guys, this is more than generous. Wow, thank you."

"Everyone, and I mean everyone, contributed. The others will be here in a couple minutes. Can I get you a drink? It's Wedding Happy Hour!" Brooke clapped her hands.

Will spoke for the both of them. "Thank you all so much. We are truly blessed to have all of you in our lives."

Brooke clinked her glass. "Toast time! To my wonderful friend and her even more wonderful husband. Congratulations on your marriage. I wish you a lifetime of love. Here's lookin' at you, kids."

CHAPTER TWENTY-TWO

"COME ON! WE CANNOT BE late."

"Take it easy, *Wilfred*." Catherine applied a last touch of lipstick and grabbed her purse. "How do I look?"

"Wonderful, now let's go," her husband replied, never glancing up from tying his left shoe. "It would be incredibly rude to arrive late to a party thrown in our honor."

Overman speak already? They had only been in Naperville for one day. "Really? I did not know that. I guess I left my bale of hay at home. Besides, you are lucky I'm even stepping foot into that sexist shithole."

"At least we didn't get married there."

"Maybe we should have blown up the picture old chubby Priscilla took of Elvis serenading us for our official wedding portrait. Bet your mother would have loved that!"

"Oh, shit. I knew there was something I forgot."

"Seriously? The Elvis photo?"

"No, no, no. Mom had asked if we had a picture of the two of us, but I couldn't find any and forgot to ask Morgan to take one."

"At the zoo? Somehow, I don't think that is the kind of photo Blythe Overman requested. She probably wanted it done by Annie Leibovitz."

"Here you go, sir." The driver handed Will a set of keys. "I had it washed this afternoon. Have a good night."

"Thanks, Manuel."

Will started the Mercedes and tore down Washington toward Riverwood Country Club.

"You really need to get a grip. This is only a few family members anyhow, right?"

"Um, no. Nothing the Overmans do is just about family. It's neighbors, Overman Enterprises' board of directors, and major Chicagoland clients."

"Shit, Will. Would have been nice to know this ahead of time. Do I look okay? Is this dress good enough?" Catherine had picked it up at one of the cute little boutiques down the street from their peach apartment complex.

At the stoplight, Will took a better look. Besides the little drop of sweat sliding its way from her temple down to her cheek, she looked great. More than great, actually. Her hair was pinned up by a small iridescent butterfly, little ringlets encircling her face. Her ocean blue strapless dress fit perfectly, accentuating her thin frame. Silver high heels and matching clutch purse completed the ensemble. "You are breathtaking." For the first time that day, he could relax. What was all the worry about?

His mother had insisted on throwing them a party. She was going to get her wedding reception no matter how many objections they made. If they did not have the decency to have a proper wedding, by God they would have a sophisticated soiree to celebrate their marriage, otherwise everyone would think Catherine was pregnant. Will left out that last part when relating his mother's wishes to his wife. No need to rock the boat.

Carter snapped to attention when they pulled up, this time offering a hand to Catherine, who was busy trying to keep her skirt from riding up and giving him an eyeful as she emerged from the car.

"Oh, there you two are. Thank you, Carter." Blythe Overman greeted them with an outward smile, then lowered her voice. "Where have you been? Most of the guests have already arrived. Catherine, let me look at you." Twirling her around, like a six-year-old, the mother-in-law bristled only once, when her gaze fell upon her daughter-in-law's shoes.

"Wonderful to see you, Mrs. Overman."

"Oh, please call me Mom."

Doubt it.

Blythe straightened Will's tie. "Come now, let's get you to your party."

"The Way You Look Tonight" floated through the air courtesy of a seventeen-piece big band, as guests chatted and sipped their cocktails.

"There's my boy and his lovely bride!" Benjamin Overman snaked through the crowd to embrace his son, then turned to Catherine, kissing her cheek. "Hello, pretty lady." He gestured to a waiter who immediately brought two glasses of champagne. "I took the liberty of ordering you some Dom. I trust you don't mind."

One by one, the key players in Blythe and Benjamin's world congratulated the newlyweds, dying to check out the newest Mrs. Overman. Like being on display in a State Street department store window, Catherine withstood her first meet and greet, only unlike many musicians, most of the guests were not predisposed to being a fan. In fact, more often than not, their mouths offered well wishes, while their eyes scanned her from head to toe, evidently unimpressed with what they saw.

"The zoo? How cute, but what do you really do?"

They did not bother to hide their surprise Will Overman's bride was not a supermodel or a Harvard Law grad with her eye on a partnership. "Las Vegas? Curious choice. I didn't think people did that anymore," followed by a not-so-discreet glance to Catherine's stomach in search of a baby bump.

The men left wondering what hidden talents this attractive, but bordering on plain girl possessed, their groins stirring at the suppositions all the way to the bar. The women deconstructed her outer shell within five seconds. Lower middle class at best. No visible cosmetic procedures. Did her own manicure and pedicure for a night as important as this? Neophyte. She will be eaten alive.

Mercifully, a bell rang, and the head waiter announced dinner was being served in the dining room.

Will escorted his bride down the hall. "How are you holding up?"

"My feet are killing me, and I think my face is frozen in this goofy smile." Just like in all three performances of *Bye Bye Birdie*, she had been working hard to generate all that fake charm and enthusiasm. Blythe's "small get-together for a few friends and family" had grown to well over two hundred people. Riverwood Country Club was theirs exclusively tonight, except, of course, for the Swynedale Room, where many of the male guests escaped, no doubt themselves fatigued from the small talk. Catherine was exhausted and in dire need of a Corona. Unfortunately, this was neither the time nor the place, no matter how many times her inner self said she should be able to drink whatever she wanted to at her own party.

"Oh, look! There are Alexandra and Phillip. Would it kill them to be on time for once?" Kisses and compliments swirled around. "That vacation did wonders for you. You look wonderful." Blythe winked as she hugged the woman, mouthing "Botox" to her son. "Catherine, I'd like you to meet my sister, Alexandra, and her husband, Phillip."

"We've literally just been back from sailing the Mediterranean. Two glorious weeks." Alexandra's teeth were so white, there was almost a glare. "But, I'm afraid I have a bit of jet lag."

"How did you get your boat back here?" Catherine asked, confused.

After much chuckling, Phillip finally answered. "Oh, we don't *own* a sailboat, dear. We rented yacht with a salon, bar, formal dining area, all of the usual water toys, you know, skis, tubes, wakeboard, plus a full crew, chef, and attendant. It's really the only way to go. Quite marvelous."

"She's darling, Will!" Alexandra intertwined her arm with Catherine's. "You must sit next to me. I insist. Blythe, where's our table?"

Like some freaky stalker, Carter appeared on Alexandra's other side. "Right this way, Mrs. Von Osterburg. Please allow me." Wriggling himself right in between the pair, he proudly escorted the women into the dining room, leaving Will to his parents and Uncle Phillip on his own.

Applause greeted them, first Alexandra, Carter, who by the look on his face was enjoying this immensely, and Catherine, followed by Phillip, a step or two behind. What was this? A Tudor feast? Guess Benjamin had more in common with Henry VIII than just his garden. Catherine resisted the urge to mimic the Queen's wave with her free hand.

Once they were seated, Will, with Blythe and Benjamin on each arm, proceeded in amid cheers and more applause. Clearly, the family Overman was the main attraction this evening. The rest were merely co-stars.

Alexandra noticed Catherine's expression and patted her hand. "Don't worry, dear. It's always been about Blythe. You'll get used to it."

The mother-in-law made her way to the microphone stand. What, no heraldic trumpets? Maybe they were already booked at the Burkesville VFW. It *was* Friday night. "We are so glad you could join us this evening to welcome our Will home..." Catherine counted a full three-second pause. "...and to introduce you to our new daughter-in-law." Apparently, she had no name. "Benjamin and I hope you enjoy our little gifts, tokens of our affection and gratitude."

An unmistakable small blue box with a white ribbon sat atop each female's place setting. Even among this crowd, there were some oohs and aahhs. Catherine craned to see what the lady in the white Chanel suit was holding. A tiny Tiffany crystal bowl.

"Oh, that is lovely," said Alexandra.

Benjamin reached into his breast pocket and handed Phillip and Will two of the same cylinders that were on the men's plates. "Didn't think I'd forget about you, did you? Let's pledge to smoke them on the course in a couple of weeks."

Phillip pulled the cigar across his face, breathing in its scent. "Arturo Fuente. Very nice."

Alexandra leaned toward her new best friend. "So, since you and I don't rate anything, what say we signal the sommelier and do some damage?"

"Sounds great." This was going to be a long night.

Alexandra ordered something from Château Mouton Rothschild, winking at Catherine. "This should do the trick. So, tell me about yourself."

For the fifty thousandth time that evening, she began. "Will and I met at the San Diego Zoo."

"Stop right there! I've heard the official story from my sister. What made you move clear across the country? Wanderlust? But why? I was tired of being overshadowed by the golden child over there. How about you? What were you running away from?"

"Two moron brothers and the family farm."

Alexandra nodded. "Well, amen to that, Catherine. Welcome to the family." They clinked glasses and began drinking wine that cost more per bottle than the monthly rent on Catherine's first apartment on Peaks Island.

The meal started off with a beef tenderloin tartare with mushrooms, crème fraiche, and toast points, according to the hand-calligraphied menu with the Overman crest that sat in front of each person's plate.

Alexandra and Catherine were busy chatting about travels abroad and island life in Maine. Seizing the opportunity, Blythe barraged her son with questions about his future.

"Good Lord, Blythe. Let the man eat his lobster thermidor in peace."

Scoffing, Blythe set her sights for the daughter-in-law. "So, Catherine," she said, barging in, not bothering to wait for an opening. "Did you notice the menu?"

"Why, yes. Clarissa Derby Designs, right?"

"You are correct, but I was referring to the actual food. Does it remind you of anything?"

Catherine searched the table for help, but there was none, not even from Alexandra, who signaled her mouth was full.

Blythe sighed. "It's an homage to all the places you have lived. See, beef from the Midwest."

"Oh, and lobster from Maine. I get it. Thank you. That was very nice of you."

"Let's hope the next course isn't stuffed koala served on a bed of eucalyptus."

"Don't be ridiculous, Alexandra."

Across the table, Benjamin and Will were head to head, discussing something intensely, but Catherine could not make out what. Besides, Alexandra was on about how blue the water was off the coast of Greece.

"Dad, I really think..."

"Don't worry. It will be fine."

"Please don't."

But it was too late.

Before Will could stop him, Benjamin was at the microphone. "Excuse me, everyone. May I have your attention? I have some good news I would like to share."

That set the room abuzz. All eyes darted toward Catherine who glanced around the table, unsure of what was next.

"I am delighted to announce that my son, Will, will be

199

joining me at Overman Enterprises corporate headquarters here in Naperville."

Applause rang out through the room. Alexandra slipped her arm around her new friend's chair. "Smile, dear. You can fight about it later."

Blythe beamed while Will rose and waved. His aunt kept her arm around Catherine, *Bye Bye Birdie* smile plastered on her face.

Benjamin returned triumphant. "Well, that should send stock prices up tomorrow. See, I told you it would go over well."

Blythe stroked Will's nape. "It is exactly how it should be."

"Stop it, Mother! Listen, I said I had to talk to Catherine first." By the time he could bring himself to look at her, she was already gone.

"Where did she go, Alexandra?"

"Anywhere but here, I suspect. Really, that was quite a show. Well done, Benjamin. But what about the girl? Did any of you think of her for one second?"

"Aunt Alexandra, I had planned to talk to her before Dad made the announcement *next week.*"

"I got caught up in the moment. What can I say?"

"Boardroom. Wedding party. It's all the same to you, isn't it, Benjamin? And, seeing as you, young man, have not raced out of here to find your wife, the duty falls upon me." Alexandra rose.

"No, please sit, Aunt. I'll go."

Blythe sat, the Cheshire cat.

Alexandra shook her head. "So, she's expendable? Collateral damage in the corporation called your lives."

"Nothing you say will bring me down tonight. Our Will is coming home to take his rightful place in the family business. This is a joyous occasion." Blythe signaled for the waiter. "Champagne all around!"

CHAPTER
TWENTY-THREE

UCKED INTO A CORNER OF the terrace, Catherine sat, painfully aware of the bug light dangling above her head, tiny zaps signaling the end of another creature's existence. A warm, muggy night, the humidity had not gone down with the sun. She gazed out into the blackness. Inside, the party was in full swing without her. Will hadn't even noticed she'd left. None of the guests batted an eye. Why should they? She was not part of the business, not part of the family, not part of this world. Everyone in that room had made that very clear, everyone but Aunt Alexandra, who had escaped herself by marrying a wealthy attorney who later sold his practice to travel around the world with her. Now *that* was love.

Fog crept in from the valley Will had told her was on the thirteenth hole. He was so different around his parents, so docile and obedient. Catherine shivered slightly despite the warmth.

"Here." Will took off his suit coat and placed it around her shoulders.

She shrugged it off. "No thank you. I'm fine."

"I understand you are upset."

"If I hadn't drunk so much wine, I'd be on my way back to San Diego by now."

"Guess Aunt Alexandra is good for something. Mom never had much use for her."

"Alexandra is the only real person in that entire room. Your mother is a bitch."

"That's not fair, Catherine. She even coordinated the menu for you."

"Oh, please! Blythe planned that menu to make herself look good in front of her friends."

"Come on."

"Oh, see how clever Blythe is," she mocked. "She is so amazing! Give me a break!"

"Keep your voice down. I don't want her to hear you."

"Of course not, *Wilfred*. Besides, your mother's bitchdom has no bearing on the fact that you did not bother to discuss a huge decision that majorly affects both of our lives."

"I didn't want to bother you until I had all the details."

"What if I didn't want to move to Naperville? Did you ever think of that? Now I have no choice but to follow along like some shit-for-brains wife. What's next? Barefoot and pregnant?"

"Honey, please." He moved to hug her.

"Get away from me. I don't even want to be in the same room as you. Are you even qualified to do this job?"

"Catherine, I do have an MBA."

"Really? How wonderful for you. That's another thing you never bothered to share. Any other skeletons in your closet?"

"Can't we do this some other time? We really should get back to the party."

"Of course, Wilfred. Well, I finally I get what MBA really stands for—Masters of Bullshit Appeasement. Lead on, Master Overman." She bowed deeply and followed him inside.

While Will headed straight for the dining room, Catherine sprinted toward the front door. "Carter? Where are you?"

"Right here, ma'am." He appeared, a bit of hamburger bun stuck on the right side of his mouth. "Oh, it's you."

"Could you please call me a cab?"

"Um, yeah. I'm eating."

Catherine grabbed his lapel and pulled him close. "Make the call, you pretentious little bastard, or I will have Alexandra Von Osterburg on your ass so quickly you won't even know what hit you."

"Okay, okay. I'm on it."

Catherine cozied into the warm bubble bath, a poor substitute for her husband's arms. She supposed they were all back at the manor by now, which made her doubly glad to be here in this hotel suite's tub, in the opposite direction.

She had taken care of herself for ten years, she could do it again. Will would probably move straight into Overman manor, happy his slumming days were over for good, much to the delight of his parents. A quick, no-fault divorce, and the family would be rid of his mistake of a wife and on to bigger and better things. At least she would get some good furniture out of the deal.

Her future would once again be blissfully free of any males, working at the zoo, drinking fucking Coronas anytime she wanted. Two lousy, stupid months. That was all her great love match lasted. Barely long enough to even get used to saying the words "my husband." Another miserable failure in the shit-fest that was her life.

Wrapped up in the room's complimentary robe, Catherine opened the minibar and got to the business of reducing the pain. No doubt Will and his father were discussing their plans for Overman Enterprises, so why shouldn't she get down to business too?

"Oh, Catherine, thank God," a voice blurted when she answered the phone. "Where are you?"

"Who is this?" she asked, knowing full well Will was on the other end of the line.

"What? Honey, it's me."

"I'm sorry. Wilfred Overman does not exist in my universe. Call my lawyer." Click. *Like she had one.*

The telephone kept ringing, but Catherine refused to pick up. Time to check out now that he knew her hiding spot. She slipped back into last night's dress with its tiny sweat stain under the left boob and slid off her wedding ring, pausing for a moment to watch it shimmer in the light. "With this ring, I thee unwed," she announced to her empty hotel room and shoved it into her purse.

"Here you go, miss. Just sign here, and we will be all set." When the guy behind the counter bothered to look up, he started slightly at the sight of her. Clearly, she had had a rough night.

"I know, believe me. Don't ask. Would you please call me a cab to the airport?"

Catherine ducked into the little lobby shop filled with all the things a traveler might forget. Since her luggage was still at the manor, she grabbed makeup, a comb, and some deodorant. "Do you have a rubber band?" she asked the cashier.

"Sure. That will be twenty-two, eighty-six."

"Gotta love hotel prices." She gathered her hair into a ponytail and grabbed her bag. Suburban taxis sure took their time. Almost as bad as in Portland. At least cabs existed here. Burkesville sure as hell never had any. Her moron brothers could have used them after Quartersfests. Thank goodness the road between Elbert Farm and Skip Nagurski's house scarcely saw any vehicles, tractors more than anything.

"Catherine, what are you doing?" The huge bags under Will's eyes told her he had not slept.

"I'm going back home, to my home, that is, San Diego."

"We have to talk this out. Come back to the house with me."

"Hell no. I don't need to face an onslaught from you, your parents, and their staff."

"Mom and Dad said they would leave us alone to talk. Besides, she is out doing damage control."

"What?"

"Did you really think no one would notice you never came back?"

"Yes, actually, that's exactly what I thought."

"Well, you're wrong. Mom's been on the phone all morning letting people know you are okay and that a terrible mistake had been made, not confirming the move with you first. She's chalking it up to us being newlyweds and not used to consulting another person about future plans. She's sure everyone will understand."

"Gee, it's great news that your stock prices won't take a dump, and Lord knows it warms the cockles of my heart, but my cab is here, so I gotta run."

"Please don't go." He reached for her arm. "I know I screwed up. I spent all last night trying to find you. Called every hotel in Naperville."

"That's why I came to...where is this? Lisle? Didn't want to be found, yet somehow, here you are anyhow."

"You have to give me another chance."

"Why? So you can save face with your parents? No, thanks."

The cabbie leaned out the window. "Miss, are you coming or what? You're gonna put me behind schedule."

"Catherine, please."

"Fine, Will. You've got one hour, then I'm leaving for the airport. Give me fifty bucks."

"Why?"

"Just do it!"

Will rifled through his pockets. "I've only got forty."

"Fine!" She snatched the bills out of his hand and gave them to the cab driver. "Sorry about all of this." He grabbed the money and drove off in a huff. Turning back to Will, she said "Talking this out would probably be the mature thing to do, but you are smokin' something if you thing I'm going back into the belly of the beast for more than fifteen minutes to change, put on some makeup, and pack my luggage. And you'd better make damn sure I don't run into one or both of your parents 'by accident' on my way to the guest room."

"Whatever you want, honey."

"Don't call me that."

"I'm parked over there."

"Whatever."

The house was totally quiet when they arrived. Not even Geoffrey was in the kitchen. "See? I told you no one would be here."

"Great. One thing you actually bothered to tell me."

"Okay, I guess I deserve that."

"Ya think?" When they got to the guest room, Catherine grabbed some clothes. "Let me get out of this dress."

Will sat on the bed, left foot dangling off the side. Why did he always feel caught in between his parents and Catherine? Was she right about that appeasement stuff? But it was just easier that way, and if he didn't have a strong opinion either way, where was the harm?

She emerged, face washed, in a pair of shorts and a t-shirt. "That's a running theme in this, you know."

"What?"

"You leaving out important details. It started the first day we came here, remember?"

He nodded.

"I tried to understand, to be empathetic to your 'plight,' especially after I had spent some time with your parents. But now I am beginning to see a more disturbing pattern. When you don't want to deal with something, you simply don't tell me and hope it never comes up. Some would call that the sin of omission. You lied to me. Multiple times. Probably because deep down you knew I would never want to come back to the Midwest and most certainly not to your parents' town. And they don't want me here, you can bet on that one. Your mother kept not-so-subtly watching me out of the corner of her eye the entire time your father was at the microphone. Don't kid yourself. She is not pleased with your choice of wife."

"Oh, I know that."

"Excuse me?"

"That's all I heard last night. Had to marry someone with no pedigree. In Vegas, nonetheless."

"Pedigree? What am I, a show dog?"

"But I kept telling them they don't know you like I do. They've never seen the way your eyes light up when you first plug in the Christmas tree, or the kindness you show kids at the zoo. They've never seen you have an entire conversation with a koala right before it falls asleep for the day, you whispering, 'Sweet dreams, Maloo.' I didn't tell you about the position because I was trying to get all the facts before even thinking about uprooting our little family and moving here."

Catherine sat down opposite him. "Our little family?"

"You and me. We're a family, right? A small, but awesome one. Well, at least until I completely screwed it up last night."

"Actually, I guess your father screwed up last night."

"It was inexcusable what he did. You have to remember,

he is in marketing and is all about furthering his brand. He saw an opportunity, all those people sitting there, a captive audience, and he couldn't help himself."

"What is it with you and assholes? First Morgan, now your father."

"Watch it, he's probably got a spy cam in this room somewhere."

"Wouldn't surprise me one bit. Let him listen." Catherine elevated her voice and announced, "Benjamin Overman is an asshole!"

Will chuckled. "Not one to mince words, are you?"

"That's a shock. Don't laugh. Last night, I was ready to call a divorce attorney."

"I was afraid of that. But, I was even more afraid of never seeing you again, even if it was to say good-bye. Please don't throw our marriage away. We're meant to be together. I can feel it in my heart." Will took his wife's hand. "I don't want to do anything without you. I love you, Catherine. Always will."

She stroked his cheek. "My 'Always Will.' I cried for hours thinking I'd lost you, that you had become *their* Wilfred and not my sweet Will."

"Come here, honey." He drew her close.

"Shut it off! I can't take it anymore!"

In the study, Benjamin Overman clicked the X, closing the camera feed. "Well, it looks like we are stuck with her. And that I'm an asshole."

"But we already knew that, dear. What are we going to do?"

"Give him a job offer he can't refuse, that's what. At least if he's here, we can look out for him, even if he is still married to the hick."

"She is going to break his heart, I can feel it in my very soul."

"Then, my dear, we must be here to pick up the pieces. He's a grown man. Besides, with Tommy not interested in the business at all, what choice do we have? Buck up, Blythe, it will all work out. I have a conference call with the board. Would you excuse me?"

"Of course. Dinner at seven?"

Benjamin nodded.

"I'll tell Geoffrey."

Stuck with the farm girl? Guess there were worst things. A prostitute, maybe, or a Democrat.

CHAPTER TWENTY-FOUR

Naperville, Illinois

"How do I look?" Will fussed with his shirt collar, then grabbed his tie, attempting a Windsor Knot while craning to see today's weather forecast.

"Hey, remember when we never had to check the weather in the morning?" Catherine took a sip of coffee. "Always seventy and sunny."

"Don't remind me," Will groaned. "What time is it? Crap! Dad said the car was coming for me at seven." He sprinted out of the kitchen.

Catherine ran after him. "Here, you almost forgot your laptop."

"Thanks, honey." He kissed her and dashed out the door.

It had taken Catherine about two months to get settled in Naperville, during which time Will dove head-first into his new position at Overman Enterprises. Benjamin insisted his son acquire a general knowledge of the company before placing him into any specific position. The boss's son would be under enough scrutiny. Benjamin had no intention of throwing Will to the sharks his first year.

There was, however, a handsome salary that came with this position-yet-to-be-named. Benjamin had really used the word "handsome," like he was on some TV drama. After seeing the check, however, even Catherine had to agree, it was a very handsome sight.

Then she went shopping.

A pro at the whole relocation thing by now, setting up house was the most fun part, buying all the dishes, glasses, and, this time, decent furniture that did not come from a re-sale shop.

Although Naperville was in the Midwest like Burkesville, that was where the similarities ended. The Chicago area stretched from the shores of Lake Michigan to well past fifty miles west. "Downtown" usually referred to downtown Chicago, also known as "the city," as in "Do you work in the city?" or "Are you going into the city tonight?" Naperville had its own little downtown, but it was only referred to as "downtown" by junior high students who were not allowed to go any farther. The very few farms on the far outskirts were surrounded by subdivisions, the last vestiges of Naperville's agrarian past.

Suburbia was its own beast. The biggest change was having to drive everywhere instead of walk. SUVs routinely cut her off, all driving forty miles per hour, no matter what the speed limit. Shit, she had forgotten to get a new Illinois driver's license. Yet another thing to do.

Sometimes, Catherine would escape to the Riverwalk before finishing her errands, where she could breathe a bit, get some fresh air. Other days, like today, she had to make do walking around their neighborhood. The sofa, love seat, and end tables they had ordered for their family room were being delivered today, so Catherine only had time for a quick (and early) walk. Much to Blythe and Benjamin's dismay, the newlyweds had purchased a house on Naperville's north side, among what Catherine thought of as "normal-sized" houses.

Children were lined up at the corner of Wiltshire and

Green Valley, fleece jackets in assorted colors zipped, hoods up. It was the first chilly morning of the season, a harbinger of what was to come. An older kid stood at the front, a little apart from the rest, button-like white earphones plugging his ears. Two smaller girls, dressed in head-to-toe purple, were making their little teddy bears talk to each other. The smallest kid pushed his way in between them.

"Hey! No cuts," shrieked the first girl.

"Back of the line, fish paste," said the other. The smallest relegated his position, rejected.

"Come on, Joe. You're gonna miss it!"

Halfway down the block, Joe's smile widened. He casually glanced over his shoulder. Bus 34 slowed down, baiting him. Joe began to trot. The bus crept up. Joe sprinted, almost tripping on his already-too-big-for-him jeans. With a final burst of speed, he made it to the corner, greeted by cheers and applause.

The bus door squeaked open, and the children ascended the stairs amid shouts of "Don't forget you have piano after school!" and "Good luck on your test!"

Catherine watched the bus pull away and the parents disperse to their homes. One lived in a mock-Victorian. Another, a Georgian. She continued down the street.

"Morning," mumbled a mustached worker man, briefcase and coffee in hand. He proceeded toward another bus stop, this time a Pace suburban route to the Metra station. He was joined on the corner by a corporate suit and a balding Billie Joe Armstrong from Green Day type, with large bags under his eyes instead of black eyeliner, who was probably in advertising.

Glancing at her watch, she picked up the pace. Her luck, it would be the only day in human history when delivery guys showed up on time.

Hmmm. What to do? What to do? The house was pretty much done, except for the second bathroom upstairs that needed a quick coat of paint. Oh yeah, and they needed a new lawnmower. The previous owners had thrown theirs in with the sale, not wanting to cart it all the way to Austin, Texas, where the wife had been transferred, but Will wanted to pick a new one out himself, determined to be the one in charge of outdoor maintenance, which was fine with Catherine. It was kind of cute, actually.

Sitting at the breakfast counter, Catherine flipped open *The Naperville Sun* as she took a bite of her English muffin. Butter dripped on the column by a Larry something. School board redistricting. Mosquito season. Blah. Blah. Blah. Meeting notices. What was this? "Classics Book Club. Meet in Room 204 of the Naperville Community Center. All are welcome. Talk or listen. Your choice." Probably filled with a bunch of crazy English major women with cats. Still, it would be something to do. What time was that meeting again?

It was so suburban, she couldn't handle it. Catherine's neighbor, Joy Monohan, had invited her over for coffee. Joy's house was one of the subdivision's riffs on Victorian architecture, light blue with white gingerbread. A slight woman with thin blonde hair and large, round cornflower blue eyes, Joy was in charge of eight hundred or so grammar school children and their souls as the Director of Children's Ministry at one of the Catholic churches in Naperville. She was one of three program directors whose personalities typically followed the same patterns across the United States. Works with little kids = exuberant, idealistic. Works with junior high prepubescents = slightly sardonic, a bit weary. Works with high schoolers = questions the existence of God, becomes fan of Jean-Paul Sartre.

"Cream or sugar?"

"Milk, please. No sugar. Thanks." Catherine scanned the kitchen while Joy poured the coffee. Everything was in its proper place, not a cookbook out of line, not a stray pile of mail anywhere.

"Here you go," Joy said, resisting the urge to call her honey. She was used to referring to her RE kids with little nicknames like sweetie, honey, or darling. It was impossible to memorize all of their names, but she still wanted them to feel special. "Coconut macaroon?"

"Thanks. So, Joy, what made you get into religious-ed?"

"John Lennon."

"Really?"

"Well, sort of. I initially had wanted to be a nun, but it was the sixties, and a person barely knew what to believe, much less sign up to join. Armies were frowned upon, whether they were for LBJ or God." Joy could not possibly tell her new neighbor that after marching to protest the Vietnam War, she went to her first college party and woke up the next morning alongside an upperclassman named Pete, which promptly put an end to Joy's nunnery dreams, since she was pretty sure purity was a prerequisite. "So, I went to school. Sophomores at Marian College were required to take personality and aptitude tests to help them make the correct career choice before declaring their majors. I was hoping it was my sign from God." She looked away for a second, disappointment flashing briefly across her face.

"What happened? These cookies are fantastic, by the way."

"Thank you. Old family recipe. Anyhow, I tore open the envelope. 'Priest,' it read, in big, bold letters. Not the ambiguous 'religious life.' Not 'sister.' Not 'nun.' 'Priest.'" The test had accurately assessed her organizational and leadership qualities, but failed to recognize gender, the only thing keeping her from being a priest. "Despite all of my alleged talents, the Roman Catholic Church was not about to budge. The apostles were all men. End of discussion."

Catherine could see the hurt in her eyes. "Ridiculous."

Joy gave her new young friend a smile. "So, I decided to major in religion and try the educational side." Joy paused to take a sip of coffee. "Besides, I met Frank, so it all worked out for the best, right?"

"So what does Frank do?" *Besides blow leaves at the ungodly hour of eight o'clock on a Saturday morning?*

"He's an accountant. Works downtown. Takes the train every day."

"Nice."

"How about your husband? Will, is it?"

"Yes, Will. He has just taken a job at Overman Enterprises."

"Impressive."

"His father owns the company." Catherine knew Will would be furious if he knew she told the neighbors about his family, but Catherine figured Joy was good enough to share some personal information, so it was only fair to reciprocate. Besides, it was fun seeing people's faces when they realize which Overmans she was talking about—a not-so-subtle, holy-shit-sort of response, but Joy Monohan would hardly say that.

"So, what are you going to do while Will works all of those hours?"

"Not sure. We both worked at the San Diego Zoo before we moved here."

"Really? Love the koalas! Oh, I just wanted to grab one and cuddle it."

Catherine nodded. "I know the feeling. I used to go over to see them as much as I could, sweet little fur balls."

"Why on earth would you leave San Diego? It's perfect."

"Will's job. There's no branch there."

"I see. Well, I could always use some help with the RE kids, if you're interested in doing any volunteer work or get bored."

"I'll think about it. Well, Joy, this was really great, but I had better get going. Have to go grocery shopping. We don't even have milk in the house."

"I'm so glad we got to talk, Catherine. Stop by anytime."

That was nice. However, their conversation had brought up something Catherine had been trying to avoid for about two months now. What would she do with her time? Will made enough to support them easily, but it wasn't just about the money. She would be bored to tears sitting around the house all day. And having kids was out of the question right now. She and Will were still trying to mitigate this thing called marriage without adding further complications.

After putting the groceries away, emptying the dishwasher, and throwing in a load of laundry, Catherine plopped herself down on the new sofa and clicked on the TV. Soap opera? White trash on parade talk show? Documentary on migrant bird patterns? Cartoons? TV court show? All-day news channel with fear-mongering anchorpeople? She picked up the phone.

"Will Overman."

"Hi."

"Hello, Catherine. What's up?"

"Not much. Pretty bored, actually."

"Sorry, honey, but I'm about to walk into a meeting. Can we talk later?"

"Sure. Just one thing. I don't like Catherine Overman."

"What?"

"I don't want to be known as Catherine Overman."

"Why? We *are* married."

"I don't want to be her. She's some bored housewife I never wanted to become."

"Ooo-kay."

"I'm Catherine Elbert. Please don't be mad at me, but I need to get an Illinois driver's license soon, and I want the name on it to be Catherine Elbert."

"Whatever you want. Listen, I really have to go. See you when I get home."

Whew! That was a load of her chest. She had been thinking about it for a while—which name to use—but did not want to offend Will. Now what? Get a job? Possibly. She had never been in this situation of not needing money before. Weird. Still, there was more to working than just money. What about fulfillment? A feeling of accomplishment? Happiness?

Catherine grabbed a pen and paper. Across the top, she wrote "What Makes Me Happy?" and in the margin, numbers one through five. Number one. Will. Number two?

Three hours and four Coronas later, the list was still not complete. "Coronas" was probably not the best option for number two, since it clearly would make Catherine look like an alcoholic, even though these were the first drinks she had all week.

Two more hours. Two more Coronas. Okay, this was getting ridiculous. Not having the last name of Overman came in at number two, followed by not my family, not his family, not farms, not bitches, not this move. She quickly scratched out the last one.

Catherine sat back and closed her eyes. Where had she felt happiness? Was she really as ungrateful as Clara had told her so many times when she was growing up?

The stage!

The only time she remembered feeling truly happy was on stage.

The garage door closed. Her husband was home.

"Will! I've got it! Hey, I kinda sound like that *My Fair*

Lady guy, don't I? By jove, I think she's got it. Funny, right?" She hugged him tight.

"Catherine, what are you doing?" He glanced around at all the empty Corona bottles.

"Will, I know I'm a little buzzed."

"A little."

"I have an announcement!" She stumbled toward the television. "Will, look! Ta da! I am going to be an actress!" With a flourish, she bowed deeply.

"Where did this come from?"

"Well, I had coffee with Joy next door, and I didn't want to volunteer for her religious-ed, then I picked up groceries, did a load of laundry, then I didn't want to be Catherine Overman, then I wanted to be an actress."

"You forgot the Coronas," he said, picking up her "What Makes Me Happy" list. "Which, from what it looks like here, come in at a staggering number two, second only to me. Catherine, there are more 'nots' on your list."

"Sshh. Don't worry about that. I told you. I'm what's his name? Henry Higgins! That's it." She tried her best English accent. "I think she's got it! Jolly good, don't you think?"

"I've heard better." His wife sounded like Grandmother Overman with a mouthful of mothballs after drinking a fifth of gin. "Do you have anything for dinner?"

"I just made a major life decision! Why would I have been cooking? I've been thinking! Who do you think I am? Geoffrey?"

"You know what? I'm going to change and then order some pizza. Sound good?"

"Sure." Catherine cuddled into the sofa and fell asleep.

CHAPTER TWENTY-FIVE

*T*HIS WAS IT! HER FIRST audition. Catherine was so excited, she forgot to put the car in park and nearly rammed the BMW parked opposite her. Sure, it was just for a local theater group, but it was *good* community theater. Oak Park even. Gerry, the instructor over at her "Intro to Acting" class at College of DuPage had announced the open call last Monday and encouraged everyone to try out. He had been "Stanley Kowalski" in their *A Streetcar Named Desire* last year and assured the class of this company's quality.

Like a flashback to *Oklahoma!* try-outs all those years ago, Oak Park-River Forest High School's auditorium was buzzing with wanna-be actors mouthing lines and reciting tongue twisters to keep loose until they were called. Catherine would be reading for the part of Annie Sullivan in *The Miracle Worker*. Gerry said she nailed it last night, so the butterflies in her stomach were only Gossamer wings, rather than Monarchs.

A voice boomed through the sound system. "Catherine Elbert. You're up."

The director thanked everyone for coming and sent them off, heads full of promise. Of course, some would get their dreams crushed on Thursday when the cast would be announced, but she would not be one of them. It felt so right to be back one stage. It had to be a sign.

Thursday! Catherine jolted out of bed. After a quick breakfast of toast and tea (she was too nervous to eat much), the waiting began. This was followed by checking her email every fifteen minutes for the next three hours.

Another piece of toast, this time accompanied by a Corona to calm her nerves, was all she had for lunch. The fifteen minutes dwindled to ten. It was getting late.

Another Corona for the fun of it. When she returned to the computer, it was there.

*Thank you very much for auditioning for the Oak Park Theater Company's production of **The Miracle Worker**. Unfortunately, your talents are not a good match for this play.*

We hope you will try again next season.

Kindest regards,

Michael Ryan

Director

Damn. Here was the first rejection, one of the many Gerry the community college acting teacher had warned about. "Acting—actually the arts in general—is a gut-wrenching, bi-polar experience. It can be euphoric or soul-crushing. You have to get used to that."

Gee thanks, Gerry, she thought, and drained her beer.

One night, Will was greeted with a glass of wine, the smell of something wonderful cooking in the oven, and a passionate kiss from his wife. "Well, hello to you, too. What is all of this?"

"It's a special day. Come sit down."

He set his laptop backpack down and joined her in the dining room, where Catherine had set up mushroom flatbread and assorted cheeses.

"Wow, Catherine. You've really outdone yourself."

"With a little help from Geoffrey." She winked. "There's prime rib in the oven."

"My favorite! To what do I owe such a grand feast?"

"Okay, well, sit down. Are you ready? I got a part in *As You Like It*, the Shakespeare in the Park! Audrey, the country wench. It's only a few lines, but my character has a name and everything."

"That's fantastic! When is it?"

"Summer. Rehearsals start in April. Thanks for putting up with me. I know I haven't been very easy to live with lately."

Will lifted his glass. "To my honey, congratulations! Me thinks thou whilst make a wonderful wench in Master Shakespeare's fair play. Cheers!"

Catherine bowed her head. "Thank you kindly, good sir, for your most welcomed encouragement. Maybe my luck is finally starting to change. Huzzah!"

The telephone rang at four o'clock, jolting Catherine out of bed.

"Cat? It's Russell, your brother."

"Russell? What the hell? Why are you calling so early?"

"It's Pop. He's had a heart attack."

CHAPTER TWENTY-SIX

*T*HE MEMORY OF DRIVING OFF in Josh's car had been etched into her brain, a talisman against any foolish notions of return. The same sickening feeling from ten years ago once again invaded her stomach. Catherine braced herself and got out of the car. "Will?"

"It's okay, honey. I'm right here." He put his arm around her waist, guiding her up the stairs.

The door opened. "Oh, hey, Catherine." Russell's hair was starting to gray. Deep wrinkles had carved trenches on each side of his mouth. Working all day in the fields ages a person. "Ma, Catherine's here."

Clara came into the living room, followed by a portly, yet pretty much the same Peter. "I suppose this is the husband," she said, gesturing toward Will.

He moved to shake her hand. "Hello, Mrs. Elbert. It is a pleasure meeting you."

Clara offered nothing. "I suppose you oughta sit down. Peter, get our guests something to drink."

Our guests hung in the air.

"So, what happened?"

"Hank went out to milk the cows, same as every day. When he didn't come back, I sent Russell out after him. Doctor said he'd had a heart attack. Died instantly."

Catherine wiped a tear from her right eye. "When's the funeral?"

"Tomorrow," Russell said. "At St. Agatha's."

Clara continued. "I cleaned out your old room. Will, why don't you and Peter bring up your luggage?"

"Um, Ma? We're staying at the Mitchell House. Didn't want you to have to go to any trouble."

"Of course you are. Well, then, I guess I will see you tomorrow."

"Ma?"

"I'm tired, Catherine. I need to get to bed." Clara turned and went upstairs.

"How is she?" Catherine asked Russell.

"Oh, you know Ma. As tough as a horse. She loved him, Cat, you know that."

There was a long silence.

"Well, guess we'd better be going. Do you need a ride tomorrow?"

"No. Meet us at church. From there, we'll go to the cemetery. There's a luncheon at the VFW Hall afterwards."

"Do you mind if I say a few words at the funeral?"

"No!" Came from upstairs.

"But he was my father."

Clara came halfway down the steps. "You forfeited being a part of this family the day you left Elbert Farm for Maine. You can sit in the congregation with the rest of the townsfolk. That's final."

"Catherine Elbert!" When Kendra Mitchell saw Will she added, "I guess it's not Elbert anymore, is it? Nice to meet you, Will." She hugged them both tight.

A teenager in a University of Wisconsin t-shirt and jean shorts bounded down the stairs. "Mom, the guests in the Keats room would like more towels. Are they in the dryer?"

"Maddie?"

"Oh, you must be Catherine."

"Look at you, all grown up!" Catherine smiled. "Where's Mr. Mitchell?"

"Tea, anyone?" Kendra herded them into the kitchen. After setting out their beverages and some muffins, she sat down next to Catherine, giving her a little squeeze. "It's so good to see you. I want to hear all about your adventures."

"Kendra, where's Adam?"

"Oh, Cat, he's in a convalescent center in Milwaukee. Alzheimer's. Been about five years now. It's just me and Maddie around here now. The dynamic duo."

"I'm so sorry. How about Josh?"

"He left shortly after you did. Last I heard he was in Alaska, of all places. His cousin, Roy, is our handyman now. Does great work."

"Alaska? Well, Josh always was a hard one to read."

"Had his eye on you, if I remember correctly."

"No way, Kendra."

"Yes he did, Cat. I caught him staring at you quite a few times, but he never seemed to have the gumption to ask you out." Then she remembered Will was there. "But, never mind that. You've caught yourself a cutie here."

Will blushed and reached for a muffin.

"Cat, I am really sorry about your father."

"Thank you."

"How's your mother holding up? They must have been married for a long time, huh?"

"Almost fifty years."

All of Burkesville turned out to say farewell to Hank Elbert at St. Agatha's Church. During the eulogy, Jonesy made the crowd laugh with tales of their escapades during those fishing trips. Russell spoke for the family and thanked everyone for coming. Clara sat stoic in the front row, a little more hunched over than usual; eyes dry, refusing to cry in public.

"Good-bye, Pop," Catherine whispered on her way to take Communion, rubbing the coffin draped in white sitting in the middle of the aisle. She could not control the tears as she received the host. Clara snorted in disdain.

After all of the serving trays and chalices were cleaned and put away, the priest circled the casket, waving incense. "And so we consecrate our brother Hank to Almighty God, in the name of the Father, and of the Son, and of the Holy Spirit."

"Amen." The congregation answered in unison.

"Eternal rest grant unto him, oh, Lord," he bellowed.

They answered, "And may the perpetual light shine upon him."

"May his soul and the souls of all the departed through the mercy of God rest in peace."

"Amen."

In the VFW parking lot, the weight of her father's death and her mother's scorn riveted Catherine to the rental car's seat.

"Come on, honey," Will urged. "We have to go in."

"I don't want to face those people, any of them. It's not like I'm the prodigal son. God knows what she has told them."

Will stroked her cheek. "I'm sure the entire town of Burkesville knows what she's like and hasn't paid attention to anything she might have spewed. Besides, you don't really have a choice. People can see you're here."

Catherine dabbed her eyes with a tissue and took a deep breath. "Let's get this over with."

"Cat! I'm so sorry." Beth pulled her into a hug. Fred soon

followed, the three Schmidt boys trailing in his wake. The oldest had to be about the same age Catherine and his mother had been when they'd saved their money so they could buy Twinkies and chocolate milk after school at the Quickie Mart, following Bill Davies there in hopes of any kind of communication. Surreal.

"Cat, these are my kids Al, Mike, and Rich."

"Nice to meet you." Catherine shook their hands while each mumbled "Sorry about your father."

"Al, the last time I saw you, you were a baby." The eldest Schmidt blushed, looking at his shoes.

"And this is my husband, Will." Catherine pulled him into the group's center. "Can we sit with you guys? We've been banished from the family table." She glanced toward Clara who was receiving condolences from Molly Smith, Burkesville's drunken whore. Well, at least she was ten years ago. Hard to imagine her propositioning anyone at He's Not Here Tavern now. "I'd rather sit with you anyway." She gave Beth a squeeze.

"I can't believe he's gone. I just saw him the other day getting gas at the Quickie Mart. He was a good man, Cat."

That seemed to be the prevailing theme of Hank's funeral. Her father had slipped her money the day she left the farm for Portland and had continued sending little checks periodically throughout the years.

"So, how's the furniture business?" Will asked Fred.

"Not bad. A little down from last year, but still, considering the economy and all, doin' okay."

"Catherine showed me some of your tables and that patio set. Beautiful."

Fred Schmidt's secondary business was a godsend during the years certain crops didn't take. Every once in a while, Beth attached a picture of Fred's latest piece with her emails.

Bill Davies waived from across the room. Much to

Catherine's delight, Denise had gained about fifty pounds over the last ten years. Childbirth can do that, and there was nothing wrong with it, but she couldn't help but smirk.

"Hey, Smellbert. Sorry about your father. He was a great guy." Age had been kind to Bill. His blue eyes still sparkled, but instead of following up with some devilish comment, he told her about his children: Jennifer, a cheerleader, and Eric, the star of his Little League team.

After a luncheon of ham, fried chicken, potato salad, and strawberry gelatin, Catherine approached Clara's table. She was talking to the priest who said the funeral Mass, some new guy Catherine did not know. Father Wilhelm had passed away last year.

"Thank you so much." She shook his hand fiercely. "Hank would have liked the send-off he got today."

"Ma?"

Clara turned, her expression changing to indifference. "Yeah?"

"Can I stop by the farm before we head home?"

"Whatever suits you."

———— ⁂ ————

Catherine gave Will a tour of Elbert Farm. The World's Largest Christmas Trees. The pig sty. The cooking garden— just a patch of dirt with weeds now. The barn where Hank collapsed. They stayed in there for quite a while. Sitting on bales of hay, Catherine told Will stories of her youth in between crying spurts.

It was time to go.

"I hope you'll be okay, Ma. Take care of her, boys."

Russell and Peter nodded.

"They do, Cat, which is more than I can ever say for you."

"Kind of hard halfway across the country."

"Too busy for the family, I suppose."

"I've been on a lot of auditions the last few months. Got a part in *As You Like It*. You know, Shakespeare?"

"Now you think you're an actress?" Clara shook her head.

"I am. We are in rehearsals now."

"Rehearsals? Please. All you are is an ungrateful college dropout who wasted my hard-earned money and ran off to Maine because you saw it on some travel show."

Russell and Peter plunked down on the sofa just like the good old days. Ringside seats. Will stayed by the door in case Catherine needed to make a quick exit.

"Then you couldn't hack it there, so you flitted off to LaLaLand to play with koalas."

"The Atlantic coast is a hard life."

"Got too much sun, probably fried your brain, now you're in whatever-ville."

"Naperville. It's by Chicago."

"No kidding, missy. Are you going to pretend to be a geography teacher now and give me a lesson?"

"What's that supposed to mean?"

"You're no actress. You play at it for fun while your rich husband pays all the bills!"

"I have always wanted to do this, but you yanked that chance away from me senior year."

"Tommyrot. If you were serious about acting, you would have stayed in California with all the other wannabes."

"I couldn't stay...Will's job...You don't understand." Catherine stood dumbstruck. How could this woman have raised her, yet know so little about her only daughter? "I took a class."

"Where? At some community college? Beth told me when I ran into her at the post office the other day. What about Second City? Why aren't you studying there if you're so serious about it?"

"What do you know about acting, stuck in this shit-hole town?"

"Plenty. How do you think I could stomach the likes of you all mournful at your father's funeral when you broke his heart the day you left?"

"Pop was the only one who ever talked to me!"

"Yeah? And what did he get for it? You just as good as stole his money and went around making a big nothing of yourself all over the country without so much as a phone call! Didn't think I knew, did ya?" Clara countered Catherine's surprised expression. "Your father loved you, and you used him, plain and simple."

"I don't need this. I'm out of here."

"Run away. It's what you do best."

Catherine gathered her purse, grabbed Will, and ran out the door, slamming it as she fled.

"Drive faster!" she barked at Will, who sped down Elbert Farm road.

CHAPTER
TWENTY-SEVEN

Naperville, Illinois
Present Day

*D*ELUSIONS OF GRANDEUR NEVER DIE easily, particularly when someone once experienced even the tiniest bit of success. A small nugget of affirmation can sustain for a surprisingly long time. Catherine's theater dreams, dormant for almost eight years, had risen to the surface faster than even she thought possible. Every scene she played in acting class, every day she practiced her lines, every time she brought a smile to Gerry's face in their workshops, all of these little protons screaming "You nailed it!" or "Well done, Catherine" were attracted to her natural negativity, forming another human entity all together—Theatre Catherine.

Where regular Catherine was starved for attention because her husband worked long hours being groomed for Overman Enterprises, Theatre Catherine commanded the room at acting class. At the premier meeting of the Classics Book Club, it was Theatre Catherine who entered with a flourish, all too willing to announce to total strangers she was an actress. Regular Catherine would have slipped in unceremoniously, skulking toward the back.

Theatre Catherine sat of equal intellect among the bibliophiles, except for maybe that Spring girl who made remarks about not understanding Shakespeare. Theatre Catherine would never admit to such a thing. Regular Catherine would have been a little intimidated not having a college education like the rest of the book club and would have started second-guessing her choice to escape to Portland. Theatre Catherine laughed off the doubt, chalking Portland up as a great adventure and learning experience—Act II in the great drama that was her life.

There was no stopping Theatre Catherine once Audrey, the country wench, came into her life, although, if regular Catherine could have surfaced for even one moment, she would have had a good laugh at the irony of it. Her first role outside Burkesville was a Shakespearean hick? Hilarious! Instead, Theatre Catherine embraced the role as if she were playing Lady MacBeth, filled with importance and lust for power. Well, at least she got "lust" right.

Theatre Catherine could not be suppressed when arriving thirty minutes late to the book club dinner at the Spanish restaurant after *As You Like It*, ensuring everyone in the place was well aware exactly where she came from, regardless if it was a lie. Regular Catherine had had a small spat with her husband who needed to get home right after the performance because he had a six thirty tee time the next morning, but Theatre Catherine was helping to break down the small set.

Theatre Catherine seemed the panacea, until she was alone at home or one of her walks. When the guard was down, reality hit. Regular Catherine knew she was the piece of the puzzle that would never fit—no matter on Elbert Farm or in Overman manor—equally out of place in both settings.

Then one by one, the failures began.

Although she left each audition with the confidence and

bravado of Theatre Catherine, regular Catherine soon replaced her, wallowing in her shortcomings. In high school, all brown hair and brown eyes got her was a chance at second banana, no matter how much pizzazz Mr. Gusselman tried to coat it with. Now, it didn't even get her a call back. Catherine, theatre or otherwise, never even made it past the first round. Umpteen times, "Thank you. Next!" was all the response she received.

Theatre Catherine thank you-next'd her way to various auditions throughout the Chicagoland area, amazed at how many of the actors here had at least bachelor's degrees in theater, many from Northwestern. The "good" community theater was a way to earn your chops for them. The rest of her competition seemed to have been performing since age six.

"Thank you. Next!"

Finally, even Theatre Catherine became tired of the charade. One Shakespeare in the Park does not a career make. The rest of the time, regular Catherine cooked, cleaned, and did laundry.

"Thank you. Next!"

Pretty soon, Theatre Catherine moved upstage, coming out only for special guest appearances, like Overman Enterprises shareholder dinners.

It was regular Catherine who brushed her hair, kissed Will, who was busy reading something or another for work, on the head, and headed out for the monthly Classics Book Club meeting. Regular Catherine was starting to speak up more, having actually read the books discussed each month, rather than absorbing only the first two full pages and the final page of each chapter, while skimming the rest in between.

Regular Catherine admitted things to herself that Theatre Catherine never could.

She was a fraud.

Had been for years.

The only true acting regular Catherine had ever mastered was changing her persona with each move. Maybe none of the bibliophiles would notice if Theatre Catherine never showed up again. If Larry would only stop calling her Audrey the country wench. Regular Catherine would have to deal with him in her usual, not-so-subtle way, that was all. But Edwina Hipplewhite? Now, she was different. There would be no bullshitting her. Maybe Theatre Catherine would have one last performance.

CHAPTER
TWENTY-EIGHT

*T*HADDEUS MUMBLEGARDEN WAS QUITE PERPLEXED. Spring Pearson was staring out the window, her back purposely toward Thaddeus, tapping nervously on the table.

"I am not sure why you are so upset."

Spring refused to turn around.

"I do not even know what I did."

"Yes, you do," Spring said, her voice sounding small.

"I can assure you, madam, I most definitely do not."

Spring whipped around. "It's 'miss.'"

"Pardon me?"

"It's 'miss,' not 'madam.' I'm single and not 'of a certain age,' as you put it."

Thaddeus chuckled. "Is that what is bothering you? You think I called you old?"

"Don't laugh at me."

"Come now, Miss Pearson. Be not dismayed. It was a mere slip of the tongue. Incorrect phraseology. I meant no harm. Clearly you are not 'of a certain age,' as I so indelicately put it. I am but a fool." He took her hand and knelt before her.

Edwina Hipplewhite burst through the door, throwing her enormous bag on the table. "Good Lord! Is this what I think it is?" She clapped her hands in excitement. "Please, don't let me stop you. Oh, bibliophiles, what joy!"

Thaddeus jolted up. "No! Goodness sake, no. Why I would never…um…no."

Spring ran out of the room, small tears bubbling down her cheeks.

"What the hell just happened? What's wrong with Spring?"

Ignoring Larry, Edwina ran to comfort Thaddeus. "Oh, my dear boy. I am so sorry to have botched up your proposal."

"Miss Hipplewhite, it was not a proposal. I was apologizing for something I had said to Miss Pearson. Nothing more. Why, we are not even dating. Why on earth would I be proposing?"

"Well, then. You had better tend to her nonetheless, dear, for I am afraid not only have you previously insulted Spring, you also made it seem like the possibility of marrying her is exceedingly repugnant to you."

"Ouch! That's gotta hurt."

"Not helping, Larry." Rosemary Stevens said.

Edwina produced a tissue from her sleeve and rubbed the perspiration from her brow. "Okay, my dears, let us get this meeting underway." From the doorway came muffled, but unmistakably upset sounds. "Shall we get on with it? Okay, who is missing?"

Annie Jacobs and Sarah Anderson entered the room, both looking confused.

"What's going on out there?" Sarah hung her purse on the back of her chair.

"Oh, a terrible misunderstanding, I'm afraid," replied Edwina. "Best to leave them to work it out on their own. Quick attendance check. Rosemary, lovely to see you. Annie. Sarah. Larry. Those two out there. Where's Catherine?"

"Late as usual. Ever since she did that Shakespeare in the Park thing, you would think she just won a Tony award or something."

The door burst open. "Sorry I'm late."

"See what I mean? Greetings, Audrey. How's that job coming? Wenching paying well nowadays?"

"Not as well as I would want, Larry, but, alas, we all have to make do." Catherine took a seat behind Annie, who smiled up at her as she walked by. Thaddeus returned, dejected.

Edwina clapped her hands, multiple bracelets shaking and shimmering upon her arms. Miss Hipplewhite was fond of bangles of all sorts, from bright, bombastic circles of color to carved ebony African arm bands. Never one to shy away from accessories, Edwina looked like a walking advertisement for World Market, dressed in a different continent's style each meeting. Asian. South American. African. Even a bit of Americana for good measure. Simply put, Edwina wore whatever she damned well pleased, which was one benefit of not being married or anyone's mother. A sari one day, a Hawaiian muumuu the next. The only requisite was that it hide her girth and had some color. "With so many interesting combinations from which to choose, why would anyone want to wear drab old black?" she was known to say at more than one bibliophile event.

"So, dear ones, what were your impressions of Mr. Irving's tales? Let us start with the most famous, 'The Legend of Sleepy Hollow.' An intriguing little story, don't you think? Brain versus brawn. Superstition versus rational thought. Perception versus reality. Do you think a persnickety school teacher even has a shot with the most desirable girl in the village?"

"Hell, no." Larry snorted. "Would Bill Gates have a chance with a supermodel?"

"Probably," responded Rosemary, twirling a blonde ringlet around her finger. "He does have billions."

"Remember, this is upstate New York in the 1800s, dear ones, not present day."

"Seems like Brom Bones is the one Katrina is originally attracted to."

"You are correct, Sarah," Edwina said. "Is Ichabod realistic in setting his sights upon Miss Van Tassel?"

Annie was first to reply. "The ladies do admire his singing and dancing, don't they? Women like good dancers."

"But he's a wuss, all scared and jittery."

"Very true, Larry dear. And what about Brom Bones? What do we think of him?"

Thaddeus piped up, "Thinking and Brom Bones should not be uttered in the same sentence."

Laughter reverberated around the room.

"He does get Crane in the end, though, doesn't he?" said Larry.

"But is it Brom Bones who scares the schoolmaster, or is it Ichabod Crane himself who ultimately frightens him away?" Edwina posed the question, and then sat back, watching their reactions. Always first with a knee-jerk response, Larry was unusually quiet this time.

"It's Brom Bones. If he didn't pull the prank on Ichabod, Crane wouldn't have run away."

"True, Annie, but I think it's Ichabod himself. He gets so wrapped up in the scary stories, he freaks himself out. Brom Bones just puts him over the edge," said Sarah.

"But, it's clearly Brom Bones dressed up as the horseman," Rosemary added.

"There is no definitive proof," said Miss Hipplewhite. "A mere hint of a knowing smirk upon Brom's visage. That is all Irving gives us."

"If enough people think it, eventually it will become fact."

"Larry, you have been around long enough to know perception is not always reality," Edwina said.

"People's realities are the result of their perceptions," Catherine said, almost as an afterthought.

Edwina looked at the youngest bibliophile and made a

mental note to speak with her after the meeting. Before long, ninety more minutes had passed. "Good Lord, look at the time! Dear ones, we had best be going. Instead of our usual meeting next month, we shall celebrate Samhain with a field trip to Naper Settlement's All Hallow's Eve, where a multitude of literary specters will provide an evening of Halloween gaiety. I will email you the details. Ta-ta, darlings. Good night."

Thaddeus bolted out the door in search of Spring, who had never returned. Small conversations erupted among subsets of the book club members. Larry and Rosemary. Annie and Sarah.

"Catherine, may I have a word?" Edwina packed her books into her large, quilted bag of assorted colors.

"Yes, Miss Hipplewhite?"

"How are auditions going? Have you given any more thought to enrolling in that Second City workshop?"

"Um...well..."

"May I give you a piece of advice?"

Catherine sighed.

Edwina forged on, sensing this could be her only chance. "True art requires a genuine connection, an emotional link to something the artist holds dear, whether it be acting, painting, or writing. Otherwise, it is but a shallow representation of life, a soulless copy. A reasonable facsimile."

The tears came stronger than Catherine could have ever imagined. Edwina engulfed her with a large arm, guiding her to a seat. "There, there. Let it out. It's going to be okay, dearest."

———— ✦ ————

"Hey, you up for a little beverage?" Sarah followed Annie out of the community center.

"Absolutely. I'm working from home tomorrow anyhow." Annie had accepted Harry's offer of working from home two days a week as a way to ease back into corporate life. Besides, it seemed his team members were scattered around the country anyway, so what was the difference?

They sat at their favorite table. Sarah fingered the lid of her peppermint mocha. "So, how are you, really? You seem to be putting on a brave face."

"It's not a facade, though. At first maybe it was a coping mechanism, but since the divorce was finalized, a strange calm has come over me. I've been having a great time getting rid of stuff. The guys at Goodwill who unload your car and I are big buddies now." After her marriage to John had broken up, Annie downsized, going from a five-bedroom Tudor to a two-bedroom condo situated alongside the DuPage River, a few blocks from downtown Naperville. "Please don't take offense, but typical suburban living thing is not for me. I thought it was, but I really wasn't happy with it, even before the IVF debacle."

Sarah nodded. "I grew up in a city-suburb. Chicago was just across the street, so I totally understand. Sometimes I really miss walking to things. It gets tiring schlepping the kids and car seats everywhere. I'm looking forward to the days when the boys and I can ride our bikes down here. Nicky would be fine, but Alex is still a little small for that yet."

"That sounds like fun." Annie took a drink of chai. "I can tell you, I'm loving decorating my condo. Two bedrooms—one I use for an office—a family room, kitchen, and small dining room. Perfect. I can clean it in two hours, tops, not two hours for one floor. I'm not my mother, you know."

Annie and her mother had still not reconciled. Marian had blamed Annie for the divorce, saying her daughter drove John away with her obsession for a biological child. That was the last straw for Annie, who refused to return any of Marian's phone calls. After a while, they stopped coming altogether. She still met her father, George, for an occasional lunch, but that too, was waning. It was just as well. Annie wanted a clean break from her old life anyhow. The only constant now was work and, of course, Sarah, whose family practically adopted Annie as one of their own. She was taken in, reluctantly at first, that first Christmas after she and John split. Annie had planned to stay at home alone with nothing but a bottle of Grey Goose vodka so she could yell at the television and make fun of George Bailey and his sappy karma lesson, but Sarah would not hear of it. Instead, she and her brother, Greg, invaded Annie's condo. While Greg scooped Annie up, Sarah packed an overnight bag.

Unlike June Jacobs and the ex-sisters-in-law, also known as the three witches from *MacBeth*, who would never allow Annie to cook anything more than the green bean casserole, Sarah had put her to work right away, cutting up bread, chestnuts, and assorted herbs for the stuffing. Together the three of them produced a lovely Christmas meal that would have made Sarah's mom, Patty, very proud. They had as best of a Christmas as they could muster. It was not without a few tears, of course, for Annie's disintegrated marriage and for the mother Sarah and Greg missed so much. But they were together, forming their own new holiday traditions and that was what counted. Oh yeah, Tom Anderson was there, too, but he stayed out of the kitchen, preferring to watch football.

"So what do you think was up with Thaddeus and Spring? Are they an item?" Sarah took a sip of mocha, a small smirk curling her lips. "I can't see them together at all, can you? Isn't he gay, anyhow?"

"I don't think so, but with him, it is hard to tell. Could just be all the British slang he uses."

"Annie!" Sarah chuckled, almost spit-taking.

"I'm just sayin'. One time, I caught him checking out my boobs."

"You did?"

"It was just for a second, but then he realized I saw, and the poor guy could barely bring himself to raise his eyes to meet mine, so we talked for ten minutes while he stood there, completely averting his eyes, like my chest was some sort of holy relic. It actually was pretty funny."

"Poor Thaddeus," Sarah said. "It's like his mother raised him to be too polite and pushed him into complete awkwardness."

"And what about Spring? So timid. Wonder what kind of parents she has. I'm going to take a wild guess and vote for hippies."

"Wouldn't be surprised." Sarah checked her phone. "Well, my dear, I must bid you adieu. It's a school day tomorrow, and Tom is leaving for Boston on an early flight. Five thirty limo pick up."

"How long this time?"

"Couple of weeks. Another system upgrade. How many do they need? I don't get it, but, that's why I wrote grants and not computer code."

They hugged good-bye. Sarah drove off down Jefferson Avenue in her minivan. Annie buttoned up her trench coat against the unusually chilly September air. One lone tree stood golden, highlighted against the midnight blue sky by its companion streetlight. There would be more soon, once autumn officially began. She walked across the Main Street bridge down Water Street toward her condo.

CHAPTER TWENTY-NINE

S TILL DARK ON HER SIDE of the house, nighttime gasped its last breath, the unknown still lurking, curling itself around tree limbs, across bushes, enveloping a lone jogger as he ran past.

In the kitchen, the first rays of morning's light began to appear behind silhouetted houses, light pink at first, then turning deeper orange as it colored the sky.

She filled her coffee cup and returned to the night.

You're no actress. You play at it for fun while your husband pays the bills.

Your father loved you, and you used him, plain and simple.

Will came down the stairs, rubbing his eyes. "How long have you been down here?"

"Since three."

"Your dad?"

"That and other things. Did you know I was number three in my class?"

"I did not. Very nice."

"Not really. You see, I never tried. The grades just happened. Burkesville was such a small shit-bag school, if someone like me was number three, that tells you how goddamned stupid the rest of the class must have been."

"Really, Catherine."

"What have I accomplished these ten years?"

"Well, our marriage has to count for something."

Catherine did not answer right away. Instead, she kept staring out the front window, sipping her coffee. "I mean, who decides to be an actress at my age because she can't figure out one thing that makes her happy besides her husband? Who does that, Will?"

"I'm just glad I made the list."

"This cannot be my life. Audition, rejection, audition, rejection. I thought my luck had finally changed after *As You Like It*, but nope."

Will sat in silence.

"I quit."

Will hugged his wife, stroking her hair. "Honey, you don't have to give up. Get something to occupy your time during the day, then do auditions at night."

"Occupy my time?" Catherine pulled away. "Gee, thanks. We can't all have a Daddy that creates a position for us, can we?"

"I need some coffee."

Catherine did not follow him into the kitchen, scared of what would come out of her mouth next. Clara was right, goddamn her. She was no actress; she merely reinvented herself with each move. Clearly she was no good at it either, since she managed to screw everything up no matter which coast she was on. Playing with fire in Portland lost her the only people she considered family until she met Will. And she had used Hank for money, giving nothing in return.

Will padded past her, mug in hand. "Breakfast meeting at seven thirty."

"Okay, see ya," slipped out of her mouth.

She would apologize later.

Edwina Hipplewhite had said the only life worth living is a genuine one. Catherine rummaged for a piece of paper and wrote "What I Know For Sure" at the top.

I have no land to be bound, chained in servitude like my parents.

No family to dress me in expectations.

No college degree to define me.

I love Will. I don't love all the trappings that come with Will, but I am delusional to think we can hide ourselves away from his family, their company, and—even though I hate to admit it—the country club.

I must make peace with my past.

Reconciliation with Clara would be impossible. Her mother had made that very clear after Hank's funeral. But what about Portland? A dull, uncomfortable feeling invaded her stomach, spreading throughout her body. Guilt.

She did not care whatsoever what became of Scott Dithersby, but Patsy? Definitely. And Katie McLellan?

"Get out of here! I don't need you. I don't need anybody. Fuck you all." That was how she had treated the woman who felt so much more like a mother than Clara had ever been. Too embarrassed to phone, Catherine began writing on a separate sheet of paper, first to Patsy.

> *Dear Patsy,*
>
> *I know I am probably the last person you want to hear from, but I need to let you know how sorry I am for what I did to you. I was wrong thinking I was helping you escape a life plagued by the Dithersbys. Instead, I robbed you of something so much more important. I do not expect forgiveness, but hope that after all these years, your wounds have healed.*
>
> *I miss you, my friend.*
>
> *Catherine*

Then to Katie.

Dear Mrs. McLellan,

I am sorry about so many things. You were nothing but kind to me, and how did I repay you? By blaming you for everything I had brought upon myself. I hope someday, you will forgive me.

Love,

Catherine

She grabbed a large manila envelope from Will's supply drawer, wrote the McLellan address on it, and stuck both letters inside, sure Katie would still know where Patsy lived, even after all these years. It was just how she was.

Catherine sealed the envelope and set off for the post office.

Maple trees blazed brilliant reds and oranges, while elms burst golden yellows. Leaves of all sizes rode through the sky on gentle breezes, while the sun presided over this glorious sixty-three-degree day. Pumpkins rested on doorsteps and house stairs, waiting to be carved. Ghouls hung from trees. Graveyards sprouted up on front lawns. Catherine had forgotten how much she enjoyed Halloween in the Midwest. The purples, rusts, and golds of the mums. The front bushes covered in fake spider webs. There was mischief in the air. "Sure you don't want to come?" she asked Will while fluffing her hair.

"No, you go ahead. I'm exhausted." Golfing eighteen holes, plus cutting and edging the lawn was plenty for one Saturday. "Besides, Michigan is playing Nebraska tonight."

Never a big football fan, Catherine was grateful to be spared. "Dave and John from *As You Like It* are going to be doing Dr. Jekyll and Mr. Hyde. Should be great."

Edwina Hipplewhite had decided on another bibliophile field trip. This time, it was All Hallow's Eve at Naper Settlement, a nineteenth-century scare fest the highlight of which would be the Headless Horseman's ride through the grounds.

Catherine bent over and kissed a spent, lounging-on-the-sofa Will.

"Have a great time, honey." Will waved her off, grateful for some time alone. Work had been crazy lately. Not wanting to be accused of giving his son any special privileges, Benjamin was pushing Will twice as hard as any other employee.

He turned on the television and took a sip of his beer.

Usually, Naper Settlement was a tranquil place, an outdoor living history museum, featuring some thirty buildings, each with costumed villagers telling nineteenth-century tales of how the area had grown from a frontier outpost to a bustling, turn-of-the century community. But tonight, all was different.

The settlement was cloaked in the darkness of night, lit only by kerosene lamps and the orange glow of campfires. They were to meet at the firehouse entrance at seven o'clock. Miss Hipplewhite flounced in, encircled by a large red cape. "Glad to see you, my darlings. Is everyone dressed warmly enough? There is a bit of chill in the air tonight." Looking directly at Spring, she continued, "especially you, my sweet little waif of a thing. Would you like to borrow my gloves?"

"Got 'em." Spring tapped her right side. "In my pocket." She made sure to wear her thickest jeans and winter coat this evening, knowing the temperatures would dip into the forties by the end of the night. Although born in the Chicago area, Spring still was not accustomed to the coolness of fall nor winter's vile clutches. Come to think of it, she was cold during every season.

"All right then, let us commence with a quick tour of the torture dungeon in the Blacksmith's Shop, then it is off to Dracula's Lair."

The bibliophiles walked past the ghost pirate ship. "Look! There is a séance in the chapel," said Sarah.

"Ironic, isn't it?" Larry worked his way in between Sarah and Annie.

"Anyone want to get their fortune told?" Rosemary pointed to three white tents.

"What a pile of crap! They'll always say something like 'You are in love with someone, but she doesn't know it.' What bullshit!"

"Scared, Larry?" Rosemary chided.

"Hello no."

"Then, let's do it."

Edwina clapped her hands. "What fun this will be! Maybe she will predict what next month's book will be. Come on, there is no line."

Rosemary, Larry, and Edwina all entered the tents.

"Are you going to do this?" Annie asked Sarah.

"Why bother? I already know my future. Laundry, car pools, and nagging about homework."

Larry emerged from the tent. "See, I told you. I'm in love with someone, and she doesn't know it. I should be a fortune teller."

"Is it true?" asked Thaddeus.

"Please," Larry grumbled. "I'll go get in line for the Dracula thing while the rest of you suckers finish up here."

"Go ahead, Spring. You're next."

"No, thank you, Thaddeus. This stuff messes with my aura and personal vibe. I don't want to know my future."

"I'll go," Annie Jacobs piped up. "I've got nothing to lose."

"I'll wait for you out here," Sarah called after her.

Rosemary came out of her tent, a small smirk decorating her mouth.

"What did she say?"

"Nothing I don't already know, Sarah. Where are the rest?"

"Off to join Larry in line for Dracula's Lair."

Edwina Hipplewhite had not come out yet. Sarah wondered what that meant.

Inside one of the tents, Annie sat across from a woman dressed like the stereotypical gypsy everyone has seen in movies, complete with scarves and gold bangles. The woman moved the crystal ball aside. "Give me your hand. You have a powerful aura." The pretend-gypsy studied Annie's hand for several minutes.

"Okay, really, I need to get back to my friends. Can you speed this up a bit?"

"I see you with a little girl. A little girl with Winnie-the-Pooh sneakers and pigtails."

"You can't possibly," she said, trying to free her hand.

The woman held Annie's hand tightly. "No wait. This is very strong. You are playing at the park. Pushing her on a swing."

"Okay, I'm done!" Annie pulled her hand away and ran out of the tent, trying to compose herself before Sarah walked over.

"Are you okay? You look a bit..."

"I'm fine. Same old crap about love and prosperous future. What a crock!"

Sarah and Annie walked to join the others, reaching them right before it was their time to enter the Lair. Edwina was right behind them.

How could some fake fortune teller have known about that dream? Annie had not had it for a while, probably since that time she had fallen asleep on the train last year. It was too weird. She shivered and pulled her coat up around her.

In line awaiting "Edgar Allan Poe," Spring felt heavy breathing on her neck. She turned around right into the face of a demon in a black shroud, torrents of blood oozing from his mouth. She let out a high-pitched, eardrum-splitting scream. The demon went away satisfied, as the crowd around her laughed.

Thaddeus put a hand on her shoulder. "It's okay, Spring. He was quite hideous."

Spring was not the only one. Throughout the night, screams broke out all around the settlement as a werewolf roamed the park, a ghostly bride wandered aimlessly in search of a husband, and zombies meandered through the lines, searching for brains.

The bibliophiles were shepherded into the dark schoolhouse. A man entered, agitated. "Silence! True!—Nervous—Very dreadfully nervous I had been and am; but why will you say that I am mad? The disease had sharpened my senses—not destroyed them—not dulled them. Above all was the sense of hearing acute. I heard all things in the heaven and in the earth. I heard many things in hell. How, then, am I mad?"

Edwina smiled, whispering "'The Tell Tale Heart,' right, darlings?"

After the gentleman's wonderful performance, she gathered the book club members near the Civil War surgeon's area within the log walls of Fort Payne. "Okay, my dears, may I just say how much I love this? The best part is they are staying true to the nineteenth-century feel and the real stories these books told."

All of a sudden, horse hooves clapped over the loudspeakers, first mildly, then becoming more deafening with each clomp.

"Move away! Move away! The horseman comes!" Dutch settlers yelled, clearing a path. The black horse grunted, blowing smoke from its nostrils. It reared up on its hind legs, then shot through the settlement. The horseman threw a lit jack o'lantern across the grassy knoll, then sped off to the cheers of the crowd.

"Oh, my soul, that was frightening." Edwina fanned herself with her scarf. "Wonderful, really."

"That was frickin' awesome!"

"Language, Larry dear. This is the nineteenth century, and one does not speak that way around ladies."

"Yes, ma'am. My apologies."

By now, the bibliophiles were used to Edwina admonishing them like children and accepted it as part of her charm. "Let us head over to the Naper-Haight House. I think you will find what lies inside quite interesting."

A man dressed in black with a white wig stuck his head out the side door. "Come, come now. We have much business which to attend."

Three Puritan teenaged girls sat, wringing their hands, moaning. "It hurts. It hurts. They did this to us!" Their fingers pointed in the direction of a housewife and her slave. This was their trial.

"Innocent or guilty? You be the judge, but let me remind you, your very soul depends upon the answer." The reverend paced before the audience.

Sarah, Annie, and Rosemary yelled "Innocent!" when asked whether the women should be burned at the stake. But many shouts of "Guilty!" were heard from the other side of the room, and that was all the reverend needed for his verdict.

One of the hysterical teenagers confronted Rosemary. "You are marked with the sign of the devil. I can see it on you. Burn her! Burn her!"

The housewife screamed "Save yourself! Get out now before it is too late!"

The audience was herded out before the reverend could take action on Rosemary.

"My God, Larry. I have never seen you laugh so hard in… well, ever," said Sarah.

Larry wiped away the tears streaming down his face. "Oh, that was rich." He turned to Rosemary. "A witch? Ha! That does not surprise me at all."

"Very funny. You'd better watch it, or I'll cast a spell on you. Oh wait, you already look like a toad."

"Darlings, over here." Edwina gathered the group next to a building where it was more quiet. "That, my dears, was the most frightening of all this evening because it really happened. Which puts me in the mood for next month's selection, *The Crucible* by Arthur Miller. Won't that be fun? Well, it might put a bit of a damper on your Thanksgivings, come to think of it, once you read about those awful Puritans, but, oh well, you shall rise above it, I am sure. Besides, I guess it will give you something to be grateful for, that you are not Puritans and that alone will allow for a happy Thanksgiving, won't it? Well, okay then. I will see you on the first Tuesday in December, after you have read *The Crucible*. Ta-ta, dear ones."

A small envelope came in the mail on a rainy, November day.

Dear Catherine,

Thank you.

Patsy.

Enclosed was a picture. On the back it read the following.

My husband, Graham, and kids, Katie, 5, and Thomas, 7.

CHAPTER THIRTY

*T*HE DEPARTMENT OF MOTOR VEHICLES was packed. Almost every seat was taken. Senior citizens waited patiently. First-time learner's permit kids sat, anxious to get this over with. Workers checked emails on their phones.

The girl smiled and jiggled her way across the front of the room. Every one of the men scattered in the rows ahead turned. The stoic senior citizen in the corner. The long-faced nerdy guy in the blue pinstripe shirt. The fiftyish balding man with strings attached to his glasses like a librarian glared through bifocaled eyes. The ruddy, size-of-a-wall guy in the recognizable brown delivery uniform. And the guy who sat to the side, face chiseled like an Aztec warrior, who tried to be above the spectacle. Yet, eventually he, too, succumbed. Were they real, or had she received them for her sixteenth birthday? It was Naperville, after all.

"Sir? Sir? Right this way, please."

A man old enough to know better than to gawk at a teenaged girl, even if she did have a figure that was the real-life equivalent of a Barbie doll, was jolted back into reality, a few drops of perspiration moistening his forehead.

Where did she go? The men looked left in unison. Bob Fosse could not have choreographed them better. Now if only they could do jazz hands, the day would be complete.

What does a girl do with looks that every porn rag in the country holds dear? At her age, did she make a decision to look like that, much in the same way punk kids choose to dye their hair green and spike it in a mohawk? Or, did nature thrust this upon her, salaciously watching her cope?

If, in fact, the latter was true, Catherine hoped she was dumb and that her body was all she had. For if she possessed even a modicum of brainpower, it would be a daily challenge, having to endure all the men who would never look into her eyes or hear her when she spoke, staring unapologetically while suppressing the desire to reach out and grab them, yarn balls dangling over a kitten's head.

"Number seven hundred and twenty-eight."

Catherine rose. Time to get that driver's license.

Another letter postmarked "Portland, ME" arrived. This time, the handwriting was a bit shaky.

> *Dear Catherine,*
>
> *I had often wondered what happened to you and prayed you were well.*
>
> *Marty and I are hanging in there. Both as old as the hills, but what can you do? We're still kicking.*
>
> *I sold Christmas Bells last year to a nice young couple who said they had always loved the place when they visited in the summer and wanted to move here permanently.*
>
> *I appreciate your words about that awful week. I knew you were hurting just as much as Patsy, but she was never as strong as you, so I felt she needed me more.*
>
> *I think of you often.*
>
> *Katie McLellan*

"Hi, Catherine!" Joy Monohan picked up her last bag of groceries and slammed the trunk shut.

"What's up, Joy?"

"Not much. I was all set to sign up for that Bikram yoga class Jenny told me about. You know Jenny, two doors down? Who the heck would want to do yoga in one hundred and five degrees? Sweet Jesus, I sweat enough every night with my hot flashes! Poor Frank, I practically bury him in the blankets!"

"Joy, you slay me. Have a good day."

"You too. Enjoy your walk."

Catherine had been helping out Joy for a couple of months now, doing light office work, stuffing envelopes and such, until she could find a full-time job.

Walking down Green Valley Street, the sun ducked in and out of the clouds, a cosmic game of hide and seek. Sunlight, then gray. Sunlight, then gray. When would it make up its mind? Are you in or out, Monsieur Soleil?

She had an interview at the old-fashioned candy store in downtown Naperville this morning at ten o'clock. At two, she had a meeting with the owner of a bookstore one block down. Either job would be great. Who doesn't love candy? And books? Goes without saying. Edwina Hipplewhite would burst a gasket if she got the bookstore job. No question about that.

Catherine pulled out of her driveway. Temporarily blinded by the sun, she slammed down the visor and headed to downtown Naperville for her interview. All in after all, huh, Monsieur Soleil?

Me, too.

"Hey, Will? Want to go hit some balls?" Catherine was decked out in appropriate golf attire—pants, shoes, *collared* shirt, sweater vest, and unzipped windbreaker made by some manufacturer she had never heard of —and toted a golf bag filled with women's clubs. She even had a gopher head cover, like the little guy from *Caddyshack*.

"What is all this?"

"Well, my darling. I know you love golf and thought it would be fun if we could do it together. Maybe you could give me some lessons. Besides, seeing as it is unseasonably mild today, I thought you would like a little warm-up before the Turkey Trot."

"No joke?"

"Do you think I would buy all this stuff if I were kidding? I even asked your mom to come with me so I wouldn't screw it up."

"Bet she was shocked."

"Actually, she kept asking me which Catherine I was on the phone. Thought I was somebody else. I finally got through to her. They are going to meet us at the driving range. How about some Arnold Palmers and lunch afterward. Sounds fun, right?"

"Are you sure?"

"Listen, your parents are an important part of your life, there is no way of getting around that. I might as well try to win them over. Hey! Did I ever show you my driver's license?"

"I guess not."

Catherine ran to her purse and fumbled through its contents. "Come on. Yes! Here it is! I'm coming! Here."

He muttered "nice picture," did a double take, and then pulled her close. "I love you, Catherine."

Her Illinois driver's license was issued to one "Catherine Elbert Overman."

THE END

ALSO BY KAREN WOJCIK BERNER

A Whisper to a Scream (The Bibliophiles: Book One)

"A Bibliophile Christmas" digital holiday short story

ACKNOWLEDGMENTS

Music has always played a large role in my life, from the time I practiced singing *Partridge Family* songs into my hairbrush at age seven, through performing in talent shows, local revues, musicals, and two choirs. It motivates me, relaxes me, and definitely inspires me.

Some of my characters have their own soundtracks, melodies I have used to get into their heads. For example, listening to Peter Gabriel's "Blood of Eden" helped me see John Jacobs' point of view, which most of the time is very different from that of his wife Annie in *A Whisper to a Scream*.

Several years ago, while writing *Whisper*, I was listening to the Indigo Girls' brilliant song "Galileo." The concept of reincarnation fascinated me, but instead of multiple lifetimes, I started playing around with a character that reinvented herself each time she moved, refashioning in accordance to her surroundings until she found the true person within. Catherine Elbert was born.

If you have never heard "Galileo," please check it out on iTunes. You will not be disappointed.

As always, there are many people to thank for their contributions to this novel.

First off, a big thank you to the Indigo Girls for writing such a fantastic song.

Heartfelt thanks to my beta readers, Jan and David, and to Geraldine A. Young for her insightful book discussion questions.

Thank you to Julia Munroe Martin for being my official Maine consultant and to my aunt and uncle for having their fiftieth wedding anniversary party in San Diego where I was able to do some research as well as enjoy some family time.

Huge thanks to everyone at Streetlight Graphics for their brilliant cover and interior design.

And last, but never least, thank you to David, Tim, and Danny, the three souls with whom I have the great privilege to travel this life. Thank you for your love and support.

Karen Wojcik Berner
March 22, 2013

READER'S GUIDE

for

Until My —Soul— Gets It Right

THE BIBLIOPHILES: BOOK TWO

QUESTIONS AND TOPICS FOR DISCUSSION

By Geraldine A. Young

1. An overbearing mother and a distant father. What do you think of young Catherine's perception of her parents, Clara and Hank?

2. The seventeen-year-old Catherine describes her farm town as sanctimonious and "smug, full of hypocrisy and stupidity." Is she reacting as many teenagers normally would, growing up in a small town with "traditional values"? Or is there something different about Catherine's attitude?

3. Burkesville is a boring town with nothing to offer her except a life just like her mother's, thinks Catherine. What kind of future do Clara and Hank want for Catherine? What does Catherine envision for herself?

4. When Hank forbids Catherine to play the role of Ado Annie in the school play, *Oklahoma!*, what reasons does he give? Why does she think her parents treat her differently from her brothers?

5. Catherine's mother discusses college scholarships with her and tells her, "You're not good enough for a full ride." Catherine feels her mother is scornful of her. Do you think this is true? Does Catherine herself exhibit any scornful attitudes?

6. Are you surprised at her parents' reaction when Catherine decides to leave home for good? What has fueled her decision, and has she has made the right choice?

7. There is freedom, a job, and new friends in Maine for Catherine, a happy situation that does not last. How does her advice to her coworker Patsy destroy her friendship with her employer Katie McLellan? Do you think Catherine's advice to Patsy about Scott was genuine or fueled by self interest?

8. In San Diego, Catherine meets her new love interest, Will, at her workplace, the San Diego Zoo. How does this job help Catherine develop and grow?

9. Is Catherine right in being angry with Will for keeping secrets from her about his family? Is her reaction to Will's family reasonable? Are you sympathetic or not with her complaints?

10. Catherine returns to Burkesville for the first time to attend her father's funeral. Has her mother changed her attitude toward Catherine after all this time? Clara says that Catherine has always been ungrateful, even as a child. Do you agree or disagree with Clara's assessment of her daughter?

11. After her marriage and move to Naperville, Catherine begins to reconsider her life and to wonder what make her happy or unhappy. Does this self questioning lead to a gradual change in Catherine's attitudes and activities?

12. Catherine felt out of place both in the farm town of Burkesville and in the sophisticated surroundings of Will's home in Naperville. Why does she feel more at home in her area of Naperville?

13. How does Edwina Hipplewhite and the Classics Book Club influence Catherine's new life?

14. The title of the book is *Until My Soul Gets It Right*. Discuss what it may mean in terms of Catherine's story—her family in Burkesville, her estranged friends in Portland, Maine, and her current life in Naperville.

15. At the end of the book, to what degree has Catherine reached the goal suggested by the book's title?

Geraldine A. Young is a freelance writer (and retired English teacher) in Ohio.

READ ALONG WITH
THE BIBLIOPHILES

Would you like to start a Classics Book Club of your very own? Wouldn't Edwina Hipplewhite be proud? Here are some ideas for menus and discussion questions for the classic literature pieces found in *Until My Soul Gets It Right*.

The Legend of Sleepy Hollow and Other Tales
by Washington Irving

Food and Beverages
Sleepy Hollow is a Dutch settlement, so how about Kaasstengels (Dutch cheese stems) with some Erwtensoep (traditional Dutch split pea soup)? Apple and/or pumpkin pie would be lovely for dessert. How about some Advocaat, which is similar to eggnog, to warm up the evening?

Discussion Questions
1. Discuss the love triangle between Brom Bones, Katrina Van Tassel, and Ichabod Crane. Who do you think Katrina fancies more?

2. The story illustrates the age-old conflict between brains versus brawn. Which do you prefer in a man?

3. How does the actual story differ from the versions you have seen in the movies or on TV?

The Crucible
by Arthur Miller

Food and Beverages

Puritan fare. Serve cornbread, roasted turkey, and stewed pumpkin with ginger, butter, and vinegar. To drink, Puritans preferred beer, wine, or cider.

Discussion Questions

1. The Puritans of Massachusetts Bay Colony established a theocracy, in which religion and government became intertwined. What do you think life would be like living in a theocracy?

2. Do you think people nowadays could be easily swept up into the hysteria that plagued Salem?

3. Salem is clearly a patriarchal society. Discuss the village women and their roles. Would the witch trials have happened if more men were accused? How do you think the proceedings would have changed?

CLASSICS BOOK CLUB READING LIST

Keeping track of what the members of the Classics Book Club have discussed? Throughout the first two novels, the bibliophiles have read the following great works of literature.

A Portrait of the Artist as a Young Man
by James Joyce

As You Like It
by William Shakespeare

The Legend of Sleepy Hollow and Other Tales
by Washington Irving

The Crucible
by Arthur Miller

Read on for a sample of

A BIBLIOPHILE
CHRISTMAS

Digital Holiday Short Story
Karen Wojcik Berner

"*G*OD REST YE MERRY, GENTLEMEN. *Let nothing you dismay.*"

Of course, men need not dismay, Sarah Anderson thought. What did they have to do for the holidays anyhow? Show up? Wow, *that* was taxing.

Her husband slammed the lid of his suitcase. "I'll be back on Friday. Will you pick me up, or do you want me to take a cab?"

"If you're back on Friday, you might as well go straight to the lawyer's office."

"Christ, Sarah. That's extreme."

"Friday's December twenty-sixth."

"Christmas is this week?"

"And they pay *you* the big bucks? You'd better be here on the twenty-third. The boys would be heartbroken if you missed Christmas Eve." She lowered her voice. "You have to help me with the you-know-whats." Let Tom think the kids cared if he made it home for Christmas all he wanted, as long as he returned in time to assemble the various cars and bikes slated to magically appear under the tree on Christmas morning. That was the one thing on her "To Do" list with the initial "T" next to it, one measly task among the never-ending items marked with an "S."

"Four days? How the hell am I going to get the system up and running in only four days?" He picked up his suitcase, laptop backpack, and phone. "I've got to call Deanna and Shrevani and move Wednesday's meeting to early Tuesday."

She trailed him through the kitchen, family room, and down the hall. He stopped briefly at the front door to dial a number on his phone.

She leaned toward him. "Have a good trip?"

He merely nodded, shushing her, as he balanced the phone

between his cheek and shoulder. Picking up his luggage, he dashed outside to the waiting limousine.

Silly her, she had thought he might actually give her a kiss. "No need for formal good-byes," she muttered, slamming the front door so hard that the pinecones almost flew off the wreath.

Seven days until the big event. By this stage of the game, Sarah had already completed seventy-five percent of her list. Christmas cards depicting Santa's workshop were signed, addressed, stamped, and mailed, complete with the requisite darling photo of the boys. The tree was decorated, wrapped boxes containing cinder blocks placed strategically around it, a barrier through which two-year-old Alex couldn't pass. Since he had become mobile, Alex had spent most of the last year climbing. First, it was stairs. Going up was no problem. Watching him come down was the part that nearly gave Sarah a heart attack after seeing him tumble and land with a thud. Blood trickled over his mouth and chin from his nose banging on the last stair. Eventually, the little tyke learned how to scoot safely down each step on his bottom. After stairs, Alex graduated to the backyard fort's ladder, followed by the rigging leading to the fort's top tier. Each stage was accompanied by many "Oh, shit!" moments that required several deep breaths for Mommy and the secret desire to down a bazillion martinis to calm her nerves.

The Christmas presents had been purchased, wrapped, and hidden someplace high and safe from prying eyes. Nicky was getting older and had heard some rumors questioning the validity of a certain round fellow typically clad in red. Other gifts, like those for the extended family, were also hidden in case Alex couldn't control himself again. Last year, he had flown through all the presents on Christmas Eve like some sort of Tasmanian Devil. What did he know? He couldn't read, an oversight her sister-in-law Marjorie could not get past. "When Peter was that age, he was already reading *Cat in the Hat*."

Really? Her son could barely form a two-word sentence. He would be lucky not to flunk second grade.

The only items left on the "To Do" list were grocery shopping, cleaning, baking, and cooking. Tight, but doable. Maybe she and the boys would bake a batch of cookies together tomorrow. Anyhow, Tom would be home to occupy the kids while she prepared as much of Christmas dinner as possible before they left for the Andersons'. She was heading into the home stretch.

Sarah snapped Alex into a fresh, one-piece footie pajama. Yawning, he cuddled into her arms as they read *Goodnight Moon*. Somewhere between saying goodnight to the stars and air, Sarah kissed his damp head, a whiff of sweet honey combined with baby shampoo filling her nostrils.

"Mommy loves you," she whispered. Alex smiled and pointed at the book, reminding her she wasn't finished. After the last page, she tucked him in, turned on his teddy bear music box, and closed his door halfway.

"Hey, wanna watch Frosty?"

"Shush, honey! I just put Alex down."

"Oops, sorry," Nicky whispered. "Let's go downstairs."

They crept along, soft strains of Brahms' "Lullaby" echoing down the hall, mindful that any creak of the floor could potentially wake up Alex, whom they still referred to as "the baby," even though he was firmly into the toddler stage and would be going to preschool next year. Sarah didn't want to think of that right now.

She had to get through Christmas first.

Annie Jacobs hung faux crystal icicles on her flocked Christmas tree. The winter wonderland was beginning to take shape. Her tree. Her condo. Her life. Everything was new, from the sleek, contemporary sectional sofa to every dish in her kitchen cabinets.

Only the books remained, illustrating the story of Annie's life as much as the characters within: *Little Women*, *Peter Pan*, and the Little House series from her youth and works by the English Romantic Poets from college. Byron and Shelley sat without Keats, however, whose work had been donated along with almost all of the contents of the house at 208 W. Muirfield after she and John split up. Her ex-husband had brought her to the Keats House next to the Spanish Steps in Rome on her twenty-first birthday, their first date. No, there would be no Keats in her condo.

She had run into the ass-in-law, Ralph, at the mall a few days ago. Well, ex-ass-in-law now. Ralph had delighted in telling her that John had moved to Milwaukee to live with Melanie and help raise their baby, Michael, as Annie had known all along he would. Some days, she barely got through without that feeling of constantly being punched in the solar plexus. Others, she was grateful for the solitude and not having to keep up appearances. Working from home, unshowered and in pajamas, proved to be very fulfilling.

She was getting back on track in her position at Jones and MacGregor Public Relations. She would never be able to repay her mentor, Harry Jones, for all of the support and understanding throughout the past year. Ninety percent of bosses would have fired her. Christian, a junior member of her team had even tried to make the case for Annie's incompetence to take advantage of the opportunity to further his own career. Harry would not hear any of it and actually demoted Christian, who ended up quitting a few months later.

Annie strung beads on the branches in large swoops, white sparkling lights reflecting in their silvery strands. She stood back, admiring her work. Designer quality, if she could be so bold. Her tree was nothing like the ones they'd had at 208 W. Muirfield. In those days, their trees had been thrown together with a hodgepodge of ornaments from their travels, all of which had also been donated to Goodwill, except for the Venetian mask from Carnevale, which she kept wrapped in tissue paper and stuffed in the very back of her dresser drawer.

Sitting cross-legged on her sofa, Annie sipped Cabernet and glanced around the condo, content with what she saw—an uncluttered mix of dark browns and various greens. Earthy. Relaxing. Comforting. Six days until Christmas. For the first time, she had no shopping to do. Harry had taken care of all the company gifts. As for family, Grandma Mary had passed away the previous year, followed two months later by Grandpa Bill, who seemed to have lost his will to live once his beloved had been taken from him. The last time she had spoken to her mother was when she called to impart the news that her divorce was final.

"I don't understand how you could let yourself get so obsessed. It was only a baby, for goodness sake. Plenty of people lead perfectly good lives without children. I don't see why you couldn't have been one of them. Now look what you did. You drove your husband right into the arms of another woman!"

Annie had promptly told Marian to go to hell and slammed down the phone. Although supportive during the in vitro fertilization cycles, her father eventually succumbed to Marian's constant harping, finding it easier to go along with his life putzing around the house doing odd jobs in the winter and golfing as much as was humanly possible rather than uttering any more words in Annie's defense. That decision left Annie basically orphaned, which was fine by her. A clean break from her old life was what she needed. It was the only way to rebuild Annie McDonnell, a stronger version of the previous Annie Jacobs, who had gone back to using her maiden name as soon as the divorce papers were signed.

She had finally sold that stupid suit of armor, the proceeds of which had funded much of her new decor. It turned out to be good for something after all. She had no need for a family heirloom if she didn't have anyone to pass it down to or elders who insisted she keep it.

Her books. Her job. Her book club meetings. Those were the only things left from her old life, all blissfully John-free. He was not a reader and had never met any of the Bibliophiles, for which she was grateful.

She would have an uncomplicated, quiet Christmas.

Greg Williams tied a red bow around the slender box, which did not contain gloves or a scarf, as one would suspect, but rather Chicago Bulls tickets. Where the heck did he put the tags? Under the Santa wrapping paper? Maybe by the green foil embossed with holly leaves? Grabbing a pen, he filled out the "To" and paused. He should keep it simple. "To: Dad. From: Greg." Somehow, those four words stung. The thought of celebrating the holidays without his mother was almost too much to bear, but he had to keep strong for Sarah. His mom would have wanted that. So far, his sister seemed okay, even with Tom out of town for most of the month, but it was only a matter of time before she cracked.

Last year, Sarah almost had a nervous breakdown on Christmas morning, and Mom had to talk her down and save the day. Well, Greg's famous lasagna had helped, as well as enough wine for twenty people, even though only eight would be dining that night, two of whom were little boys. Good wine, too. But if he couldn't share it with family and save Christmas, what good was it? Besides, his mushroom lasagna, with its delectable Béchamel sauce, was the only thing Nicky would eat, which showed he had a very advanced palate for a child of his age. Clearly, his nephew took after him. Perhaps they could watch the Food Channel together the next time the kids visited. Once a month, he took care of the boys while Sarah went to her book club meeting, each time giving his sister shit about "burdening" him, all the while loving the time spent with his nephews.

Greg stuck the tag on his father's gift, careful not to smudge the writing. No one did Christmas like his mother had. He and Sarah used to joke around, calling her "The Christmas Queen." After cooking a complete Thanksgiving feast the day before, Patty Williams never skipped a beat, starting bright and early the next day decorating for Christmas. The only indulgence she allowed herself was warming turkey leftovers for dinner that night so the decorating could forge on without her having to stop to cook dinner.

The self-help books all stated the same thing—year one was the most difficult, enduring all the "firsts." The first Mother's Day, their grief had been as raw as the black dirt covering Patty's plot. Then, he had almost broken down at Steve's on Independence Day. Watching Audrey and Mason run around with sparklers, "writing" their names in the midnight blue sky, flashed Greg back to his youth. He recalled a seven-year-old Sarah flitting about, laughing as she twirled with her sparkler. He, on the other hand, had barely moved, too scared an ember would leap off and scorch his five-year-old fingers.

"Come here, Greggie. Let me show you something." His mom had lit a sparkler of her own and traced G-R-E-G in the night sky. Magic!

He wiped his eyes and reached for another gift to wrap.

"Knock. Knock." Gingerly balancing one cup on top of another, Annie let herself into the Anderson home. "Pick-me-up time! Figured you might need a beverage break."

Sarah greeted her wearing a flour-covered apron accented with smears of red and green frosting.

"You look like Betty Crocker threw up all over you." Annie set the drinks on the only unoccupied square of the kitchen counter. Cookie sheets, bowls filled with icing, empty food-dye tubes, cooling racks, parchment paper, and oven mitts took up the rest of the space.

"Auntie Annie! I did this one just for you." Nicky handed her a sugar cookie snowman with three eyes, a combination mouth/nose, and four green buttons, one of which looked oddly like a penis.

"Thank you, honey."

Sarah darted toward a cabinet. "I'll get you a plate."

"Annie! Annie! Annie!" Alex kicked his feet and waved wildly in his chair, sending frosting flying halfway across the kitchen. "Cookies! Cookies! Cookies!"

"Hey, bud. See you graduated from a high chair into a whatever-that's-called."

"Booster seat," Sarah interjected.

"A booster seat? High-five me, big man!" Annie couldn't help but laugh. Such chaos. She smiled, grateful they weren't in her kitchen.

Sarah eyed her peppermint mocha like Golem coveting the ring. She grabbed it, savoring its minty goodness.

Annie took a seat at the kitchen table. "So, are you ready?"

"This is my last big 'To Do' besides cooking for Christmas Day. I even have my shrimp marinating for tomorrow's appetizer."

"Well done. Hey, where's Tom?"

"Supposed to be in at eight o'clock. Or is it eight thirty? Something like that."

"Hope he gets here okay. I heard there's another storm about to hit the east coast."

"Oh, crap. Really? I haven't even turned on the TV."

"Crap! Crap! Crap!" Alex glommed onto his new word. Nicky giggled.

"Oh, shit! Alex, no!" Sarah put her hand to her mouth.

"Shit! Shit! Shit!"

"No, Alex! Nicky, stop laughing. You're encouraging him. Go upstairs and get cleaned up, please. Thank you."

"Shit! Shit! Shit!"

Sarah wiped off the toddler's hands and untied his bib, careful not to drop all the cookie crumbs on the floor.

"Shit! Shit! Shit!"

"Alex, honey, that is not a good word to use."

"Mommy said."

"Honey, Mommy made a mistake. Please don't use that word again." Off went Alex, climbing the stairs in search of his brother. Sarah rejoined Annie. "That should assure me a Mother of the Year nomination. Tom's always harping on about polite society and the deterioration of the language. If he hears Alex yelling 'shit'…"

"He will laugh his ass off, just like Nicky. That was a precious moment. Best thing that's happened to me all day."

"Aren't you supposed to be at work?"

"Ahh, the beauty of working from home. I can get out of the condo anytime I please. Besides, most everyone took the week off. Harry's actually encouraging it. Very European, don't you think? Joyeux Noel. Buon Natale. Frohe Weihnachten. How about Polish? Boże Narodzenie."

Sarah laughed. "How do you know that?"

"Choir in high school. We sang this international piece that blended 'Merry Christmas' in eight or so languages."

"I didn't know you sang." Sarah smirked and pushed Annie's arm. "Sing something."

"Why do people do that? If you find out someone's a heart surgeon, you don't ask her to perform an operation."

"It would be kind of awesome for a doctor to break into surgery and crack somebody's ribs right in front of you."

"Not for the patient. Take it easy, Sweeney Todd."

"So, what are you doing tomorrow?" Sarah took another sip of mocha.

"Not sure." Annie shifted in her seat.

"What about your parents?"

"I have no desire to sit there drinking sherry with those two while…" Annie closed her eyes and sighed. "You might as well know. John moved to Milwaukee. One big, happy family now, I guess."

Sarah reached across the table for Annie's hand.

"I ran into the ass-in-law last week. Couldn't keep his mouth shut about it. How John and Melanie brought the baby—little Michael, that's his name—down for Thanksgiving. Never seen John happier, he said." Tears dotted Annie's cheeks.

Sarah got her some tissues. "You absolutely must come here for Christmas. I insist."

Annie blew her nose and tried to compose herself. "I can't. Don't want to spoil your holiday. Besides, I am planning on spending both days snuggled up with a bottle of Grey Goose in front of the fireplace."

"Vodka is not a satisfactory holiday companion."

"I think many people would beg to differ, Mrs. Anderson. Don't worry about me. I'll be fine."

"But—"

A loud thud came from upstairs, followed by a wail.

"Mom! Alex tried to climb my dresser!"

"Oh, shit!" Sarah got up to run, then glanced at Annie.

"No, you go! I'll let myself out."

Seeing Alex toddling down the hallway, rubbing his head, Sarah yelled for Annie to wait a second, but her friend had already gone.

ABOUT THE AUTHOR

Karen Wojcik Berner grew up on the outskirts of Chicago. After graduating from Dominican University with degrees in English with a writing concentration and communications, she worked as a magazine editor, public relations coordinator and freelance writer. A two-time *Folio Magazine* Ozzie Award for Excellence in Magazine Editorial and Design winner, her work has appeared in countless newspapers and magazines. She lives in the Chicago suburbs with her family.

To learn more about Karen, please visit her website at www.karenberner.com.

Made in the USA
Charleston, SC
10 September 2013